I0589468

COOL
SHORT STORIES
By
Don Kirk

If you like the macabre, the gruesome, the grim, or ghastly, and you like to get in the head of eccentric characters who are a tad off balance and extremely unpredictable, this book is for you. If you like Hitchcock, the Twilight Zone, or Tales from the Crypt and you have a healthy but morbid sense of humor, this book is for you. If you're not squeamish, sensitive to blood and gore, or weak of heart or mind, and you love a good mystery, this book is definitely for you. And if you look forward to the dead of night to devour a good book when the shadows grow frightfully long and dance strangely across your bedroom ceiling, you should definitely buy this book.

OTHER BOOKS BY
DON KIRK

AVAILABLE FROM THE PUBLISHER

Welcome to Redrock Canyon Territory

Barbed Wire, Windmills, & Six Guns

Western Ballads and Poetry

Discovery Bay

Erika

Hinsdale: The Summer of '58

COOL
SHORT STORIES

BY

DON KIRK

Cool Short Stories
Psychodramas With A Twist

Copyright © Don Kirk 2006

Published by
SWEETWATER STAGELINES™
An imprint of
THE OLD WEST COMPANY™
5118 Village Trail Drive
San Antonio, Texas 78218

ISBN-10: 0-9654341-5-X
ISBN-13: 978-0-9654341-5-7

Horror / Science Fiction

Printed and bound in the United States of America

SWEETWATER STAGELINES™
SAN ANTONIO, TEXAS

COOL
SHORT STORIES
By Don Kirk

They're coming to take me away, ho ho, he he, ha ha. To the funny farm where life is beautiful all the time—That 1966 song by Napoleon the Fourteenth frequently plays over and over and over again in my tortured mind. It always seems to be there, torturing me, in my crazed mind—*And I'll be happy to see those nice young men in their clean white coats. And they're coming to take me away, ha haaaa*—That "ha ha" resonates in my head, reverberating far out into the universe, into infinity. But no, it's that "infinity" that's *in* my brain, my thoughts never daring to leave the bony bounds of my hard skull—until now. I found that my ugly glob of gray matter was unbounded in its potential to dream, to hope, to love—and to tell thoroughly demented tales of Gothic terror. I pulled out my ancient dust-covered dictionary and wrote down this definition with a dull No.2 pencil:

> **Psychodrama**—n. 1. A psychotherapeutic technique in which people are assigned roles to be played spontaneously within a dramatic context devised by a therapist in order to understand the behavior of people with whom they have difficult interactions. 2. A dramatization in which this technique is employed. 3. An event, social interaction, *or narrative* that manifests psychological forces or problems.
>
> — *The American Heritage Dictionary of the English Language.*

I learned that in the 1930's, Jacob L. Moreno conceived and developed a technique to explore the inner conflicts of troubled individuals and, as an extension, writers conceived dramatic stories that delved into the psyche of men. Dr. Moreno informed us that the, "Psychodrama is a transliteration of a thing done to and with the psyche in action. Psychodrama can be defined, therefore, as the science which explores the 'truth' by dramatic methods." Hopefully some of these stories do just that as they entertain.

I found these bizarre short stories in an old ringed notebook dating back to the early 70's (yes, I have been "mad" for many years it seems), and many appeared to fit the definition of a psychodrama. Some were hand written and had never been read by anyone. Others had been typed on a *Royal* portable typewriter I took with me to college way back in 1966—the end of the age of innocence and the beginning of a new world-shaking drug culture. Because I'm a poor typist, I doubt that I ever showed anyone these type-written stories either—maybe I didn't want them to know who I really was. Some of the stories are only a few pages long, others considerably longer. I also included in this work a prose version of two thirty-minute teleplays I wrote long ago, and other more recent works. It's clear that I had an interest in Twilight Zone-type twist endings, which work well for short stories. My writings also seem to exhibit a morbid sense of humor like the Tales from the Crypt. Some are spiced with humor and others are laced with social commentary, but either way, the reader will never know what to expect, and I hope that, at the very least, some of these twisted stories will be a pleasant and enjoyable surprise.

And just maybe, reading these cool short stories, you can discover the inner conflicts that torture *my* mind (and maybe yours) and by playing psychiatrist, you can enlighten me, ever so gently, what my problem must be and then tell me, hopefully, that I'd be on the road to recovery if I would just scribble down some more of these horrific mind searching psychotherapeutic stories for you to enjoy. What? You mean, so you can get *inside* my head? Ha, ha, ho, ho, he, he, no chance, they're coming to take me away, ha. haaaa…

— 22 July 06

CONTENTS

Grave Sight

By Don Kirk

BUNKETY-KLUNK. Suddenly I felt the buckboard jerk to a stop. A horse whinnied. Clouds of dust filled the air. Old Doc Harvey jumped to the ground with a solid thud and shuffled his feet to the rear of the wagon. I listened attentively as he carefully slid the sweet smelling, freshly cut pinewood coffin to the edge of the old weathered wagon bed. I heard the four leather handles stretch painfully as the pine box was pulled free of the dusty graying buckboard. The casket floated right smooth, rocking rhythmically, toward Cemetery Hill.

Reverend Thomas was there, so was Martha Willingsworth. She was sobbing, tear drops soaking her dainty silk handkerchief. The bone box was carefully laid to rest on the ground next to a freshly dug six by three.

I knew much of the town had showed up to see the buryin' and say their final good-byes. Those conversing were talking in strained whispers, afraid they might wake the peaceful sleep of the dead. I could hear the rustle of Madam Kinsley's black cape and the tick-tick of Old Man Crabtree's gold pocketwatch, which was always in his waistcoat pocket. I had once sent a message with his telegraph key at the railroad depot. I messed up on some of the Morse code, but Old Man Crabtree straightened it out for me.

Reverend Thomas cleared his throat. His throat had to be full of a lotta stuff I wish not to describe here. All sounds and whispering stopped except for the rustle of dry leaves flirting around in the cool morning breeze. I waited quietly, listening to every sound— the crickets and sparrows and fluttering butterflies—but chills suddenly ran up and down my spine. I shuttered and I shivered and I suddenly came to my senses as Reverend Thomas began to speak in a low raspy voice. I couldn't pick out every word, but I knew he was a-readin' from the Good Book. I never could learn to read a lick myself, but Aunt Carla used to read me chapter and verse while we sat in front of the cook stove. The reverend spoke on, "so it is with high regard and admiration that I place in the hands of God, this fine young man who so epitomized the hopes we have for our young men. Men, we hope, will make this town their future…"—I could imagine the townspeople standing still—actually a-rocking from one leg t'other—with their heads bowed, well, except for my little sister Anna. She would never bow her head at prayer meetin's on the Sabbath—"…Having proudly taken over his father's dry goods store after the violent death of his father at the hands of the notorious Henderson Brothers Gang, our dearly departed Farley Madison took care of the business, making it grow and prosper, only to be heartbroken when his loving wife Catherine fell to consumption not more'n a year later."—Oh Catherine, what a wonderment she was. She could settle up a blackberry pie that would please the likes of a hound dog. She was somethin' true, always there to help anyone in need. Reverend Thomas had finally arrived at the end of his long eulogy. I was glad of it. I heard the shuffle of feet in the dry dirt. The townspeople, all my friends, well most of them, were turning away and hurrying down the hill as storm clouds began to well up to the south; dark clouds building, rising, coming from nowhere in particular. Doc Harvey slapped the reins and his buckboard jerked forward and creaked back down the hill, but sister Anna, I was sure, just stood there, tears sliding down her rosy little cheeks. Aunt Carla, her eyes barely visible beneath her black veil, grabbed the tiny hand of little Anna and tugged on it.

"Time to go, honey. Farley's going to a good place."

"Where is that, Aunt Carla?"

"A good place, far from here. He's gone now, way up there in the heavens."

Little sister Anna and Carla Bloom left, but I remained. I could smell the sweet aroma of thistle blooms.

Floating again, the pine box rocked unevenly. The drop rope grated across the corners of the box as the box was lowered into the grave. I heard dirt slide down the sides of the six-by-three. The air was still and stale. Dust filled the air and traveled on the curling air currents. Another cold chill ran up and down my spine. A shovel of dirt thudded on top of the wooden coffin. I watched as dirt sifted through the cracks between the box's boards, blocking the last rays of light. Another thud and another, then there was darkness, absolute darkness. I couldn't see the nose in front of my face. It was black as coal tar. There was an eerie absolute silence and calmness to my very soul, but a new tenseness sprang throughout my body. I was closed in. I was finally six feet under—in my last resting place. Dirt spilled in around me, packing tight against my coffin. Just silent darkness—still as a mouse. I began to wonder what else could be lurking inside this dark, black as night, pine box. I still wore my buckskin shirt, my well-worn Levi's, my trusty pocketknife given me by my paw on my fifth birthday, and my boots, oh, my boots! They're not on my feet. They're not there! Oh, here they are, lying softly under my head. That's good, but now my feet are bare, left exposed, my toes a-stickin' out there a-gettin' cold. I felt naked. And my hands and fingers and my eyeballs, all exposed to the elements. Just outside my box in the dirt are grubworms and pill bugs and cinch bugs and and termites.TERMITES! My God! Those little white-bodied critters with the big appetites. I can hear them chewing already! Eating their way inside—to me! Thousands of 'em swarming about, eating their way inside, to ME! Oh God! And what is that I hear buzzin' about? It's a fly, a big green-winged horse fly buzzing about my face. It's landing on my nose! I can't wiggle it off; I must get it to fly away. It's gonna lay eggs on my nose. Get away! It's gonna lay eggs and then they'll hatch and maggots'll crawl up my nostrils. Oh God! Maggots! Slimy, crawling maggots. I must swish away that fly. I've got to get it off my nose. Oh, there, it's flying away. Good. But where is it now? I've got to get it out of here before it lands again. Shoo away fly. Shoo away. I can't see it. I don't hear it buzz. Is it crawling on my feet, crawling up my leg? Go away.

I can't move my arms. I'll be very still, very very still. I listen, but I don't hear anything, nothing at all. Absolute silence. My heart, I can't hear my heart. It's not beating! I can't feel the hot, red blood pumping through my arteries. I feel nothing. That spoiled meat, I shouldn't have eaten it. I knowd better, I knowd it might have gone bad, but I was terrible gut-shrunk. I carried it in my saddlebags for too long. It had been fresh beef, not jerked. They had cooked it over the campfire, those drovers, they had offered it to me, but I hadn't time to eat it, so I saved it—saved it for far too long.

There's a hindrance, my veins, they feel all stopped up? The mortician had shot that painful, stinging embalming fluid into my veins. It surged wildly through my body like a prairie dog forcing his way through the ground—stretching my vessels, scraping my arteries from the inside like a bumble bee forcing his way through a busy hive. Oh, God! There's no sensation in my fingers, or my nose. There's no movement. There's no pulse in my fingers or ears. Nothing. Nothing but those damn termites chewing outside. They can't eat through my clothes, CAN THEY? I DON'T THINK—oh, I'm talking too loud. Shoot, it's quiet in here, too quiet, when all I can hear is myself thinking. I'm rather glad those termites are making all that racket, munching and munching and smacking their ugly little lips.

Hey, you know, one of my legs, I think it's shorter than the other. Just a little bit though. I can feel that it's shorter. I know it. Just like I can feel the earth moving. I feel almost weightless, like I'm a-floatin' free. No, that's crazy. That can't be.

Look there, an earthworm, gobbling its way through the loose soil, winding around and around, never going in any particular direction. I've disturbed his home; his little tunnels might cave in on him now that the soil is so loose. How horrendous, he might smother to death. And I hope his little body don't get stuck with wood splinters from my pinewood box. Hey, would you look at that! There are flowers up there on my grave. Sweet smellin' thistle blooms. Gee whiz, the sky is bluebonnet blue today and not a single fluffy cloud in the sky and the wind is scampering like ocean waves across the yellow prairie grass. Oh, those sweet smellin' thistle blooms.

I see now why cemeteries are put on a hill. Sos the rains will drain away and not lift the coffins outta the ground. Thank God for that. I'm safe here. WON'T EVER GET WET. DON'T TALK SO LOUD! I can hear myself talking. STOP THAT!

My eyes, hey, they're closed! I thought they were open! Gee willikers! And pickers and chiggers and rigours. Ha! Sticklers and frog stickers. And whiskers and chins, and cheeks and handlebar mustaches and porkchops. There is nothing to do in here. Oh I sense there is someone over there. Over there, in another grave, in another pine box just a few feet away! Gosh, who could it be? I wonder if he knows I'm here? How long has he been there? Maybe I knew him in my other life. Maybe he died by the gun, or by disease or just by old age. It couldn't be Doc Harvey; he's still up above, or Martha Willingsworth. Maybe it's Martha's husband:he fell off a loaded wagon and was run over by a wagon wheel. And Clem Sutterman had heart trouble; maybe that's him. We used to play checkers on a barrel in front of his general store. I remember the checkers were made of slices of corncob. I didn't think he was a very good player, but maybe he just let me win. I could break through this box and dig a tunnel over to him and we could play checkers again. Boy, wouldn't he be surprised to see me! Ha, when I knocked on his door—his pine box—I might wake him, or scare the ever lovin' devil out of him. Ha!

Let's see now, I need something to break through my box, a hatchet, a claw hammer—but none here. I know! I'll start peeling on the wood with my fingernails and chip my way right through it. The grain runs lengthwise, it'll be easier to scrape this way. And if I reach over my chest with my left arm, I can scratch the wood near my right shoulder. Hum, they sure don't leave you much maneuverin' space in these here boxes. Where will I put the dirt I dig out of the tunnel? I don't want to shovel it into my coffin, that's for sure. Well, there ain't no real problem, I don't reckon the dirt's packed tight around my box. I can push it aside to make room for my tunnel. The earthworms will keep it loose and make it easy for me. Stay here earthworms!

I must get started.

Is that someone calling me? I think I hear someone, maybe in the grave next to me. But it's not Clem! It's a woman's soft voice. Just four feet away, just four feet. She's next door! That's right. She's next to me! Just four feet away! I can see her. Oh God, she's beautiful. It's my Catherine! My darling Catherine! I miss her so. CATHERINE! Is that you?

"Yes darling, I'm here."

Monster in My Room

By Don Kirk

IT'S LATE AT NIGHT, quite late, a time when few cars scurry along the streets, when nothing stirs except the hoot owl. The moon is only half full, ready to catch anything that might fall into it. It's a warm night, the cicadas hum incessantly and the mosquitoes are gorged from their evening's dinner. The sky is cloudless, the Milky Way visible to all who take the time to look for it. There is no sign of a thunderstorm, no mysterious breeze whistling through the trees.

Just an ordinary night.

Unless you live on some far off south-sea island, your nights are probably like this one; nothing special ever seems to happen. How, indeed, can something strange happen without the obligatory "Shakespearean thunderstorm" rumbling ominously with huge water droplets hitting the windows, tree limbs banging against the window panes, and lightning turning the night sky into day—all there to foretell impending doom. It's a requirement for the foreshadowing of terror in storytelling, but that's not what's happening in our story because—

It's an ordinary night,

in an ordinary household.

We have an apartment house in a suburban neighborhood in Anytown. The house isn't unusual or weird or even haunted. It isn't up on a hill overlooking a motel. And the family living in it is quite the garden variety suburbanites: a devoted husband, a loving wife and their "cute-as-a-button" five-year-old daughter. She has her own bedroom, her crayon drawings pinned to the flowery wallpaper, a box of fluffy teddy bears in the far corner, a few toys hiding under the bed, and a couple of half-dressed Barbie's on top of the dresser. Quite ordinary I'd venture to say.

And, well, let's just get on with our story. You know the household.

It's two A.M.—not twelve midnight—and a streetlight—not moonlight—shines into the bedroom window. The dainty little pink curtains don't blow at all because there is no breeze. Suddenly—well not "suddenly", since this was an ordinary night—more like, casually, the little girl wanders into her parents bedroom and tries to shake her mother back into this world:

"Momma, Momma, wake up!"

"Uh, huh?"

"Momma wake up. There's a monster in my room."

"Uh, what Honey?"

"Momma, there's a monster in my room. Please."

"What are you doing out of bed?"

"Momma, he's big an ugly and glows in the dark!"

"Who sweetie?"

"The monster, Mamma."

"There's a monster in your room?"

"Yes, Mamma, please…"

"He glows in the dark?"

"Yes, Mamma, he's big and ugly and glows in the dark."

"Did you try to scare him away?"

"Oh, Mom-eeee, I'm scared." The sweet little girl snuggles her face into her mother's breast.

"Honey, there's no need to be afraid. He's probably gone now. You go on back to bed now. Mommy is very tired."

"But Momma, he's still in there."

"Go on," says Mother sternly, "my bedroom's next to yours. You can call me if the monster gets too close. I'll come running, sweetie—I promise."

"NO! I'm not going back," replies the little girl, tears welling up in her eyes, "Can I sleep with you, Mamma?"

"No darling, but I'll go back to the bedroom with you and take a look." Mother is not willing to give in completely. She knows her daughter is a "kicker"—tossing and turning and kicking all night—and she knows she wouldn't get any sleep if she let her daughter stay—and then worse, it would then become a nightly ritual.

Mother yawns and pulls down her warm comforter. Sitting up, she nestles her bare feet into her soft, cuddly house shoes. She reaches for her housecoat, stands up, and fights to get her arms into the sleeves.

"Mommie, I'm not going in there."

"You'll be fine. There's no such thing as monsters."

The scared little girl quickly jumps into her mother's bed.

"Okay honey, I'll go look in your room first and see if the awful monster that glows in the dark is still there—and you, dear, don't you go to sleep on me, not in here. Not in my bed! You hear?"

"Yes, Mamma."

Mother ties her housecoat and carefully makes her way into the dark hallway on her way to her daughter's bedroom.

The little girl pulls the covers up to her chin and waits. She lays there attentive to the room, her eyes wide, fixed on the open door, trying to see into the murky darkness. A sliver of light streaks across the hallway wall—and then nothing else. Seconds pass; minutes pass. The little girl continues to stare intently at the open doorway.

Before long an hour has passed, maybe more. The sweet little girl sits up in bed and tugs on her father: "Daddy, Daddy, wake up, there's a monster in my room."

And so our little story ends there with no more to be told, for there was no "Shakespearean thunderstorm" and thus no reason for anything out of the ordinary to occur. Maybe Mother just fell asleep in her daughter's bed while she waited for the monster to show itself. Or maybe…it did.

The Inanimates

By Don Kirk

THE ATMOSPHERE had been calm and without the slightest breeze, but dark menacing clouds were beginning to swell overhead. Beautiful rays from the sun, like torch lights from Heaven, gradually decreased in number and the colors of the landscape became deep saturated hues of blues and greens and yellows in a surreal light. Then the blackest of blacks overtook the landscape. On a hilltop visible in the distance, silhouettes of people stood around a coffin perched on a stand as the clouds continued to close in overhead. The wind began to blow and the people began to turn and walk away. There was an eerie, yellow horizon beyond the dark clouds and flashes of bright light charged the sky with electricity. Something glittering, in what little sunlight was left, marched over the hill. Coming closer, and closer, was a row of huge silver forks, knives, and spoons.

Marching forward, steadily approaching, they were coming closer—rows and rows of forks, knives, and spoons—coming closer. They were attacking. An army of dinnerware bent on annihilating everything in its path. They seemed upset about something. The eerie pounding and clanging sounds of the looming silverware was suddenly broken by the rat-tat-tat of machine-gun fire as white smoke swallowed the atmosphere. Dark-red blood oozed from the forks and knives and spoons as they fell to the left and fell to the right, clattering harmlessly to the earth.

Oh, that irritating clatter. What the hell? My eardrums are exploding with an awful clanging. What is… that's what it is, that confounded alarm clock!

The two little silver bells on the top of the wind-up clock clattered violently.

Who the Hell set it on a Saturday? No, wait, this isn't Saturday. Damn, it's a frickin' Monday. Jonah reached over, straining to find that little slide switch on the back of his alarm clock, the one that would stop the clapper from beating the bells to death. He moved it, or so he thought, but the clock kept on clanging. He took the backside of his hand and raked it across the nightstand with abandon. The old timepiece took flight like the Wright's airplane, flying across the room, and colliding with the sheetrock wall. The inconsiderate, clangorous monster slowly died an unappreciated death allowing the room to return to its cheerful early-morning quiet.

Jonah lay there, cussing this dreaded Monday—fifty-two every year—thinking of the things he must do this day. Unfortunately, it was the same mundane things he had to do last week and the week before that.

All I gotta do is jump up quick, he thought to himself. *Just jump. Don't think about getting up. If I think about it I can't get up, I'll just lay here.* Jonah knew that from past experience, he was always thinking about something else when he actually got up, like the letter he had to file this day in bankruptcy court—there, he was up, on his feet.

Damn if it didn't work, he thought. Standing there in brightly colored boxer shorts, he kicked the alarm clock with his right foot, sending it back into the wall, and then he looked back to the bed to find Megan still sound asleep. *The friggin' alarm didn't faze her, didn't screw up that beauty sleep of hers, not one bit.*

Making his way to the dresser in his bare feet—across a ceramic tile floor that felt like glacial ice—Jonah changed direction at midcourse and found himself in the bathroom. He flipped on the glaringly cold florescent light over the sink and stared at his sullen face, *another lousy Monday, fifty-two in a year. When will it ever end? Day in and day out*—Jonah raised his leg to the toilet tank and slammed the flushing lever down with his foot. The lever snapped off and hit the floor with a resounding clang.

"God damn it! Cheap-ass crap."

He turned to the mirror over the lavatory sink and looked at the foggy, repulsive image of himself.

"No one should have to shave first thing in the morning," he grumbled.

"Huh, honey, what's that?" came Megan's voice from that dark space that was the other room—the room with that repulsive alarm clock.

Jonah stumbled back into the bedroom to retrieve a pair of socks from the dresser. He pulled on the top drawer's knobs, but the drawer edged sideways and jammed before it could be fully opened. Pulling hard on the knobs, Jonah forced it the rest of the way with an aching screech. A knob broke off in his hands.

"Damn! No one should have to get up on a Monday morning."—Jonah kicked at the dresser and stubbed his toe—"Ahhh, God damn!"

"Honey," uttered a voice from the bed, "Is anyone in your family sick?"

"No. Why do you ask?"

"Oh nothing, I had the weirdest dream. I think you were in it wearing a black suit at a funeral…"

"Ouch, damn it!" bellowed Jonah, as he stubbed the other toe on a leg of their double bed with the sagging mattress. He dropped onto the bed. It sagged even more. "I'm gonna cut the friggin' legs off this sorry-ass bed, make kindlin' of it! Burn it 'til there ain't nothing left but smoke and ashes."

"You can chop it to pieces with the biggest axe you can find *when* you get us a new one, dear."

Jonah re-entered the bathroom limping.

"Megan, MEGAN! Where're those new razor blades I bought last Saturday? I know I put them in here somewhere? Honey? YOU HEAR ME?"

"Don't know, dear." Megan turned over in the bed and buried herself in a cozy comforter.

"What are they doing here in the medicine cabinet?"

"Don't know, dear," came her muffled voice.

This wasn't Jonah's day. Monday never was. In fact, it was just last Monday that he got drunk and smashed up his car. Totaled it. He wasn't hurt, except for a few bruised ribs and superficial wounds, but his car went to that junkyard in the sky…and he had no insurance. And on the Monday before that, he had an argument with his wife's T-bone steak—it was too tough he said, gristly and overcooked—and he twisted his silverware in knots and threw each piece across the room. And that act broke the curved sheet of glass on the front of the china cabinet and shattered a few pieces of Megan's wedding china.

"Damn it all! I just bought this," cursed Jonah as he slammed down his shaving cream. He had pressed on the button and no white foam had oozed out. The bathroom was now saturated with sticky steam from the scalding water left running for so long.

"I'm out of shaving cream!" blasted Jonah.

"Honey, you can use soap," came the distant voice of Megan as she reluctantly threw off the covers, put on her pink terry-cloth robe, and made her way to the kitchen to fix Jonah's breakfast.

With some difficulty, Jonah forced a thin, new double-edged blade into the old *Gillette* razor. It was his father's razor, and probably his father's before him. The mirror, having completely fogged up, irritated Jonah and with his finger he maliciously slashed across his reflection. He turned off the torrid water and twisted the cold-water handle. Only one drop of water fell to the drain.

"Oh hell, what now?"

Jonah slowly lathered up the hand soap, finally accumulating enough to place on his sleepy, cheerless face so he could begin the usual regiment of shaving off his tough whiskers.

Carefully pulling the razor across his face, Jonah began to pay particular attention to the watchful reflection in the mirror that was starring intently back at him. He raised his chin to expose his neck, drawing the razor across the taught pink skin.

"Ahhh, mother!"

The sharp razor blade cut deep. Blood oozed from a painful gash.

"Damn, damn, damn!" was heard throughout the dark house as the razor, now in several pieces, slid across the tile floor. Jonah grabbed the whole toilet paper roll, breaking the holder as he violently pulled on it, and then wadded up a bundle of the toilet tissue, trying futilely to stop the bleeding on his chin. "You can have it all, the whole friggin' world."

"MEGAN!" roared Jonah, "To hell if I'm goin' to work today, damn!" He turned off the hot water and picked up the empty shaving-cream can in order to throw it away, but found, instead, as he pressed his index finger down on the valve, lots of bright glistening-white shaving cream billowing forth. He looked into the mirror again and stared with frustration and disbelief at the way the world was treating him. Jonah looked beyond his reflection and focused on the glass, and to him there seemed to be a smirk on the face in the mirror. The mirror was laughing at him! He was sure of it.

"Damn you, mirror!" he screamed.

Suddenly, a crack zigzagged its way across the mirror like ice breaking on a frozen pond. Jonah's eyes dilated in a fearful realization, but it was too late for him to react and the entire, oversized, mammoth mirror fell forward, falling slowly, deliberately, toward Jonah. He saw the image of himself in the mirror as it shattered into hundreds of pieces. As the mirror crashed down upon him, a shard of glass imbedded itself in Jonah's bared neck. He choked and gurgled and blood gushed from his pitiful mouth like a West-Texas oil well. Jonah grabbed at the glinting sliver of glass and tried to pull it free. A powerful spurt of blood shot into his eyes. Jonah's cynical eyes rolled back in his head and he fell backward, and twisting in agony, he collapsed face down across the open toilet bowl. A haunting laughter filled the room as bright crimson blood dribbled into the toilet water creating little radiating waves that clashed with each other. Then the room felt a calm, peaceful silence. The bathroom and the bedroom, in fact, the whole house seemed to be relieved, freed from its tormenter.

The toilet bowl suddenly flushed itself. It gurgled and hissed and the bloodstained water circled around and around and disappeared down a four-inch hole leading to another world.

Jonah lay slumped over the toilet bowl. His legs, twisted gruesomely, lay lifeless across the white-tiled floor. Shards of mirrored glass reflected the fractured world around it. And through the bathroom door, the bedroom still lay in darkness except for a ray of light coming into the room from the hallway. The eerie silence was finally broken by words that Jonah would never hear:

"Honey, breakfast is ready."   ★   ★   ★

Air Pocket

By Don Kirk
(Based on a Teleplay by Don Kirk, 1981)

OUR STORY BEGINS as two young dark-haired boys and a cute little golden retriever bound gleefully along a well-worn dirt path winding serpentine-like through a forest of tall trees. The boys, John and Richard Tucker, are spirited third graders who have just been released from school for the day, somewhere around 2:30 in the afternoon. They each carry a load of heavy schoolbooks and a ringed notebook with ruled paper and a clear plastic pouch chock full of No. 2 pencils, a leaky fountain pen, a red plastic pencil sharpener and a stick of chewing gum. The brothers do everything together; they are as close as any two brothers can be. John is barely ten months older than Richard, but that ten months makes him a good deal taller than his brother—it also makes him the boss.

"Come on Rick, you're falling behind!" shouts John.

"I got more papers to carry than you," retorts Richard.

The two boys come running out of the woods and approach a large body of standing water surrounded by dense foliage. It's the local swimming hole. The playful young golden retriever runs gleefully after them. A heavy rope of twisted strands of hemp hangs from the sprawling limb of a large, very old, oak tree and the grass on the bank is trampled down from over use. The boys stop beside each other and look out over the pond. The affectionate retriever sits down quietly beside them. It too surveys the pond and then looks up at the boys, waiting calmly for their next move.

The boys stare at the large stretch of beckoning water. The surface is smooth as glass, not a disturbing ripple in the surface, not the slightest breeze.

"Let's go in," says John.

"Mom said for us not to swim in the pond."

"Oh, that was just for last week," counters John, "This is another week."

"But," worries Richard, "that boy that drowned—"

"Oh, it's safe," John interrupts. "We've swimmed here lotsa times, hadn't we?"

"Uh, yeah."

"Well then?"

"I don't see none uh the other kids showin' up," counters Richard.

John throws down his burdensome schoolbooks, sits down on a big algae-covered rock and begins to remove his favorite white and black tennis shoes. The golden retriever jumps in joy and spins around, apparently he can't wait to go swimming either.

"They'll be here," says John. "You don't wanna be the last one in, DO YOU Richard?"

"No," replies Richard as he sits down on the edge of the bank to remove his worn shoes—shoes that have traveled untold miles around the small town of Bakersfield and have been with Richard through all of his adventures. Richard looks out at the water. It looks a little scary to him. It's a swimming hole apparently devoid of life, not a floating lily pad or jumping frog in sight.

"I got you beat," yells John as he pulls off his shirt and darts for the huge oak tree with the hanging rope.

"You started before me!" yells Richard. He hurries up his undressing—first his shirt then his jeans—and jumps to his feet and comes running. "I ain't gonna be last."

The golden retriever jumps into the water; he isn't going to try the swing.

John swings out over the water and at the apex of the swing, he lets go, falling, falling, falling, until he cracks the water's glassy surface. He makes a big explosive splash like that of a hundred-pound cannon ball. Richard climbs up on one of the oak tree's largest overhanging limbs. He grabs the returning pendulum and pushes away from the tree, swinging out in a huge arc, but he swings past the point where he's supposed to let go and the rope begins its swing back. Clinging tightly to the rope, Richard stares down at the deep, dark, creepy-looking water.

John, floating there in the pond, looks up at Richard with a devilish grin. "Come on Richard, let go!"

Richard, apprehensive, finally releases the rope with his fatiguing hands. To Richard, the fall seems like an eternity. Time slows down—he falls down—down—down, and finally, plunges through the water's surface, disappearing in the flash of an instant as if a bullfrog has reached out with its long, quick-as-lightening tongue and gobbled him up and swallowed him whole.

Richard finds himself in the dark depths of the haunting pool. His cheeks, ballooned out as if he has two oranges in his mouth, tries to hold his breath. His hair trails behind him as he sinks, deeper and deeper and deeper. Richard looks up to the surface and tries pulling himself up with his arms. He kicks with his feet. Can he make it before he runs out of oxygen? He can see sunlight flickering on the surface of the pond and rays of light dancing in the darkness of the depths below. *Am I close? Will I make it? I must not take a breath yet*, thinks Richard. Suddenly something grabs Richard, pulling him downward, away from any chance for survival. Richard fights for his dear life, his arms and legs flailing wildly. Panicked, he pulls free, propelling himself upward. It has been his brother John tugging on him, John not aware of the peril he was putting his brother in.

Richard's head breaks through the surface. He gasps for air, sucking the fresh oxygen deep into his lungs. John pops to the surface, a mischievous grin on his face.

"Why did you do that?" bellows Richard.

John just laughs.

The legs of the two boys move like a pair of scissors below the surface as they try to stay afloat and not sink into the deep dark depths of the spooky pond.

John and Richard—and their golden retriever—splash around in the water, having the time of their lives. Their long day at school is a forgotten memory; their homework, it can wait.

John swims to the shoreline and climbs out of the pond. He

makes his way onto the old oak tree once again, and swings out on the rope, a rope that has been there for generations. Thousand's of kids have probably enjoyed that two-hundred-year-old oak tree as it grew there quietly beside the alluring crystal-clear swimming hole—a pond that begs for company on this hot, sultry day. John drops into the water, barely missing Richard who is still floating in the water. With his arm, Richard shields his face from the splash. The powerful shower of water quickly recedes and Richard looks around for John—but he isn't anywhere to be seen. Everything becomes terribly quiet. Richard keeps looking, keeps waiting, but John doesn't reappear. Richard becomes as anxious as a cat lying next to a rocking chair.

"John?"

Suddenly the water erupts beside Richard. John's head comes splashing through the surface, his hair covering his eyes. Richard's eyes widen with astonishment and John wipes his soaking hair from his face:

"Richard! Richard!" babbles John in excitement. "I found something. You gotta see it!"

"Where?"

"Just down there, under the water," replies John. "Come on. It ain't far. Take a deep breath and follow me." John pulls on Richard, dragging him under. They both disappear below the surface of the water.

The boys swim downward. Down, down, down they go. The refraction of the sunlight on the water's surface projects patterns of undulating shadows on the silhouette of the two descending boys.

John and Richard swim down to the opening of a large corrugated drainage pipe that's projecting through the muddy, algae-covered earthen wall of the pond. John motions Richard to come in with him. Richard begins to panic and shakes his head. He strains to hold his breathe, the good air is dissolving into his lungs, leaving only the harmful carbon dioxide behind. John grabs him and pulls him in. They disappear into the pipe.

John and Richard swim through the large pipe against a current that spins them around like a washing machine and disorients them. They no longer know which way they are swimming. They swim toward a small round disc of light. The disc grows in size and they find themselves at the end of the pipe, and to their surprise, it is sticking out of a hill. A small amount of water dribbles out of the pipe. They find they can breathe and no longer seem to be under the water's surface, even though patterns of light from above still dance on them. Their shorts drip with water as if they have just climbed out of a swimming pool. The drainage pipe's opening is some distance above the ground so John has to turn around so he can climb out feet first. He grabs hold of the bottom edge of the pipe and then drops to the ground and then looks up at Richard.

"Come on Rich-ard," says John, "Don't be a scardy cat. I'll catch you." John raises his arms to catch his brother. Richard carefully turns around and lowers himself down, holding on to the pipe's edge, his feet dangling, searching for solid ground to stand on.

"I gotcha. Drop. Drop!" commands John.

John takes a step backward and lowers his arms as Richard drops to the ground. John makes no attempt to catch him.

John laughs and says, "Never trust nobody."

Richard then gets up from the ground, finds himself covered in muck, and glares at John. John grins back with his usual devilish grin. Richard turns to look at their discovery. John looks too. They stare with wide-eyed wonderment and a bewildered expression.

Sitting in front of them, wrapped in an overgrowth of aquatic plants, is a small town street that looks different from what they were used to. It looks abandoned. Dark green algae covers the ground with vines running thickly over and around the buildings. An unadorned country house with a front porch sits across from a one-pump *Conoco* service station. A general store with a sign that reads *Winn's* and a café called *Harrold's* lies just beyond. Painted on the screen door is the picture of a yellow-haired girl holding a loaf of *Wonderbread*. The aquatic plants are trampled down along the road in front of the buildings. Just beyond the buildings, the landscape disappears into nothingness. There is no horizon. The ground and sky merge into a soft-blue, shimmering cyclorama without edges. Waves of shimmering sunlight flow across the scene. It is eerily strange and mesmerizing to the boys. There are no birds chirping, or crickets, no sounds at all. It's as silent as the sounds of an underwater world.

John looks at Richard with amazement, his eyes wide with astonishment. "Wow!" he exclaims.

Richard tries to take a step and finds that his bare feet are mired in the mud. He works to pull his feet free. "Yuck!" His feet are tangled in the vines.

"Come on Richard, let's check it out."

John moves toward the little town and Richard follows, dragging the stringy vines after him.

John approaches the side of the country house and passes below a ladder that is leaning up against the side of the building. John stops at the front window and peers in. Richard joins him, cupping his hands around his eyes to block the reflection so he can see inside. John goes to the front door and puts his hand on the doorknob. He turns it slowly, ever so slowly. The door snaps free. John slowly pushes the door open and steps inside. Richard follows close behind, very close behind. The room is all neat and tidy as if someone is living there. There are no cobwebs or dirty floors as you would expect to find in an abandoned house. Old books snuggle neatly on a bookshelf and knickknacks sit quietly on a shelf over the door. A large rocking chair sits waiting to take someone into its arms and lull him to sleep. The room is bright and cheery and rays of light filter through the windows, softened by the loose weave of sheer muslin curtains.

John approaches the dining room table. The table is set with china and silverware. John picks up an elegant cut-glass drinking tumbler and examines it: the colors of the rainbow are refracted through it.

"Wow! Neat huh?" says John as he hands the tumbler to Richard.

"Yeah," replies Richard as he stares intently at it, his face looking warped through the cut glass. "Neat-O!"

John then blurts out, "Look! Look! Over here." Richard comes running over to the bookshelf. On the shelf is a stack of comic books, all from the 1950's, *Superman*, *Spiderman* and even *Batman*. There are *Uncle Scrooges* and *Archies* and even *Jugheads*. John grabs up the stack of comic books and turns to Richard:

"We've hit a gold mine, look, *Donald Duck* and *Casper the Friendly Ghost*! First editions, they're worth millions and millions of dollars! We're rich! Wow! Wait'll the kids at school see this!"

Puzzled, Richard says, "But those comic books aren't ours."

"Finders keepers, losers weepers," replies Richard.

Suddenly, the excitement of the moment crashes to a halt as a bright light moves across their faces and across the wall and then disappears. John quickly returns the comic books to the bookshelf. He dives to the floor and crawls to the window. Richard is left holding the water glass, so instead of jumping to the floor, he carefully takes the glass back to the table, sets it down in its original spot, and walks to the window and kneels down. They both peer out of the window, confused and afraid about what might be happening.

Through the window, the boys can see across the street to the service station where an old white Chevy convertible with a red stripe along its side has driven up next to the gas pump. It has a badly bent-up chrome grill and smashed headlight. A pretty middle-age woman with a beehive hairdo sits in the driver's seat motioning toward the office in an attempt to get the attendant's attention. She is loud and boisterous as if she has been drinking too much.

The boys look at each other in bewilderment.

"Come on," says John, "let's get outta here. There's people in this town!"

They get up and head for the door. John peers around the doorframe of the open door.

"Let's go," says Richard, "I'm scared."

"Okay, follow"—John remembers something—"Wait!"

John heads over to the bookshelf and grabs up the comic books—as many as he can carry—and returns to the front door.

"Okay Richard, all clear, let's go." John rushes out the door and Richard follows, but as they try to slip around to the side of the house, they hear the woman calling out: "Hey, you boys!"

Richard stops in his tracks, but John continues around the corner out of sight.

The woman leans forward, putting her elbows on top of the car door.

"Come here, son. It's all right."

John looks out from around the corner of the house.

"You too son, I won't hurt you. My name's Aunt Marietta."

Both John and Richard step out into the street, but walk together, standing shoulder to shoulder. John strains to hold the comic books behind his back.

"Well now, you boys are new here aren't you?" asks the lady who's wearing a hefty amount of makeup and black eyelashes as long as porcupine quills.

The two boys turn to look at each other and then nod a slow "yes."

She picks up a silver liquor flask off the seat and says, "Well— welcome. Would you boys like a drink?"

"Uh, no ma'am."

"Okay then, have it your way." The woman turns away, starts her car, and drives off. She apparently has forgotten about the gas she needs. The boys stand alone in the street, dumbfounded.

From down the street comes a young boy rolling a hoop with a stick. He runs behind the hoop, keeping it rolling almost straignt down the street. He passes John and Richard, paying no attention to them. The two boys stare in amazement.

"Boy, we're gonna have to try that when we get back home."

Suddenly, there is the sound of splashing water from above. The boys look up in the sky to see the feet of their golden retriever as it paddles frantically around in circles on the surface of the pond.

"He's looking for us!" says Richard in amazement.

"Huh?"

"Come on." Richard turns and heads for the ladder that was leaning up against the side of the house. He reaches for a rung and begins to climb.

"Wait Rich, I can't go yet. My comic books will get wet!"

"Leave 'em!" says Richard.

"Just wait a minute. I have to find something to put them in to keep them dry."

John runs away from the ladder and disappears around the building. Richard looks back up toward the surface of the pond and continues to climb. The golden retriever continues to paddle just above him. Richard reaches for the dog, and after some effort grabs a leg. The dog sticks its head into the water to see what's pulling on it.

Richard thinks he hears John's voice calling out, "Richard! Richard! Rick!" as the dog wraps his snout around Richard's arm and pulls him to the surface of the water. The golden pulls Richard toward the shoreline. Richard crawls on shore, exhausted, and sits next to their clothes and schoolbooks. He tries to clear his head and ears of water and then he looks out over the pond. He looks down at John's clothes and then back at the pond. The retriever barks at the pond like it's an unwelcome cat, and then trots back to Richard who wraps his arm around his dog. The golden retriever looks out over the pond, tilting his head as if bewildered. The pond looks calm and quiet; it seems harmless, the surface smooth as glass. Not a ripple, not a wave, not a splash. And nothing in the woods is stirring, not even a bird or squirrel or lizard—

Suddenly, something pops up through the water's surface and a glint of sunlight is reflected from it. The golden retriever jumps to its feet and barks with joy. Richard stands up to get a better look. It's a stack of comic books wrapped in cellophane. A sigh of relief comes over Richard. The dog jumps into the water and swims for the bag. He paddles and paddles, gradually coming closer and closer to the shinny plastic bag. It carefully takes the bag in its mouth and turns back toward the shore.

Richard takes the bag of comic books from the Golden and it returns to his side. They stare silently out over the water. And wait and wait. Nothing stirs and nothing else pops to the surface. Richard can just make out the little town shimmering just below the surface of the pond and the town seems to have a new resident: the lady in the white convertable has a passenger—and it's John.

Be Quiet Now, Dear

By Don Kirk

MARY LOGAN SAID *her husband's business was headed for bankruptcy. A Chapter 7 would shut his doors, they'd have to move, and their two girls would have to be taken out of school. Isn't that awful dear? And Mildred Henner is going to get promoted over me and she doesn't deserve it. I've been there twice as long as she has. She kisses the boss's behind and I won't do that. Honey, could you get my hand cream for me, it's on the bedroom dresser and could you make me some hot chocolate and then…*I couldn't get her out of my mind. I couldn't get her voice out of the deep recesses of my throbbing head. She was driving me craaazy!

I closed the coffin lid down on her lifeless body.

Her sweet little mouth was closed—shut tight.

She was dressed in white. I had placed her soft blond hair neatly over her shoulders. I had matched her favorite red pumps with her white pearl necklace that I had placed carefully around her soft inviting neck. It was dark now, the moon was full and she was quiet. I shoveled a bit of mother earth on top of her. I dug in for another spade full and threw it in the grave; it washed over the vaulted casket lid. I slung another shovel, and another, and another. She wasn't speaking to me now. No, not any more. Talk, talk, talk, jabber, jabber, jabber—she was always talking. She talked while we watched a movie, while we ate out, while I tried to do my morning constitution. She talked—and only *she* talked. When we went out with friends they could never get a word in edgewise—the spaces between sentences were as thin as a knife's edge. She even struck up a conversation with strangers on the street—and kept talking until they walked off. I could never pull her away. She said that was rude, *don't push me*, she said. She flirted with every person that came within speaking distance and eventually ran off everyone she ever met with her talk, talk, talk. I often tried to pull her away and she'd just say, "I'm having fun. Don't mess with me." At restaurants—during the entire meal—she conversed with people at the *other* tables and I had to do my best to keep the managers from throwing us out on our ears. She, to say the least, embarrassed me. She was like an alcoholic: obstinate and inconsiderate to others like a drunk would be,even though she rarely actually took a drink. And when she did take a drink, there was no difference in her behavior. Her blood *was* alcohol.

Finally, I quit going places with her.

I tried to spend my evenings in a different room from where she usually was—at opposite ends of the house—but I could still hear her blabbing on the telephone for hours on end.

And the worst of it, she talked in her sleep. Bla, bla, bla—every friggin' night.

Well she's not talking anymore.

And she's not flirting with men anymore—she can flirt with the worms for all I care. Though I'm sure her talking would eventually run *them* off. But no, she can't talk now; she can't talk ever again. Her sweet little mouth is closed tight. I know because I used a curved suturing needle and laced her lips together. Her plump little lips sewn together tight as a Victorian corset. She won't be blabbing to anyone—anymore.

I had kept her for awhile tied down to a dining room chair, a chair I had to nail to the floor. She squirmed, squealed, and glared at me with those vicious, dagger eyes, but I took care of her. I fed her soup through a straw as long as I could, but she wasn't happy—because she couldn't gab.

I threw another shovel of soil on her coffin. The full moon gave me just enough light to finish the job. The other guests in the cemetery, I wondered what they thought about their new company. She was pretty, I admit that. Definitely pretty, but she had a mouth on her, backed up by an intolerance of others. It was her way and no other way. Dare you suggest an alternative, dare you disagree with her, dare you disobey. She believed in unquestioning obedience, loved to give orders, and yet she didn't want anyone to tell *her* what to do. She even supported government control over our lives like any good right-wing liberal, and yet she defied anyone who disagreed with her. I couldn't figure it.

I threw the last of the dirt on her grave and patted it down. I neatly placed the grass sod back on top, but I didn't know what I was going to do with the rotting corpse that now lay beside me, the one I had removed from the coffin so my lovely wife could have a new home. The corpse was the remains of a woman, Charlene Dauer; that was the name chiseled on her headstone. But now, what was I going to do with this wrinkled-up carcass? Maybe I could dig up another grave and put her there? But then what would I do with *that* corpse? Put it in still another grave? That would be a never-ending task, something I wasn't up for. I had better things to do in the evenings.

Weeks had passed and I had decided to remarry—though it wasn't with the good graces of a prist or judge: we simply lived together—happily. I had finally found the ideal woman. She was quiet and unassuming; she was undemanding. She, frankly, didn't ask for much. I could live in my house in peace. I put down the mystery novel I was reading and turned off my bedside-table lamp. The moon shone brightly through the bedroom curtains as I rolled over to my sweet loving new wife and put my arm around her, around Charlene—around her lovely decomposing body. I said "Goodnight Darling" and she didn't say a thing. The perfect woman.

The Dogcatcher's Catch

By Don Kirk

CAGES RATTLED, dogs barked. A cute little snow-white kitten was curled up in a corner of a huge steel cage; a cage built for a German Shepherd or Doberman. In fact, circling an adjoining cage, with head down, distraught and hungry, was a tall, lanky, black Doberman with brown markings. In another cage, a tiny flat-nosed Pekinese sat calmly sniffing the air and then licking its paws.

Without warning, all the cages tilted and the animals were thrown sideways and then thrown to the front as an invisible force jerked them around, forcing them against the walls of the cages. The cages were made of steel wire mesh so heavy and closely woven that escape wasn't possible, even by the little white kitten. The cute thing was scared. What had happened to her mother? She was now in an environment she had never experienced before, though most of life on earth was still new to her. Only minutes earlier, the kitten was romping through tall green blades of grass where she had fun sneaking through it and surprising her mother. She could remember her mother's warm body. And she was so hungry, but her cries for help were not heard. Where was mommy?

Suddenly, there was the crash of a small cage against another. A whimpering old hound dog, with his large floppy ears and sad face, was shoved into a smelly cage on the back of the beat-up flatbed truck. The cages, stacked two high and in two rows, clattered loudly and incessantly. The hot air of a Sunday afternoon in June blew the fluffy white hair of a very frightened kitten. On the top of the cages lay a tin roof to shade the animals. A spare tire hung on the rear of the truck with a black plastic cover that read "VACCINATE AND RESTRAIN YOUR PET." Above the words of advice was a portrait of a cheerful cat and dog cuddling up to one another.

"Where's mommy?" the fearful kitten wondered out loud.

"Horror, horror," spoke a deep pathetic voice.

The black, long-snouted Doberman looked around to see who had dared to speak—but then no other words were said.

The truck again started forward, the invisible force now pulling all of them to the rear. The Doberman was almost knocked off his long spindly legs. *Bang*—The old Ford truck backfired, choking black smoke replacing the clean air.

"Oh, my aching carcass."

"Who said that?" demanded the Doberman, a dog known by his fellow pack members a "Dobie."

"You speaking to me, sir?" asked a small but heavy looking dog with a black and white coat and long brown drooping ears and the saddest of eyes.

"You!"—Dobie focused on the new member of the outcast— "You! You know you mustn't speak around humans."

"Fiddle on that. What does it matter anyhow, we're all hamburger," responded the distraught Basset Hound.

"Don't you mean 'dog meat'," blurted out a sleek, pure white dog with black spots—a large Dalmatian about eight hands high.

Dobie's pointed ears perked up as his long snout turned to see who else had chosen to break the animal code.

"Yeah, dog meat grilled over a hot fire," continued the Dalmatian. "We're on death row, mates."

The cute white kitten curled up tighter; the Doberman noticed.

"Hay, watch it buster," snapped Dobie. "See the kitty. She heard you!" Dobie turned to the kitten, "It's okay little one; he was only joshing you. He's a mean, inconsiderate old dog. Pay him no mind."

"You can take that to the bank, Little One," asserted the Basset Hound, his long ears flopping every which way. "We're all gonna be fine."

"Don't sugar coat it pal," exclaimed the Dalmatian. "We're toast, like peanuts roasting in an oven!"

"Stop with that or I'll tear the arteries out of your pitiful neck," threatened the Doberman. "Can't you see the Little One is scared out of her mind?"

"I never did like felines no how," responded the Dalmatian. "They're a pain in the arce. And the little ones, they're real messy. Cute, humph!"

"You two cut it out, I can't take this bickering," interrupted the Hound. "It only makes my migraine worse. And this buckboard ride isn't doing my body a bit o' good either. I got rheumatism in every bone in my pitiful body. Even in my aching canines."

"When was the last time you cleaned your canines on a good T-bone, old man!" snapped the Doberman.

"Barf on your own turf, nose job!" retorted the Hound.

The little, long-haired Pekinese spoke for the first time: "You boys aren't related are you, 'cause you both musta been kicked out of the same litter."

"And who are you, Lady Flat Face?" barked the Dalmatian. "Did someone drop you out of a ten-story window face first?"

"What's eating you Mr. Downer, fleas or just life in general?" barked the hound.

"Buster, in case you haven't noticed, this ain't no ride to Disneyland,"—and looking to the primping Pekinese—"and you madam, ain't goin' to no dog show."

The Ford truck jerked to a halt again. A large fat man with a belly that was causing him to walk with an arched back, climbed laboriously from the cab. He unhooked a long staff with a loop of cord on the end and lumbered into a fenced yard where he met a middle-aged lady.

"The thing's here, officer, in the squirrel cage. I caught it with a bowl of milk."

"Nice job, lady."

"It don't have no tags, and don't look like it's eaten in a long time."

"Ma'am, I'll take care of that scrawny alley cat for you, don't you worry."

The four caged dogs—and one frightened little kitten—watched as the dogcatcher opened the cage and caught the cat in his noose. It was a calico with a white coat splashed heavily with black and brown; quite ugly except for the large white whiskers and piercing, emerald green eyes. After some doings, the cat was dangling from the catcher's pole, spread eagle, scratching at thin air. The tenacious dogcatcher brought the squirming cat to the cage next to the Dalmatian's cell and forced it inside.

The Dalmatian was the first to speak, "My, my, a cat's gettin' her due."

"Enough," blurted out the Basset Hound, "go find a dog house to climb in! Ain't you got no respect?"

"Right you are," agreed the big black Doberman.

The new cat on the block, surrounded by mean old dogs, arched her body and raised the hair on her back. The dogs all stared at her and showed their teeth. She stared back with her piercing emerald eyes, ready to take them on.

The tension was broken as Little One raised her cute head and whimpered, "Meow."

This drew the attention of Emerald Eyes, the calico, who raised her head and peered at this sad, lost and homeless, white furball.

"What's that sweet thing doin' here?" demanded Emerald Eyes.

"You askin' us?" jeered the Dalmatian.

"Meow," whined Little One.

"It'll be all right sweetie."

"Don't you know where we're headed, missy?" barked the Hound.

"It's not a fun place," spoke Lady Flat Face.

Emerald Eyes looked over at the female canine that was licking her coat with her tongue and asked, "You going to a dog show?"

All the other dogs snickered.

"My white hair is shedding something fierce! There's no hope," mumbled the Dalmatian.

"Quit your complaining, Mr. Downer!"

"Quit calling me 'Mr. Downer'? My name's Firehouse!"

"Well, whoop-dee-do!" exclaimed the Basset Hound.

Firehouse continued, "Do you fellas know that my grandfather worked for a fire station. And my ancestors were coach dogs."

"Coach dogs, what in tarnation are they?" asked the Hound.

"Their job was to walk alongside horse-drawn coaches and fend off any highwaymen who tried to rob their master."

"Well!" spouted the Doberman proudly. "I'm a pure-bred German guard dog, also trained to protect my master."

"Well, where's your master now?" interjected the Hound.

The proud Doberman with his smooth coat and docked tail, looked at him with dejected eyes and turned away.

The kitten, white as snow, clawed the cage until it got the attention of Emerald Eyes: "Oh honey, when we get out of here, I'll help you find your mother."

Dobie looked at Firehouse, "What's she talking about, gettin' outta here?"

"She don't know nothin'," said Firehouse, "just an annoying thorn in my tender paw."

Emerald Eyes circled the cage once and lay down. Her eyes stared out at the passing street scene. Her deep light-green eyes began to glow weirdly. Looking into a cat's eyes, you always knew they understood more than they let on. Now it seemed as if this cat was going to do something more than we knew it could do—

Seemingly out of nowhere, a scrawny tomcat, with tail high in the air, entered a crosswalk at the street intersection up ahead. Half way across the street, the cocky cat stopped for a moment and turned to look at the dogcatcher's truck barreling down on it. Brakes began squealing and smoking, locked tires bounced off the pavement and all the animals were thrown to the front. Another car swerved, finding itself in front of the skidding truck. The crunch of metal cut through the air. Radiator antifreeze spewed into the air like Old Faithful at Yellowstone.

The animals slowly came to their senses, wondering what on earth had happened—except Emerald Eyes, she knew. They poked their noses through the wire mesh in an effort to get a peek at what was happening up ahead. The truck's hood was bent upward and steam engulfed the scene. The fat dogcatcher was conversing—well, arguing—with the other vehicle's driver, his arms flailing violently.

"Now's our chance!" screamed Emerald Eyes.

"What are you doin', cat?" demanded Firehouse.

Emerald Eyes pushed her paw through the wire mesh, curled it inward, and quite easily pushed up on the bar latch. The door came open. The alley cat climbed onto the outside of the cage and made her way over to Little One's prison cell. The little kitten jumped with excitement as Emerald Eyes opened her cage. Little One sprung out of the cage and fell onto the pavement. Emerald Eyes jumped down and pushed the kitten with her nose to see if she was okay and then climbed back up the cage to release the Doberman. The other dogs watched in amazement.

"Forget what I said about cats," said Firehouse.

Emerald Eyes went to pick up Little One by the nape of the neck. Just then Dobie saw a car racing toward them. He made one big leap and grabbed Emerald Eyes by her neck and pulled them both aside as the car zoomed by.

"Phew, that was close," sighed Hound Dog.

"Hey, what about us?" barked Firehouse.

Dobie turned his head back to the "boys" and then back to Emerald Eyes who was strolling with Little One down the street, their tails high in the air. Then he looked at the dogcatcher still arguing with the driver. Dobie stood up on his hind legs and reached for the latch. Pushing with his black wet nose, he raised the bar, and the door came open. The no-longer-sad-faced Basset Hound, jumped free, carefully trying not to jar his tired old bones. Dobie looked over at Firehouse. Firehouse stared back silently. Dobie moved toward the cage, jumped up, and in a single move, released the latch. Firehouse grinned.

They all scurried down the street toward the felines and came up on each side. Firehouse spoke: "Little One, all of us will help you find your mama!"

The cute little kitten looked up at Firehouse and smiled. They all walked into the sunset, all their tails wagging, even the Doberman's little knob of a tail—

And then a twenty-ton *ReadyMix* cement truck ran over all of them—

Cute stories are for cute kids.

Henry

By Don Kirk
(Based on a teleplay by
Richard Kirschenbaum & Don Kirk, 2001)

IT WAS 1974 and the Vietnam War was winding down. Nostalgia was growing for the days of rock & roll and ABC had launched a sitcom called "Happy Days" loosely based on George Lucas' hit movie *American Graffiti*. While the rest of the country was caught up in nostalgia for those glorious days—its music, it's culture, its clothing—a lonely man by the name of Henry Hayward was having his own adventure with the past.

Henry Hayward sat in the driver's seat of his 1941 Buick; its red leather seats and chrome dash made it quite handsome looking. But it was only partially restored, a work-in-progress, a long work-in-progress. The dull pearl-white classic was in a closed, two-car garage located at the back alley of a lot with a modest 1940's wood-frame home. The wood-frame garage had exposed wall studs that revealed that the outside walls were covered with clapboard siding. A large collection of old movies recorded on videotape were shelved on the garage wall. There was a sizeable collection of mechanic's tools: socket sets, screwdrivers, crescent wrenches and engine rebuilding tools. There was an old round-topped refrigerator where Henry kept a stock of his favorite refreshments—*Cream Soda, A&W Rootbeer, Delaware Punch, Big Red*—and the usual sundry of dusty garage junk, stuff that hadn't, and probably never would be used. Only an estate sale would rid this garage of its burden. Hanging on the wall was an old café clock circled in pinkish neon tubing. Its long black hands pointed to 11:35. A *Farmer's Almanac* calendar showed the date to be Friday, June 13th. Henry was relaxed as he watched a video of an old movie on an antique black & white television set that sat on a tall stand in front of his car. He had the driver's seat reclined and could barely see over the steering wheel. Sucking through a peppermint-stripped straw, Henry drank a *Big Red* out of an original glass soda-pop bottle. *Big Red* was his favorite carbonated soft drink. Henry Hayward, an average man lost in his past, wore a black leather jacket and brown, pleated slacks. He had the windows of his Buick rolled up: apparently it was a bit chilly late at night in this un-insulated garage.

Henry was thirty-nine years old, weighed in at a hundred-seventy pounds, had dark brown hair that looked almost black, and he had lifeless brown eyes. He stood at five-foot, eight-and-one-half inches, and considered himself to have extraordinary good looks, but the rest of the world would likely not agree with that assessment.

Henry began to nod off in the middle of the movie, but quickly came to his senses to find himself witnessing—through the closed right window—a young guy and girl smooching in a parked car to his right, a black 1955 Mercury. Henry found himself peering into a drive-in movie theatre in the 1950's past, the heyday of the outdoor drive-in. The young man, 22 years old, good looking, obviously from old money, sat in the driver's seat of the Mercury trying to get more than just a sweet kiss out of the young lady in a pink cashmire sweater who sat in the passenger seat. She was a beautiful wide-eyed brunette not yet out of her teen years. Henry stared, thrilled at the scene he was witnessing. The cute inexperienced girl tried to push the boy away, but he wouldn't quit. The young man began to get rough with her. He put his hands around the girl's exposed neck. Henry sat up, intent and concerned about what was happening. He could not hear her screams through the closed window. It all appeared quite unreal. The young man squeezed tighter, the girl loosing her ability to fight back. Finally she went limp. The preppy boy had choked the life out of her; her life draining into oblivion, or maybe into a glass bottle, or maybe just catapulted straight to Heaven. Henry heard only the soundtrack of the movie he was watching, the movie story continuing as if nothing had happened. Henry stared at the murder scene, mesmerized as if he had just watched another movie on the other side of a glass partition—until the spell was broken—

Judy Tremain—Henry's live-in lady friend, cute, in her thirties, wearing a short white pleated skirt, and dedicated to her older boyfriend—broke the spell as she came through the side door to the garage. Judy motioned to Henry to come to dinner. Henry stared, then came to his senses. He nodded to Judy. All traces of the outdoor drive-in scene were gone. The movie was still playing on his TV screen in front of the car just as before.

Henry and Judy sat across from each other at a modest dinner setting in an unadorned dining area off the kitchen. They engaged in what Henry considered mundane conversation:

"Jan says we can move into her house next month when she leaves—"

Henry continued to eat stringy spaghetti—with a couple of greasy meatballs thrown in—without saying a word.

"Oh, it's so pretty out there," fantasized Judy. "Birds, and rabbits, and squirrels. You think you can find a job up there, Henry?"

Henry looked up, his mouth full, a noodle hanging down several inches from his lower lip, "Uh, yeah."

"We can finally have a place for the kids to play."

Henry froze in mid-eating, "Kids, what kids?"

"Y-o-u k-n-o-w!" said Judy cunningly. She smiled sweetly and twisted her fork in her plate of spaghetti, then brought the gob of food to her mouth.

The next evening Henry tried to repeat the frightening vision he saw the night before. Did it really happen? Or was he only dreaming a nightmarish tale. Late at night, back in his garage where he liked to spend his evenings after Judy had gone to bed, Henry put the tape back into the VCR. On the edge of the cassette was hand-lettered: MURDER IN A HOUSE ON SIXTH STREET. Henry liked thrilling tales of horror and mayhem. As a child he enjoyed watching old movies on a Saturday night, back when the local networks would show the monster movies and sci-fi films all through the night. He and his sister would stay awake as long as they could to see as many movies as possible, but his younger sister would never last—sound asleep long before the last movie ended, but any movie *Henry* started, he had to finish, no matter how bad it was.

Henry fast-forwarded to the scene where the vision had appeared before, but he stopped the tape near the end of that scene. Henry grabbed his *Big Red* with his long peppermint-colored straw and climbed back into his classic Buick. He looked out of the corner of his eye to the closed right window where he saw the vision before, but nothing seemed to be happening. No vision, no replay of the murder he witnessed the night before. Had he only been dreaming? Henry, impatient, got out of the car—spilling his drink on the floor—and rewound the tape further to the beginning of the scene and tried again.

Henry Hayward took a sip from his *Big Red* as he watched the movie again—and again he glanced over repeatedly to see if anything was happening in the passenger-side window. Finally, there it was: a young man put his hands around a girl's neck and choked the life out of her. The young man then calmly, nonchalantly, got out of the car and walked toward the refreshment stand. Henry leaned over trying to see the face of the young man as he walked away between the cars, but he saw only the back of his head with its dark brown hair. Then he noticed the white, pin-stripped shirt and an unusual waist belt: a wide black leather belt with serpents stamped on it. Henry looked back to the black Mercury. The dead girl's head lay against the top of the seat, staring straight at Henry:her beautiful fresh face, eyes wide open, her mouth parted slightly as if in a comfortable sleep. Images from the drive-in movie screen flickered on her once luminous, now less-than-serene face. Henry stared in a trance for moments, maybe minutes, maybe more, but then reached over to roll down the window. As he slowly turned the crank, the window lowered and the drive-in-scene disappeared revealing only the wood studs, and a lawn chair hanging on the garage wall.

Henry climbed out of his Buick and left the garage by the bi-fold doors, leaving the TV and the garage light on, just a bare incandescent bulb hanging from a rafter. He was dumbfounded by what he had just seen. Was he going crazy? This was no dream—dreams rarely happen twice and never in the same way. Henry closed the doors and latched them. The light from inside was choked off, leaving him in a world of darkness.

A plate of food was lifted from the dining room table. Judy placed the dish by the kitchen sink along with the rest of the other dirty dishes and walked to the living room.

"Henry, you've been so quiet lately. What's wrong dear? Henry?"

Henry paid no attention to her as he took a small cast-resin statue off of a nick-knack shelf. It was of an ape sitting on a stack of books by Darwin, the ape contemplating the white human skull it held in its hand. Henry sat down with it on his favorite leather, arm chair—well, except for the seat in his '41 Buick—and stared intently at the statue. Judy pulled up the matching ottoman and sat down on it facing Henry, her knees together, her elbows on her knees, her cupped hands holding her chin up.

"Henry? You spend too much time in that garage. Henry, look at me, are you depressed about something?"

Henry finally responded: "See this ape. He's deep in thought."

"Henry Hayward, you need to see a doctor," scolded Judy. "Jan's got one you can call." Henry didn't reply. Judy, disgusted, got up and left the room. Henry got up from his chair, returned the statue to the shelf, and quietly, without a word, retreated to his '41 Buick in the garage. This was his world.

Henry was convinced that what he had seen was real. It must have been, he wasn't crazy, he was aware of the world around him; he could react to it. He didn't hear voices in his head; he was sure of that. Henry put in the VCR tape, fast forwarded it to the same scene in the movie, jumped in the car with his *Big Red* soft drink, and as he watched the movie he kept glancing over to the passenger window to see if the vision would re-appear—but nothing happened. He became frustrated as if he hadn't gotten his nightly fix. He was irritated as if things weren't going his way.

Henry jumped out of the car and rewound the tape, repeating the entire process, and still nothing happened. Henry grabbed another video cassette that still sat by the VCR; one that he had watched last week, a thriller called *Night Sweats*. He attempted to repeat everything he did the first time he saw the vision, down to the way he poured his *Big Red* into an old soda-pop bottle, the way he moved his seat all the way back, the way he adjusted the rearview mirror so glare from headlights wouldn't hit it even though he was just in his garage. Henry became tired and about ready to give up for the night when the vision appeared for the third time: the young man put his hands around the girl's neck and choked the life out of her. The murderer then calmly, nonchalantly, got out of the car and walked toward the refreshment stand. Then a security guard passed on the far side of the 1955 Mercury apparently looking for gate crashers. He was in his forties, with week-old whiskers, and wore a greasy baseball cap. He was probably the one that did all the maintenance chores at the drive-in and he was the one that, during shows, enjoyed trying to catch non-paying customers—especially teenagers hidden in a car's trunk. His flashlight scanned the interior of the black Mercury, but just missed illuminating the inanimate dead girl's face. The security guard didn't notice that anything was amiss; he saw only the back of her head. Henry frantically reached over to roll down the driver's window to alert the security guard of the girl's condition, but as the window retracted, the image of the murdered girl in the car was again replaced by the garage wall. Henry quickly rolled the window back up, hoping—but the vision was gone; he saw only his own reflection in the window. Henry climbed out of his '41 Buick, drink in hand, and walked around the front of the car to the right side. He stared for a long time at the narrow empty space between his car and the garage wall.

Henry lay on the living room couch, hands behind his head, focused on the ceiling. An old *Hunter* ceiling fan turned slowly and Henry listened to the drone of the motor as it laboriously tried to get its five wooden blades around one more time. Bluish moonlight was sliced up in long strips as it forced it's way through the Venetian blinds. Henry turned over on his side, curling up into a fetal position—and fell asleep.

The young man put his hands around the pretty girl's neck, squeezing tighter and tighter, and choked the life out of her. The young man then calmly, nonchalantly, got out of the car and walked toward the refreshment stand. Henry opened the driver's door to his Buick, climbed out, and found himself in a 1950's drive-in. He *was* there in the past. There was gravel on the ground. There was a movie playing on a big outdoor screen. Cars—a mustang, a Ford Fairlain, a '49 Cadillac Coupe de Ville and many other classics, all in a row, their noses pointed up toward the screen. In that drive-in, where a horrible crime had just occurred, Henry crossed in front of his Buick, the movie playing on the screen behind him and the mono soundtrack echoing, out-of-sink, through hundreds of tinny speakers. He then crossed in front of the black '55 Mercury with its white side-walls, polished chrome hubcaps, powerful waterfall grill that looked like the grinning metal teeth of a monster, and approached the passenger side of the Mercury. His figure blocked some of the rays of light from the projector, his shadow projected on the bottom of the big outdoor screen.

"Out of the way, buster!"

Henry bent over and peered into the window to view the dead girl. He saw the back of her silky brunette head. She looked peaceful. Henry reached in to touch her, but paused, and pulled back. *This can't be real*, he thought. *I'm not here. Wake up. WAKE UP!"*

"He'll be here any minute; we've got to go," said the character on the screen.

"If we don't find the murder weapon we can't prove anything!"

"Sixth Street will become a Hell, a neighborhood of dead people."

The girl's murderer looked back at the theatre screen, trying not to miss too much as he bought a small box of popcorn and a large drink in a paper cup at the brightly-lit refreshment stand. He appeared to be the only customer there. The clerk placed his purchase in a cardboard tray; one of those with four round holes that expand to hold the cups tightly and a rectangular place for a bag of *Doritos* or a plate of hot cheese nachos. Henry stood up, looked toward the snack bar and then back at the dead girl. The murderer began his walk back to his car, the light from the movie flickering on him. Henry tried to open the passenger door to the Mercury, but the door lock was down. The gravel of the drive-in crunched under the murderer's feet. Henry reached through the open window to raise the lock. The young, innocent looking, murderer lifted the drink cup out of its cardboard holder. He passed another car; a guy and girl were necking, oblivious to the movie. The murderer returned his drink to his tray. A *Big Red* logo was printed on the paper cup. Henry looked toward the refreshment stand, looking for the murderer, but he was blinded by the glare of the projector light as movie images danced on his face. He then pulled on the door. It snapped open slightly, only very slightly, and the girl's body slid toward the door. If he opened it more, the girl would fall out, if he didn't open it wider, the security guard would surely not see her. Henry looked to see if the security guard was approaching—he did last night in the garage—there—there he is, his flashlight moving back and forth, pointing into each car. Henry ducked, and then sneaked around the front of the Mercury and back to his car, quietly closing the driver's door. The Security guard came by the far side of the Mercury, scanned his flashlight, but again he did not see the dead girl. *I must catch this murderer*, thought Henry, *while he's young, before he kills again and again, becoming a dreaded serial killer.*

Henry found himself awakened by Judy. It was late in the morning, very late, causing another argument with Judy.

"Wake up Henry. You sleep all day and watch movies in that awful garage all night. You don't spend any time with me."

"Huh, what?"

"You don't get your work done—"

"I'm sorry honey, but—"

"But what, Henry? Do you know I'm here? It's me, your—"

"It's you, my Judy—"

"I don't know what I am to you. I've had enough, entirely enough. I'm packing my bags, this is it; I'm going to Jan's. For all

I care, you can live in that worthless garage for the rest of your worthless life!"

Henry stared at himself in the bathroom mirror.

Later that day Henry found himself looking in the store windows downtown. He was ambling aimlessly when he noticed his own reflection in the display windows instead of the dressed-up mannequins he was looking at. He stared at his reflection, in deep thought, in another world, not that of most of us. Henry didn't seem to notice that the display in the window was of a Victorian suited man with a black beaver top hat, long tailcoat and a large axe. The axe was raised over his head; he appeared ready to chop off the head of a beautiful maiden in a white linen dress. Henry realized he was in front of a wax museum and turned away ever so slowly and stepped into the street. Out of the corner of his eye, Henry saw something that got his full attention: a pin-stripped shirt and a wide, black-leather belt with serpents stamped on it. Henry turned to look only to see no sign of the man who was wearing this familiar outfit.

Henry cruised down main street in his dull white 1941 Buick with its red upholstery and chrome fenders, but he was oblivious to the cityscape passing before him.

He pulled up to a large Greek looking monstrosity with Corinthian columns that were totally out of proportion to the tiny pediment. He hopped out of his Buick and hurried up the long row of steps to the city library. He entered the smoked-glass front door where his reflection appeared only for a moment—the reflection slipping aside as the door was opened.

Henry cranked a roll of microfilm through a mechanical viewer. The light of the microfilm flickered on Henry Hayward's obsessed eyeballs. Henry stopped the microfilm on a cinema advertisement for the week's drive-in movies. Scanning down, he saw *Murder in a House on Sixth Street*, the second feature in a double billing. The first feature was entitled: *Night Sweats*. Could this be? Henry rolled the microfilm to the top of the newspaper's page. The Kansas City Star was dated Friday June 13, 1957, the same day of the month that Henry first saw the image in his window of the girl being strangled.

Henry returned to his car—and as he climbed in—he saw a man behind a column in front of the library. The man seemed to be watching him. He was wearing a pin-stripped shirt, but his face was in shadow. A chill ran up Henry's spine. Had the murderer come into Henry's world, upset that Henry was interfering in his life?

It was late in the evening as Henry opened the front door of his home with his key. Etched on a brass plate by the door was "157 SIXTH STREET." The porch light was on, not its usual state. As the door creaked open, he saw two large suitcases with a ladies pink jacket lying on top.

"Judy? Judy?" called Henry in mounting panic.

Henry heard footsteps and let out a sigh of relief. Judy walked into the room—across a worn, squeaking, strip-wood floor—carrying more "stuff" in her arms. She was halfway dressed up. Not her usual state.

"I'm outta here, Henry. I'm gone. Be good. Don't mess up," said Judy as she grabbed her two suitcases, her pink jacket, and walked out the front door. "And don't forget to brush your teeth."

Henry turned to peer out the open door. A car drove up with a very young man in the driver's seat. A lone streetlight shone down harshly on the young man, his face in shadow. Judy climbed in and they drove away. After a moment, Henry turned away without a word and walked down the hallway, lit only by a bare bulb overhead. His shadow moved across the white wall in the opposite direction—toward the front door.

Henry Hayward came through the kitchen door into the garage, with one of those small Kodak Instamatic cameras you could get at any K-Mart in the '70's. He pulled a large monkey wrench off of his pegboard wall of tools, and placed both items on the passenger seat of his car. Henry was careful about details now. He checked the time on the clock on the wall. He pushed the "play" button and started the second feature, *Murder in a House on Sixth Street*, at the same time he had seen it scheduled on the old microfilm: 11:30 p.m. Henry hopped into the car with his drink and settled back to wait. He glancd to the right ever so often to see if anything had appeared. The "special" scene of the movie soon appeared on the TV screen. Henry quickly looked to the right. The vision had indeed re-appeared! The young man put his hands around the girl's neck and choked the life out of her. The murderer then calmly, nonchalantly, got out of the car and walked toward the refreshment stand. The security guard passed on the far side of the 1955 Mercury looking for gate crashers. His flashlight scanned the interior of the car, but just missed illuminating the dead girl's face. Henry turned to the right and looked out the rear window to see the murderer returning to his Mercury. The murderer held in his hands a cardboard container with a large drink and a small box of popcorn. Henry watched as the murderer got in the car and continued to watch the movie, the killer seemingly unconcerned that someone might discover the dead girl. Henry waited until the time was right. He picked up the flash camera. He wanted a picture of the young murderer. He wanted proof, something he could research in old high-school yearbooks. He could find this murderer who had been haunting him and turn him in. Henry reached over to roll down the window, but stopped short for fear of losing the vision—fear of being transported back to his garage. Pressing—ever so slowly—on the little plastic button, he fired off the camera's flash. Whoosh! The flash reflected in the window like an exploding atomic bomb. And as it faded, Henry saw his own reflection in the window, staring back at him.

Henry pulled his razor across his three day-old whiskers. There were deep shadows around his eyes. A white-towel hung around his bare neck. Looking intently at his face in the bathroom mirror, but just past him, standing behind him…Henry suddenly froze as he saw the image of the murderer also reflected in the mirror.

Henry couldn't make out his face; it was blurred by condensation on the mirror. Had the killer come to get him? Henry turned but saw only an empty white-tiled bathroom. He stood there, dazed, his razor still held high near his face.

Henry pressed on the little plastic button again—the young murderer saw the camera flash going off. Outraged, the murderer jumped out of his car. Pulling the open car door out of his way, his silhouette raced across the front of the Buick—the movie playing in the background—his head obscured by the top of the windshield. He reached the driver's window of Henry's car. Henry's heart started pounding and a surge of adrenaline flowed through his veins. The murderer began pounding on the window. Henry awkwardly, hurriedly, tried to take another picture—the flash went off, but not at its intended target. Henry fearfully grabbed the monkey wrench that sat on the passenger seat and was poised to strike the killer. He held the wrench high. Everything seemed to move in slow motion as the irate young man pounded, pounded, pounded violently on the window. The glass suddenly shattered into a thousand little pieces. The image of the murderer disappeared with the falling glass, and was replaced not with the garage wall, but—

—with an abandoned, wind-swept outdoor drive-in. It appeared to have been boarded up for some time: a few remaining speakers dangled from their galvanized posts, a ramble of weeds had choked out the gravel and the movie screen was torn in several spots with pieces of canvas dangling like a puppy's folded ears. Henry stepped out of his car; there was a crunching sound as he stepped on the broken glass scattered on the ground. Henry stood there looking at the huge, faded-white theatre screen. He was completely alone, no one else was there. A hawk screamed overhead, an eerie piercing sound like no other. The sun rose over the barren horizon. It was daybreak.

Henry came out of a *One–Hour Photomat* with prints of the film he had shot the night before. As he hurriedly ripped open the package, pulling out the 3 by 5 glosssies, flipping through them, hopping to find his photo of the young murderer, he walked into the street headed for his car. His peripheral vision alerted him to a vehicle bearing down on him. A 1955 black Mercury—the murderer's car—quickly approaching him—coming straight for him! The car loomed large with a huge row of glinting silver teeth, coming closer, in minute detail, in slow motion. Henry found himself jumping aside, the photos flying everywhere, floating through the air, and then finally caught by the air turbulance of the passing car.

Henry stood there on the hot concrete pavement watching the car recede in the distance, stirring up street dust and orphaned trash as it got smaller and smaller until it was barely visible.

Henry kneeled down to pick up the photos, clutched one of them, and stared intently at it. It was a shot of the camera flash reflected in the car window. *Damn!* The murderer was still not discernable. The murderer had come into Henry's world to stop him. He was sure of it now. He had come to stop Henry from exposing his dirty deed. If only Henry hadn't gone into *his* world.

Henry suddenly awakened from a deep sleep as salty sweat ran down his brow. He wiped his forehead. Moonlight slicing through the Venetian blinds disfigured his face.

It was well after dark as Henry drove his Buick into the abandoned drive-in, his headlights flashing across the screen. He pulled up next to a dangling speaker, rolled down his window and reached down, pulling up the heavy steel speaker by the cord. Grabbing it with his right hand, he raised the window an inch or two with his left hand, so the speaker would hang safely on the window. Hopefully it wouldn't break the window. Henry turned the volume control knob slowly to the right, but he heard nothing. The knob came to a stop and wouldn't go any further, still no sound. Henry sat in his Buick staring at the blank screen.

Henry took a drink of his *Big Red* and dug into a box of popcorn. Suddenly a beam of light hit the movie screen. A bright, glaring light shone blindingly in his rear-view mirror. Henry adjusted his mirror to send the light elsewhere. A shadow created by the headlights, danced on the front dash as a vehicle approached from behind. A car crawled up to Henry's left side stopping even with his car. Henry, looked first in his rearview mirror, and saw only his young eyes reflected there as he remembered them many years before. Then, carefully, cautiously, Henry turned his head to the left to see who was in the car that had just arrived—

It was Henry, himself, thirty-eight years old, sitting in his classic,'41 Buick. Henry was seeing himself! How could that be? He turned his head back to the front. The movie, *Murder in a House on Sixth Street*, was playing on the big screen. He looked at his watch; it was 11:40. Henry had to face a horrible reality; thoughts welled up deep in his mind—churning round and round, making his brain ache something fierce. His eyes stared into a hollow emptiness that was his own mind. His sweating eyebrows raised up just the slightest. Henry Hayward slowly turned his head to the right, ready to take on the whole truth. He saw, sitting next to him, the murdered girl, her beautiful luminous face, her eyes wide open, her mouth parted only slightly—but limp and lifeless. Her dead eyes stared right at Henry; piercing deep into his soul. Henry's face, blank, motionless.

A flashlight beam raked across his face.

Henry saw the security guard looking at him in the window.

The horror of it—

The flashlight beam continued to scan the car until it revealed the dead girl.

The Cyst

By Don Kirk

WHEN I FIRST NOTICED IT on the side of my big toe, it was the size of a peanut, but then it grew to the size of a pecan, and became red and sore to the touch. I could no longer wear my shoes. That left me without my beloved tennis—a daily activity that relieved the stress of my job as an accountant at Marburger and Jones. The aching discomfort finally triggered a concern that maybe I had broken my toe. It was time to see a doctor. I put on a pair of sandals and drove to the nearest medical clinic.

After signing in and waiting a half-hour, I was led into a sterile, plastic-coated examining room where a nurse took the usual blood pressure, temp, weight, and medical history. And after another extended period of flipping through two-year-old magazines (Field & Stream, Architectural Digest, and Golf Digest), the doctor—it turned out to be just a middle-aged physician's assistant—examined the mysterious bump. It took just seconds for him to declare a verdict.

"It's not broken, Mr. Tibble. It's just a ganglion cyst."

"A what?" I asked.

"A gelatinous mass, a sac of jelly-like fluid. It usually occurs in a joint or tendon sheath and is caused by repetitive motion."

"Like playing tennis?"

"Yes."

"It looks awful," I replied.

"Does it hurt?"

"Aches at times, even throbs; I have this urge to scratch it."

"It itches?"

"No, not really. I just have this *urge* to scratch it."

The overweight assistant lowered my bare foot letting it rest on the cold steel step of the examining table.

"Well," he said, without inflections, "we can do one of three things: cut it out, use a syringe to extract the fluid, or hit it with a Bible."

"Hit it with a Bible?" I asked as I tried to imagine how this would be done.

"That's the way we used to solve the problem."

"With a Bible?"

"It breaks the cyst open and the fluid is quickly absorbed back into the tissue. You can do it yourself, but I can't officially recommend it to patients. There's the possibility you could break a bone in your foot."

"Break a…no, I wouldn't want that."

"Or you can wait, do nothing. If you refrain from using the joint, the cyst will eventually diminish in size, the fluid re-absorbed in a few months, but recurrence can be expected."

"It'll come back?"

"Yes," the physician's assistant replied soberly.

"You're sure it's not a broken bone in my toe? You don't think I need a second opinion? I don't maybe need to see a specialist?" I wasn't sure how far to trust a physician's assistant. In the past I had older white-haired doctors with thirty or forty years of practical experience, but now, as they retired, they seemed to be replaced by something called PAs. I had no idea what kind of formal training and practical experience was required before they could legally dispense medical advice. He did wear a white lab coat and had a stethoscope hanging around his neck, maybe that made him qualified.

"It's not broken," he said as he took hold of the big lump and moved it around under the skin. "See, I'm sure of it. A broken bone wouldn't move around like this and you wouldn't be sitting still while I pushed on it."

"Just a ganglion cyst then?"

"Just a ganglion cyst. I'll send you home and we'll see what happens. Do you need anything to alleviate the pain?"

"Pain? Uh, no, I think I'll be fine," I said, not sure that was the right decision. Pain? Was there going to be PAIN?

He marked up my medical record and stood up. "Okay then, that's it. Keep pressure off the tender site as long as it remains swollen. Stay off your feet as much as possible, don't wear tight shoes, and by all means, don't play tennis for a while."

"I won't," I replied.

He made a beeline for the door. I didn't think they should let lowly PAs wear a white coat and sling a stethoscope around their necks.

Well, that was it, I had come to the doctor for nothing. It's embarrassing to go to the doctor and not have anything seriously wrong with you, just flat embarrassing.

I returned home and lay down on the couch, putting my feet up on the armrest. I stared at the cyst. *Very common, nothing unusual*, the PA had said. I sat up and felt the big knot on my toe and tried to move it under the skin just as the PA had done, but it didn't move all that easily and I felt as if I shouldn't be messing with the mysterious bump—I was sure the thing didn't like for me to play with it.

Almost two weeks had elapsed and there was still no reduction in the cyst, in fact, it had grown to the size of a walnut. I was beginning to hate it. It was raking on my nerves, changing my routine. I kept in bed more than normal, and wearing sandals left my feet cold. It was time I returned to the clinic.

Without hesitation, the PA suggested: "Let's excise it. It's a minor procedure; we can do it here in the office. Make a little incision and pull it out; a couple of stitches and—

"You'll perform the procedure?"

"No, Dr. Garvy N. Nyfe will do it."

"Garvy Who? Are you sure—"

The physician's assistant quickly left the room. I had become attached to the little walnut on my toe. It was part of me. I feared I might miss it. No I wouldn't, not on your life. Shoes again, real shoes, that's what I wanted.

Dr. Nyfe came into the room and introduced himself. He was taller and heavier than his assistant, and seemed even more hurried. He gave me a "local"—a nice word for a big, long needle with the sting of a red wasp—and left again. I waited in the non-descript cubicle, trying desperately to read the wall of graduation certificates. I was soon to go under the knife—with Dr. Carving Knife at the helm. I couldn't bare to watch and looked away—

I looked back at my foot and saw a gauze bandage neatly covering the wound. I carefully touched it; there was no walnut, no pecan, no peanut. The terrible, aggravating, ganglion cyst was gone! It was finally over, I thought, but to my chagrin, the insanity of it all had only just begun.

A few days later, I returned to my job, but things didn't go so well. My calculator did not always agree with my penciled estimates. I would add up a column of numbers and subtract them to verify my addition, but all too often I was not getting that comforting "0.00" on my calculator. And the boss pointed out some simple math mistakes I had made. I could not discern where I had gone wrong. And worse, I turned in a major client's records only to get a scathing report about my work. Apparently, there were numerous inconsistencies, the kind that brings the IRS down on a client. My boss came to see me.

"Tibble, you're the best accountant I've got—"

"Yes sir, Mr. Marburger?"

"But you haven't been up to your usual high standards."

"Sir?"

"You don't seem to be with it, Tibble. Are you getting a good-night's sleep?"

"Yes sir, why yes sir. I'm fit as a fiddle."

"I don't know, Tibble. How about you take a few days off?"

"But I, I'm fine—"

"How's your toe, Tibble?"

"It's great, not bothering me at all."

"Well, something is, Tibble, I don't want to see you back in here until next week. Regenerate those brain batteries of yours." And at that Mr. Marburger turned away and sauntered out the open door scratching the back of his head.

I sat at my kitchen table playing with some simple algebraic equations, a little hobby of mine. I was trying to determine the odds of winning the state lottery if I bought five tickets, or ten or fifteen, and if the extra money, paid out over a year, would be worth the improved odds. But I was having a hard time deriving the equation needed to arrive at the solution. This was normally quite easy for me, but even the answer to Jack's selling twenty-eight apples at twenty-five cents a piece and having started with four dozen, which he had received by trading away six watermelon he had paid a dollar each for—how much profit did he make? Three dollars, was that it, no, one-fifty, no—I had to see a doctor about my mental acuity. Mr. Marburger would never let me come back this scatter-brained.

They wouldn't let me keep my jeans with their zippers and metal brads, but luckily dressed me in green scrubs instead of one of those peek-a-boo hospital gowns. I was taken to a large room on an upper floor of a medical building where a large band of windows wrapping two sides of the room revealed a magnificent view of the city. But my eyes were drawn to the thing standing alone in the middle of the room: a large, ominous-looking machine of George Lucas proportions. A huge, time-portal-like ring stood tall at eight feet. Two technicians in crinkled white lab coats approached me and directed me to a narrow cushioned table that extended out from the machine.

They gave me earplugs, had me lay on my stomach, strapped me down, and locked my head in a rigid position. I was then propelled slowly by electric motors into the gaping "donut hole" of the CAT-scanning device. "Computerized Axial Tomography" they called it, completely painless and easy they said—

"Stay perfectly still, you can breathe, but don't move. It'll take about twenty minutes, just relax. You're not claustrophobic, are you? Don't answer that. We'll be done in a jiffy. H-o-l-d it."

I strained not to move, afraid to ruin the pictures, but their "jiffy" was quickly turning into minutes that seemed like hours. I was becoming anxious. Panic was taking over. Then the table I lay on stopped moving and there were no more metallic hums or clicks. I was relieved, but I heard no one say I could move. There was an eerie silence in the room punctuated only by the computer hum of a hard drive or fan motor. What had happened? Was anyone still there? I'd had enough and wiggled myself out of the confounded contraption and sat up.

I turned, and could see, through a window into an adjoining room, three men huddled at a computer work station. They starred intently at the monitor. I walked through a door where I could see the screen image with its colored slices of my brain, but I could not see the men's faces. I stood there, feeling stupid, chilled in my oversized scrubs.

I cleared my throat.

One of the men turned toward me. "Hi, Mr. Tibble, I'm Doctor Abbott. How have you been feeling lately?"

"Pretty good, well, I feel weak sometimes and a little mentally confused. Is something wrong with my scan?"

"Everything's just fine, but we're going to have you come back." The very tall Doctor Abbott looked distinguished and important, a blue-stripped tie pulled tight to his pencil-thin neck, and a black handlebar mustache plastered on a placid face, he looked much like a British aristocrat, missing only the walking cane and bowler hat—maybe there wasn't enough room for the bowler between his head and the ceiling.

"What's wrong?"

"I think we've got some kind of machine malfunction. It'll take some time to fix."

"What's wrong?" I repeated.

"Step over here." Dr. Abbott pointed to an area of the brain scan that appeared without tones of gray. "It's clear as a bell. There's no tissue density, nothing there."

"Nothing there! How can that be?" I asked.

"That's what we don't know."

"But you're the expert! So I've got a hole in my brain?"

"No, of course not, there's nothing wrong with your brain."

"You sure?"

You can get dressed now and we'll call you when we've re-calibrated our CAT."

"Sure, that's…that's just dandy."

"Everything will be just fine, Mr. Tibble, don't you worry."

Everything will be just fine, that's what he said. I wasn't so sure. Had I been irradiated at some time in my life, maybe when I was a curious little baby crawling around in the dirt absorbing uranium or plutonium or some kind of imported killer bacteria—maybe I'd eaten a nasty mind-altering mushworm? I had led my brain to a near panic state when the phone rang. I grabbed it. It was Doctor Abbott. He wanted me to come in for more pictures.

After another scary trip into that donut thing, and as I was being led out of the room, I overheard two doctors I had never seen before as they sat on their stools at the computer.

"This can't be."

"Can't be."

"Never seen anything like it."

"Nothing like it."

I pulled away from the nurse and interrupted their cerebral consultation. "What is it, doctors? What's wrong?"

"I'm Dr. Morgan and this is Dr. Larryton and Dr. Curlita, renowned neurologists. Could you sit down, please?" One of the men had a mop of black hair and the second was wiry thin with an unruly hairdo; the third was fat and balding. I sat down and stared at them. They were a sight.

"How do you feel?" asked the mop-headed Dr. Morgan.

"I'm okay I guess."

"Any nausea, vomiting?" asked Dr. Larryton.

"No."

"Your temporal lobe, there's a vacant area there too."

I suddenly felt woozy and weird-like, like I was going to pass out. The nice nurse tried to hold me up.

"You're fine, just an anomaly. We think the CAT needs further adjustment."

"Further adjustment? What do you mean further adjust? I do not be-lieve it! And, and what do you mean by an, an-homely? Is something wrong with me? I...I think this could be bad!"

"Why do you say that?"

"I have another cyst growing on me."

The two doctors stood up together, each holding canted coffee cups about to tip over like tanker trucks on a tight corner.

"You've another cyst?"

"Under my arm…here, look."

Larryton and Curlita walked over to me and stuck their faces into my armpit. I leaned back. I was afraid they were going to spill their hot coffee on me. They hadn't yet drank from their monogrammed vessels. Their eyes stood wide and curious. They felt the lump and pushed and pulled on it and then walked away from me and huddled together in a corner speaking quietly so I couldn't hear them. I strained to hold up my arm; they had not told me I could take it down. I made out a few of their words, all medical sounding stuff—probe the left ceremonial hemisphere, shock the medulla oblong thing, drain the parrot-cranium fluid, probe the encepha, maybe an infection, staph-lo-cock-us—I did not understand a word of it—then the three doctors turned around and walked back to me.

"We need to admit you to the hospital."

"What?" I felt my stomach turn over.

"We don't mean to alarm you, but we need to do some exploratory surgery."

"But, but, what's wrong?"

"We'll do a biopsy, then we'll know for sure."

"A biopsy?"

"Uh, we need to take a tissue sample to see if it has metastasized."

"Muh-tas-duh-sized? Is it imported germs? Cancer?—"

"Oh no. Cancer no, we don't think so, and if it is, it's likely to be benign. So don't worry, you'll be just fine, trust us."

"How can you say I am fine when you do not even know what is wrong with me. You have no idea what is going on with my body—do you?"

"After the biopsy, then we'll know."

The rough popcorn texture of the white ceiling came into focus. I then noticed the blue glow of a television set sitting on a table in front of me. I stared at a red, polka-dotted tie dancing on the screen and then focused on round spots of light on some balding man's skull. A lady sitting next to him called the man "Dr.

Phil." Doctor? Did I know him? Was I in a hospital room? It sure looked like one. I reached under my left arm. The cyst was gone away. "Oh boy," I said, because the ugly, aggravatin' cyst was all gone.

A tall, big-boned nurse with dirty-blond hair tied up in a beehive came into the room.

"How you doin' Mr. Tibble?"

"Is it over?"

"Yes, Mr. Tibble. You're going to be just fine now."

"Mr. Tibble! Who is Mr. Tibble?"

"Why, you are."

"Oh…you know what, nurse? The cyst under my arm is gone?"

"Yes, Mr. Tibble, it's been gone for a long time now."

"When will the doctor come?"

"When he finishes his rounds, but first, it's time for your group session."

"My what?"

"You know, it's your favorite time of the day."

"It is?"

"Yes. With Johnny and Glen and Sarah—"

"I, uh, I don't know Johnny and Glen and—"

"Here, Mr. Tibble, your notebook, you can work on your addition tables, two plus three…you like to do your arithmetic don't you Mr. Tibble?"

"Yes."

"That's good."

The nurse turned to walk out when I suddenly spoke up. "Uh, Miss Clippit, what about this other cyst, this one on my wrist?"

"Oh, dear, no, be careful with that. Don't pick at it or push on it. It must be left there."

"But Miss Clippit, it aches and throbs sometimes."

"Don't play with it."

"It itches sumpin' ter'ble, Miss Clippit. I just wanna smash it against the table."

"Don't you dare hit it, you'll get a very bad headache."

"But I don't like it."

"It's your friend Mr. Tibble, you need it and you must take care of it."

"Why must I, Miss Clippit?"

"Because, it's your brain—what's left of it."

The Contrarian's Husband

By Don Kirk

SHE WAS EXASPERATINGLY CONTRARY, a contrarian of insidious proportions. We were married for thirteen years and she never once did the same thing in the same way as myself. If we walked into a shopping mall and I walked through the right door, she'd walk in the left door. If we walked into a restaurant and I headed for a booth by the window, she'd walk to a table. If I placed a throw rug on the floor parallel to the wall, she'd want to lay it perpendicular. If I put my pencils in a cup with the erasers facing up, which I always did, she'd turn them over so the eraser was facing down. For her, the points *had* to be up, wanting me to skewer myself and die of lead poisoning, I was sure. Why else would she want them up? I never could understand why she insisted on doing things in just the opposite of my particular propensities. Was it intentional? Was she trying to aggravate me on purpose? Actually, I didn't think so. I figured she was from a parallel universe where everything is a mirror image of this world, a world that was wrong side out. For example, I hung my shirts on hangers with the fronts facing to the left—I've always done it that way—but she hangs my shirts always facing to the right—that's the way *she's* always done it. Fair enough: *You hang your clothes in your closet your way and I'll hang my clothes in my closet my way. Okay?* Well, she does do the washing and hangs the clothes, so I can't complain if my closet is full of shirts turned both ways, can I?

One day recently, we were sitting across from each other at the dinner table and she had her fork to the left of her plate and her knife and spoon on the right. I had my fork on the right and my knife and spoon on the left. Her drinking glass was on her right, mine on the left. The illusion of a mirror image was apparent to me. Everything looked perfectly symmetrical and correct.

My wife spoke up, "Honey, your silverware is on the wrong side; the fork should be on your left, the knife and spoon on the right, and your glass, it too should be on your right."

"But dear," I said, "you know I'm left handed; this way I won't have to reach across my plate to get a drink."

"You can switch after we start eating," she replied.

I retorted, "And then you can switch your glass to match mine."

"But I'm right-handed," she challenged.

"I'm not moving my glass if you don't move yours."

She got up and left the room.

I had had enough, no more contrarian from another universe. She made a living at it—keeping me in a continuous slow burn. It was time I developed a perfect plan to rid my world of her presence. I could put my pencils the way I wanted them, the carpet parallel to the wall, the coffee cups in the kitchen cabinet, facing down. Finally, I could be at peace, she could be at peace, the universe could be at peace, and no longer would she be burdened with my "opposite nature." So I planned a trip out West in our van. We often took such trips and this one would seem no different to her, only this time, she wouldn't be coming back.

We came upon a historical museum of mining based around an actual nineteenth-century gold mining operation in Nevada. Tours were available down into the mine, deep down. We took the tour, riding down in the original wire cage that was lowered by steel cables released slowly by an electric winch. When we reached the bottom we found tunnels dripping with water that ran off in all directions. The hard-rock miners dug wherever the veins of gold led them. Dim light bulbs were strung on wires along the ceiling. As the tour guide led a small group of us, I hung back to take pictures and encouraged my wife to stay with me.

"Here, let's go this way," I said, "This tunnel returns to the main route just down the way."

And she says, "Okay, but I'll take this tunnel."

I said, "Sure, meet you there."

What she didn't know was that I had examined the tunnel plan in the museum gift shop and took a mental note of the tunnel routes. I told the truth about which tunnel would return to the main route and she took the bait, hook line and sinker. She did what a contrarian would do, just the opposite. The tour-guide, his tour group, and me—but minus my lovely wife—returned to the surface, and we said our "goodbyes" and tipped our guide. Then, the guide flipped a switch that turned off all the lights in the mine—to save electricity, I'm sure. I wandered over to the cage and, with my pocketknife, covertly cut the alarm-bell wire so that anyone down below couldn't call for the cage. It was my last act of desperation on the last tour of the day, on the last tour of the weekend. Perfect timing. No one would be going down again until next Monday.

I sat down in the museum's coffee shop and ordered a hot, black coffee—unleaded. I had actually done it. I was proud of myself. It was finally over. My lovely Contrarian would never find her way out. She was done, history, finito. A sigh of relief and newfound peace came over me. I left a healthy tip—I was feeling good—and returned to the van with my plan to report my wife's disappearance to the police on the next day—after I had spent a quiet cozy night in a motel watching the television programs I wanted to watch, eating what I wanted to eat, and taking a shower when I pleased—

But as I returned to the parking lot and unlocked the driver's side door, I heard a voice staight from Hell: "Honey, where have you been?" My jaw dropped, my blood turned to ice. My wife was sitting in the passenger-side seat, all smiles. Yes, the contrarian, there she was, in my car, alive and apparently doing just fine.

I tried to calm my frantic heartbeat and hide my mortification: "Why, I've been looking for you, Hon! Where have you—"

My lovely wife broke in: "The tunnel was a horizontal shaft straight out of the mountain. I just followed the ore-car tracks."

"You did, Oh God, I…I thought you were lost. The management went back down into the mine. They looked all over for you. When they didn't find anyone, they said they didn't believe I had come in with anyone."

"Well, no matter, come on lets go, they're closing the place."

"Sure Hon, sorry I took so long."

We drove on, I didn't say much. I was turning things over in my mind. I wasn't going to bring her back home, not this time, no sir-ree. Another opportunity would present itself, I was sure. The West was still wild and woolly with plenty of open space that was dry and desolate—and isolated—to the far distant horizon. And the desert was punctuated with tall mountains with very cold, freezing air and high cliffs and deep rivers. I had choices; I would have opportunities.

We were making our way through Death Valley, two hundred feet below sea-level, closer to Hell than anywhere in the U.S.; the perfect final resting place for my dear beloved wife. It was twenty sizzling degrees above the one-hundred-degree mark. Our A.C. was blasting full tilt and I was looking in anticipation for a good vantage point to take a photograph.

"Which road should we take, Hon?" I asked, "This road to the left looks good, it'll take us up the valley," and she quickly replied, "Right fork, I like the right fork toward the mountains."

"Maybe you should look at the map," I said.

"Oh, you know I can't read a map. I have no sense of direction, that's what you tell me."

"I do. You wouldn't know west even if the sun was setting."

She said nothing; a sullen mood overtook her.

"Okay Hon, six of one, half a dozen of the other, we'll take the right fork."

We took the right fork, and as we came over a hill, I pulled to a stop and grabbed my camera.

"Honey, I want to get a picture of our van coming over this rise with the snow-capped mountains in the background."

She said nothing; she probably wanted me to take a picture in the *opposite* direction.

I turned off the key and put the emergency brake on.

"Honey, you take the driver's seat and drive back up over the hill and I'll get a shot of our car as you come back over the rise."

"Okay, but you drive back there and *I'll* take the picture," she insisted as she took the camera and climbed out of the van and closed the door. I beamed as I turned around and drove back up the rise and disappeared over the hill.

And I kept driving. I wondered what she would think when I didn't return? How long would she hold the camera to her face waiting for me to come over the rise? Out there alone, it would be eerily quiet with scary-looking critters scurrying around her feet on the scorched desert sand, and she would be standing in one-hundred-twenty-degrees of burning heat with no shade to the horizon. Before I dropped her off, we had taken a dirt road well off the main paved road, not even marked on the map. I doubted that anyone traveled this route on a regular basis—

Suddenly, my radiator began to overheat and steam rose out of every crack and crevasse of my hood and radiator grill. I pulled over and raised the hood and waited. I had to let it cool before I could remove the radiator cap and add some of our drinking water. A few minutes later, a beat-up dull-red 1950's Ford pickup truck came barreling over the hill behind me and passed me by, but then its breaks took hold, slid on the gravel, and came to a fishtailing, dust-cloud stop. The pickup began to back up: the driver was apparently stopping to see if I needed help. He came to a stop just ahead of me and the passenger door flew open. A hand holding a camera appeared—and out jumped my wife!

"I got a great picture of you broke down on the road," she said excitedly.

"Uh yeah," I was in shock and overcome with fear, "My engine overheated, dear…can't drive it…the radiator, I…I'm sorry Hon…"

"Mr. Sawyer, picked me up," she said.

"Great."

The passenger door was pulled shut by the unseen Mr. Sawyer, and the pickup tore off down the road.

"He lives out here?" I asked.

"Got a couple goats in the arroyo at the foot of the mountains."

"I see. Lucky he came along."

"Lucky."

I grabbed the water jug out of the van and asked my dear darling wife, "Do you need a cool drink before I pour the rest into the radiator?"

"No, I'm fine." Of course she'd say no; she'd never in a million years agree with me, not me. No, she was fine, she said, cool as a calculating cucumber.

I wiped the sweat off my tortured brow.

"Would you like the guided tour by one of our knowledgeable summer students or would you like the self-guided tour?"

"Self-guided," I said unwaveringly and plopped down the admission price. I started to turn away when—

"Here sir, your brochure, numbered points of interest, descriptions of the rooms, a full-color map—"

"Thanks," I said as I grabbed the brochure and dropped it in the nearest trashcan.

I had just purchased two tickets to the famous Winchester Mystery House in San Jose. It was an immense Victorian home that looked as if it would be a great place to visit. It was six acres of rambling house, one hundred sixty rooms—can you believe it—stacked room upon room four stories high, spilling off in every conceivable direction. The brochure said the mansion had 2,000 doors, 10,000 windows, forty-seven fireplaces, numerous blind closets, secret passages, and 40 stairways, some leading to absolutely nowhere. It was the perfect place in which to get lost. Even the original owner and her servants had to carry a map to find their way around. It had been designed—and added onto continuously—by the eccentric Sarah Winchester in order to baffle the evil spirits that haunted her. She felt that her husband's making of guns would bring the rath of the dead. I hoped the house would baffle my dearest, lovely, endearing wife.

She and I climbed the steps to the tall double doors at the entrance. I grabbed the silver doorknob and pulled the right-hand door open, it squeaked thrillingly—a haunted house where any-thing could happen. Ghosts and goblins and spirits of the dead to take one away—far away.

"Oh, this is great, honey," I said, "the ornate entrance hall. Look at all the doors, thirteen to be exact. Which one shall we try first?"

"This one."

"How about we start with the left one first," I suggested.

"No, this is fine."

"Okay, lead the way. Six of one, half a dozen of the others."

I followed her into a narrow hall that twisted and turned up steps in one direction and then down another. There were doors everywhere. I opened one. There was just a wall behind it, no room there at all. I climbed a short run of stairs with thirteen steps that went to the ceiling and stopped dead with no access to the second floor. Turning around, I returned to the hallway. It broke off in several directions, and my curious, self-absorbed wife was nowhere to be seen. How wonderful.

Now to get out of here. My wife had nary a chance. Ennie-meenie-miney-moe, I took the middle passageway. I looked for a window so I could get my bearings. Through one door and then another I went. There, a window, I peered out. All I could see were other rooms, windows, skylights, and tiled rooflines that jutted off in every direction; I couldn't see the countryside beyond and any distinguishing landmarks. I continued on, climbed another long, winding set of stairs to get up higher—maybe a tower window to get my bearings—but the stairs lead to a tiny room with no windows and no other doors. Maybe lady Winchester had indeed outsmarted the evil spirits; I couldn't see how they could have circumvented this perplexing labyrinth of rooms. I was beginning to feel the need for the brochure with the map, but I had thrown it away so my wife couldn't get her hands on it. I made my way back down the stairs and opened a small door on a landing that led into a bathroom. There was my wife, my lovely wife—calmly adoring herself in the sink mirror.

"Honey!" I said. "I thought I had lost you."

"I'm just fine. Are you having fun dear?"

"I am, I am," I choked on my heart. "This place is great, like a huge House of Mirrors at a carnival."

"Isn't it though?"

"It is, dear." I turned out one of the doors.

"Honey, stop!" she called out. "You need to come this way."

"No Hon," I said, "I'm sure that's not right, the door is only four feet high."

"You can duck through it."

"That's okay, I'll go this way."

"Have it your way," she said, and climbed through the tiny door.

"Good riddance," I mumbled. I knew I had a very good sense of direction; I knew I could get out of this torturous maze without worry. I exited through another door into a hall at the end of which was a large white-paneled door. I grabbed the copper knob and opened the door; it led into a large linen closet. I closed the door behind me and tried another door, but it was locked. I returned to the door I had entered and found it had no doorknob on my side; it was a door that opened only one way—placed there I'm sure to keep evil spirits from following Sarah Winchester to her séance room. I tried to get my fingers on the edge of the door to open it, but the crack was narrow and the latch secure. Looking around the room, I could see no other way out. There were no doors or windows. I opened a linen cabinet and, low and behold, in it was a small door no more than three feet high. I crawled through it and found myself in a hallway at the end of which was an imposing door with a large glass windowpane that glowed brightly with light. Finally, I had found an exterior door. I opened the door and stepped out…no floor there…falling…falling…I crashed through a skylight and landed in a basement room. Shards of glass showered down on me cutting my face and hands. I started to get up, but checked my move: there had been a sudden sharp pain in my leg. I was sure it was broken. I looked around the room; there were no doors, not a one. I cried out with a wimpy "help" and then mustered the energy to yell louder. No one responded. The tour groups, where were they? I looked at my wristwatch: five-thirty. The museum was closed. They were friggin' closed! They wouldn't find me until tomorrow. Ahhhh, a protruding leg bone sent sharp pains to my brain, bright red blood dripped on the wood floor. I lay there feeling completely helpless. Then I heard something: a floor creaking—footsteps! My wife, my pretty, loving wife! She's wandering around in the house somewhere; she'll find me. I heard a door hinge squeak. *She's here!*

But she wasn't.

Hours passed, maybe more. I no longer felt any pain in my leg. It was much better now. I heard the sound of pounding hammers and then saws cutting through wood. Help was coming; they were cutting their way to me. I'd be rescued at any moment. I tried to scream out, but my throat was horse, it hurt something fierce when I tried—*but I must, I must let them know I'm here.* It was getting dark; I could no longer see my hand in front of my face. The hammering continued incessantly. The house's evil spirits were all alone with me, I alone with them.

Outside in the parking lot, my wife threw a nice brochure with a full-color map of the Winchester Mystery House on the passenger seat, turned the key in the ignition, and drove off.

The Department Store

By Don Kirk

MOTHER WAS LOOKING at the nice string of pearls at the Jewelry counter of *Rosenbloom's*, an upscale department store in New York City. It was the Christmas holidays and all was joyful and colorful and brightly lit with red and green. The music of Christmas came from everywhere and nowhere in particular. Men in goatskin jackets and woman in fur coats scurried about as if they thought the end of time was soon to arrive. Shopping bags were brimming full of things—silly, foolish things, nothing of real value, nothing the recipients of these gifts ever wanted or would ever have a need for. Some of these gifts would be returned the day after Christmas when many other yet unsold items would now be on sale—and would surely then be sold. Without these inane purchases—a full twenty-five percent of annual retail sales—the American economy would surely collapse.

"Mommy, lets go see the toys," begged little Annie Stillworth as she pulled on her mother's arm.

"In a moment sweetie, we'll see all the toys. You can pick out your favorite to take home, but just one."

"Yes Mommy, let's go." Annie pulled hard.

"I'm coming dear." Mrs. Stillworth lay the string of pearls she was ogling back down on the beveled-glass countertop a bit too hard and the clerk threw her a derisive smirk.

Up the shiny chrome elevator to the second floor, the two girls went, Mrs. Stillworth in her gray pin-stripped suit and little daughter Annie in her pretty white Christmas dress, a dress accentuated with bright cherry-red shoes and a matching red purse. The high-ceilinged hall was filled with pretty things: elegant clothing on beautiful cream-colored mannequins wearing carefully styled hairpieces, high-tech electronics, and huge high-definition television screens covered with green holly and red bows. A festive atmosphere it definitely was, carefully designed to get the customers to buy, buy, and buy some more. And then, too, the plush carpeting laid out in each department was there to snare and hold the victim like a sticky spider web. Mrs. Stillworth had been lured to the kitchenware department where she fondled the fine crystal wine-and-liquor bar set. She popped the crystal with her index finger; it pinged expensively.

"Mommy, this is not the toys; I can't play with these," said Annie as she cradled a wine glass loosely in her hand.

"No dear, here give me that, you'll break it," scolded Mrs. Stillworth as she grabbed the crystal from little Annie. Annie's self-absorbed mother went on about her dallying as Annie looked up at her scornfully. She then noticed that her mother no longer had hold of her hand. She was finally liberated, free from her mothers long-fingered shackles, feeling free as a child running naked in a field of wildflowers, unencumbered by the huge weight that had, for much too long, been attached to her little wrist.

Annie wandered cheerfully through the bustling store, a forest of ladies fine silk stockings moving about her like disembodied wooden stilts. She looked way up to the finely clothed mannequins with their faces forever frozen in time. She hopped on a big *choo-choo* train that tooted down a plastic track. *Whoo-whoo* went the train whistle; *clang-clang* went the bell. Annie hopped off at the depot and opened a little white picket-fence gate and entered a yard full of colorful toys. A two-story gingerbread playhouse stood tall in the middle of the yard. She entered the little house and climbed to the second floor, peeked through each window, played with the little kitchen furniture, and played with every colorful, tinkling, jangling, talking toy she could find. Finally, she set down in a huge pile of cuddly teddy bears—and fell asleep.

Annie woke, bleary eyed. Rubbing her winkers with her little fists, they opened a little wider. She looked around and climbed from the pile of teddies. The huge room was now dimly lit; a few small pools of light dotted the floor. It was so quiet, one could have heard a pin drop. The glistening silver, metal, and brass made nary a squeal. Annie ran across the granite floors in her shiny red patent-leather shoes and they clicked on the floor sharply. She ran up one aisle and quickly down another.

"Mommy, Mommy, where are you?"

She inadvertently kicked a big, buttoned-eyed brown teddy bear lying on the floor, it spoke with lonely despair: "I'm so soft, won't you play with me?"

Alarm began to show itself on little Annie's face. She found the big glass front door and pressed her face and hands up against the cold glass. She peered out at the dark, empty street where colorful neon lights danced on the wet pavement. A crumpled trashcan rolled down the sidewalk and a mangy basset hound confronted a scrawny black cat. The cat raised its hackles. The dog cowered, whimpered, and quickly retreated. A vagabond wandered aimlessly up the street picking up cigarette butts. Was it still burning, he hoped. And the beer cans, maybe a drop or two of life-sustaining alcohol remained.

Terrified little Annie pounded on the window. "Mister, help me! Help meeee!" But her desperate voice went unheeded and the homeless man disappeared around the corner as orphaned sections of the daily newspaper tumbled past the doors. Annie turned away from the window sad and dejected. Her head down, she began to cry. The mannequins, all well dressed, seemed to stare sadly at poor little Annie. Annie looked back at them, the figures of men, woman and children dressed up for the holiday season. A little girl mannequin was dressed in finery much like Annie's. Annie walked up to the mannequin dressed in a very pretty green dress with matching purse.

"Are you lonely?" Annie asked.

The mannequin stared back at her with its big turquoise glass eyes.

"What is your name?" asked Annie.

The mannequin just stared blankly at her.

"Your name will be Sharon. Is that all right?"

Sharon was unmoved.

"I like your pretty green purse. May I have it?" Annie reached for the emerald-green purse with the pretty pink roses on it, and pulled it free from the mannequin's arm.

"Your skin is smooth, but so cold and so hard. You're made of plastic aren't you? But that's okay; I like you. Want to play?"

Sharon seemed to reply with a tiny little smile.

"But I can't play with two purses," continued Annie, "here you can have mine."—Annie placed her red plastic purse in Sharon's hands—"It has a powder case and lipstick and tissue in it."

Sharon gazed curiously back.

"Who's the boy with you? Does he want to play to? Can he play with us?"—Annie ran over and got a baseball and a big wooden bat and put it in the little boy's arms.—"Here, you can play baseball. Would you like that?…Fine. Sharon and I will cook dinner while you play."

Annie drug a little kitchen set over to Sharon. Annie retrieved little pots and pans, plastic plates, and dinnerware. She grabbed up all the colorful plastic food she could find: mash potatoes, carrots, apple pie, pizza. Sharon's eyes seemed to gleam with joy.

The night passed quickly and soon the lights in the store came on one department at a time. Fluorescent tubes in the glass counters ignited and began to hum. Christmas music filled the air.

There was a noise at the front door. A key turned, the latch snapped open, and a security guard dressed in a blue uniform with brass buttons pushed open the glass doors. He walked down the main aisle, his rubber-soled feet clopping on the granite floors, the sound echoing about the room. He put his ring of keys in his vest pocket and then noticed that some of the glass cases were broken and shards of glass were scattered about the floor. As the security guard walked toward the telephone hanging on a nearby column, his attention was brought to a row of mannequins posed as a well-dressed smiling family with three children. He stopped short and backed up a step. He peered at a little boy with a baseball and bat cradled in his arms and then noticed a little girl mannequin with a pretty green dress and cherry-red purse. He knew that wasn't right and removed the red purse and placed it in the hands of the little girl mannequin standing next to her—the one with the white dress, red shoes and emerald-green purse.

Redemption In a Watery Grave

By Don Kirk

JAKE STOMPED HARDER ON THE BRAKE. The wheels were locked up and skidding on the pavement. The car was inching forward toward the edge. Jake grabbed the emergency brake between the seats and pulled hard. The car jerked, but didn't stop. Skidding forward, it slid closer to the river's retaining wall. He looked in the rear view mirror to see a black Mercedes Benz pushing against his bumper with unmerciful intent. The Benz driver shifted into a lower gear. What had Jake done to deserve this? Why was the driver so bent on taking his life? Jake was in a new, white cadillac Seville that was fogging up. Bulldozing the brake peddle was doing no good. Jake put the transmission in reverse and stepped on the gas; the engine roared. The tires just spun and smoked on the pavement. Jake was loosing ground, fast. Suddenly his car tilted forward and the rear wheels came off the pavement; the engine raced. Jake saw the Mercedes come to a stop. *Get out now*, Jake screamed to himself. Jake opened the door, but something slammed it shut: a wood piling. Jake knew he was going down; at least a fifteen-foot drop into the river. He was going over; it was going to be a horrible fall and a terrible splash. *It isn't the fall, but the stop that kills you*, he thought. Jake snapped on his seatbelt for the ride down, and braced his feet against the floor and his arms against the steering wheel. The car nosed down, and over the edge it went. Jake was now airborne; he felt weightless, loose objects in the car were thrown violently around him. He saw blue sky and white puffy clouds and nothing below him but air; the horizon line rose upward. The fall seemed to take forever, taking on a dreamy, ethereal quality. "Just a dream, time for me to wake up," Jake mumbled out loud. The car tilted further forward; Jake slid forward in his seat, his feet thrust against the firewall. BAM! His jaw slammed shut and broke a few finely-polished gold fillings. The car plunged into the water. Water began to flow through the radiator grill and then through the firewall around the steering column. The engine sputtered and stopped. The sedan seemed to float on the surface for a long moment. Jake tried again to open the door, but the water had already trapped it shut, and the car began to sink. A big bubbling gulp of air burst around the car. The waterline rose on the windshield. Water seeped under the doors. The sky—the whole world—was disappearing above him. The car was descending slowly; foamy bubbles rose around the vehicle like soap suds in a bathtub and streamed up past the window. Water spewed through holes in the floor and oozed around the dashboard radio as if it was a glob of pure evil bent on getting at Jake. *Stay calm; wait it out,* screamed Jake within his tortured mind. What had he done to deserve this? His muscles tightened; he was afraid to take a breath. How far down would he fall? How deep was the river? How long would it take to reach the bottom? Jake prayed to God for a shallow river. The sedan's plush pristine-white interior was filling with murky water. Air bubbles streamed upward just outside the window, released from every joint in the body panels. The water was lapping on Jake's lap; his heart was pounding fast now, fear rising exponentially. He tried to think, how was he to get out alive? What must he do? *Think! Do I open the window now or wait until the car hits bottom?* He tried to compose his thoughts. *Don't panic, don't panic,* he repeated these words to himself, but that didn't seem to help. His breathing was rapid and heavy, his heart about to blow out of his chest. *Relax, take a deep breath; there's plenty of air.* The icy water was now soaking his shirt. The car was canting further forward. *Seatbelt! The seat belt, get it off.* Jake reached into the freezing cold water and searched for the release button. He fumbled with the latch—*the button, where in hell was the button?* His heart raced. Then something to his right got his attention. Something was in the car with him—in the passenger seat—a person, a woman, all dressed up nice, but with a reproachful frown plastered on her face. It was Jake's ex-wife. Pretty and innocent, her sweet lips a bright luscious red. Then her cursed scowl turned slowly into a gratified grin. *No, no!* Jake stared, terror-stricken. He knew how he had mistreated her. She appeared happy to see him drowning. She was relishing his dire situation. He fiddled with the belt lock. His ex-wife raised her left hand; her wedding ring twinkled. Then she put her hands around her own neck and squeezed hard. She was mocking Jake with a scary pantomime that wasn't funny. *No, no, you're dead. I squeezed the life out of you a long time ago.* Jake watched as she pulled a deck of playing cards from her purse. He looked down, fidgeted with his lap belt. The rising water was pressing him tight against the belt. His ex-wife pulled one card at a time from the pack and threw them into the swirling water. Jake fidgeted with the belt. *I'll never go to Las Vegas again, dear. I promise I won't.* Jake grinned insincerely as he said this. There, the button, Jake pushed on it, the belt snapped loose. The wife's uplifted mouth dropped back down as the playing cards continued to swirl around in the water. Jake rose in the seat, becoming buoyant as the water quickly filled the cabin and tried to force out his life-sustaining air. The car fell further and further into the black ink of the lake's depths. Rays of flickering sunlight became thinner and weaker, no longer able to reach any further into the murky depths of Hell where Jake felt he was destined. Darker and darker became the world above, the world Jake was leaving behind. He wanted to forgive all his trespasses. He wanted to make things right. He wanted his ex-wife to forgive him. He had wanted to get back all the money he lost at the casino. Was it too late to correct his mistake? Bundles of greenbacks began to eradicate themselves from the black bag on the passenger seat, the turbulent water sending them tumbling. *You can have it all back. Just let me out of here!* Jake's face was turning blue. The icy water was numbing his fingers and legs and trembling face. *Open the window, now's the time; do it now.* Jake pushed on the electric window's rocker switch—lock—unlock—lock—nothing happened. The electronics were fried, short-circuited by the river water. Jake's breathing quickened. Water now lapped on his chin. He tilted his head back trying to keep his mouth above the unrelenting cascade of water. Trapped in the rear of the car was probably a bubble of air. He had to get there, but the headrest was blocking his way and he couldn't see: it was dark, muddy water. U.S. currency swirled about him. He ran his hands under the headrest looking for the release catch. *Where? Where was it?* He found it, lifted, and pulled the headrest free. Jake floated back over the seat and slid into the air pocket. Yes, there was more air there, a big bubble of air several feet in diameter. It gave him more time to think, to work out a plan. Jake tried hard to get his brain signals to flow, tried hard to clear the cobwebs of his mind. The cold water was affecting his thought. *What, what do I do? First I'll...breathe easy, don't panic, calm down.* Then Jake felt another presence. He turned to see another figure in the back seat with him; it was the Flamingo's casino boss dressed in his finest evening suit. *No, no, you're dead too. I shot you with my Glock. Go sway!* The boss glared at Jake with vengefullness and shook his head disapprovingly. Jake begged, *take it, take it. You can have it back. I'm sorry I took the money.* The casino boss smiled. Jake looked away. How long was this little fishbowl of air going to last? Suddenly the car hit the muddy lake bottom and clouds of thick mud rose past the windows. Jake was sinking into a muddy abyss, soon to be swallowed up by a bottomless world of pitiful muck. The car, ever so slowly, settled into the choking weeds and rocked onto its left side, and as the tail end dropped down into the mud, trapped air in the trunk rippled into Jake's life-giving bubble giving him a few more precious seconds of life, a few more seconds to be saved, a few more seconds to confess his sins, a few more seconds to think about what he had done with his life. Had he finally gone too far? You can steal a candy bar from the dime store and get away with it. You can lie about the condition of the car you're trying to sell and turn a profit. You can cheat on your wife and maybe she won't find out. But can you steal from the mob and live to tell the tale? Jake glanced again at the casino boss there in the back seat with him. *You won't get me. I'm getting out. I'm not giving up. I have time. I won't die in this watery Hell. Go away!* Jake could hear a gurgling sound; water was quickly seeping into his bubble of life making it smaller and smaller and smaller. Only seconds had passed, but it seemed like hours. The stale air was becoming harder to breath. Jake was feeling lightheaded; he was breathing his own carbon monoxide now, very little oxygen was left. Jake had to get out now, right now. He struggled to remove his soggy shirt and pulled off his shoes. With his head pressed against the ceiling, and no where else to go, the water licked at his nostrils. This was it, now or never. Jake took one last deep breath and then grabbed the front seat and pulled himself over it. He groped in the dark for the door handle, found it and pulled, but nothing happened. He ran his fingers across the windowsill and found the locking knob and pulled up on it. He grabbed the door handle again and pulled, but the door wouldn't budge. Jake rammed his shoulder against it, nothing happened. The door was pressed against the muddy river bottom. Jake swam over to the passenger-side door. The car suddenly started to shift: it was rocking from the river currents. The car—and Jake—would slide deeper into the bowels of Hell. Jake flexed his legs and with all his might, kicked at the window. It shattered. The first time ever that the breaking of glass felt exhilarating to Jake. There was a sudden pressure change in the car and filthy, slimy muck rushed in. Jake pushed through the mud and swam out. *Which way to the surface? Which way was up?* The blackness and bitter cold had disoriented him. If he just took off, he might find himself swimming horizontally, or worse, going downward. His lungs were quickly consuming his last gulp of air. Then he saw bubbles rising upward from the car. Jake felt his bare feet on the hard metal of the car's roof and bent his knees and pushed off with as much effort as he could muster. He held his arms at his sides and paddled desperately with his feet—natural buoyancy would take far too long. And up he went. He could see light flickering up above, but his lungs were cramping up, his throat tightening. He wanted so badly to take a deep breath. He felt very weak. *How far, how far must I go?* He paddled on. The surface, life, a future, didn't seem to be getting any closer. Air, air, Jake had to take a breath, he had to; he was in excruciating pain;

no longer could he wait, no longer. He opened his mouth—but just then broke through the water's surface. Fresh air engorged his lungs. He took another deep, gasping breath; it smelled so sweet and fresh, full of living things, trees and grass—wondrous aromas he had taken for granted. *I made it! I made it! I'm alive. I beat those assholes! Ha. But, the money! It's still in the car. I must go back to get it. I must because it's mine, all mine! I earned every damn penny of it!* Jake dove back down into the murky water, the smell of greenbacks still more alluring to him than fresh air. He found the car and reached into the broken window. He felt around for the black bag and clasped his hands around the handle. With the other hand, he grabbed a few bundles of bills floating about, and quickly returned to the surface. Welcome sunlight glared into Jake's eyes, and as a wash of water cleared them, he could just barely make out the riverbank. Two men in brilliant, pin-stripped suits stood on the bank with pistols drawn. Then a heavy-set shadowy figure standing behind them came forward, melting between the two goons. It was a wispy, almost transparent image of the casino boss. He cracked a self-satisfying grin.

A tall-slender figure then began to appear next to the fat man. It was holding his hand lovingly. As the ghostly image became clearer, Jake could see she had a delighted smile. It was Jake's dead ex-wife.

My Darling Tilley

By Don Kirk

THE SUN WAS SETTING on a long stretch of desert road in Nevada and the Hamptons weren't going to make it to California this evening. It was beginning to rain and the blackness of the night was closing in on them. A neon sign flickered up ahead through the rain-spattered windshield, it read: SAND'S MOTEL. $12.50 SINGLE.

"Tilley," said Harold suddenly, "wake up. I'm going to have to stop here. We're not going to make it to Bishop, this motel will have to do for tonight."

Tilley raised her head from Harold's shoulder and rubbed her eyes. "What?"

"This is it. Get your shoes on. It'll be fine."

"Tonight?"

"Sorry, Dear."

Harold turned his black '49 Packard into the motel and stopped in front of the office.

"I'll get the best room they've got, their honeymoon suite."

Tilley looked at the row of small pink cabins with peeling white trim, and each with its own little carport. "The honeymoon suite must be around the back," she said sarcastically.

"You folks, going west?" asked the hotel manager.

"Yes, it's our honeymoon."

"Well, I'll be danged!"

"Sir?"

"We ain't never had honeymooners here before."

"No?"

"Not never."

"Is the water hot?"

"Yes sir, you betcha, give it about fifteen minutes. I'll light the pilot light for you."

"That'd be nice."

"The wall heater is already lit. I keep it at sixty."

"Okay if I turn it up to seventy?"

"If you're a mind too."

"How much then?" said Harold Hempstead as he pulled out a money clip chock full of Ben Franklins.

"Two a yuh, how many days?"

"Just tonight thanks."

"That'll be sixteen fifty."

"All I have is a hundred dollar bill. Can you—"

"Oh, no sir, I ain't seen that much—"

"I tell you what, I'll trade you this sterling silver money clip for a special night in your fine motel."

Harold pulled the clip from his folding money and handed it to the motel clerk to examine it. The clerk turned it over and eyed it carefully. "You got a deal, mister."

Harold signed the register and returned to the car.

"He took my silver money clip for payment," said Harold. "I bought it in Mexico, only worth about fifty cents. It'll take a week for the paint to wear off and we'll be long gone."

"Oh Harold, you can afford to pay him fair."

"Yes, but getting away with not paying him is the fun of it."

Harold drove his car into the carport and unlocked the door. He fumbled for the light switch; a floor lamp by the window came on. In the dim, dust-filled air, he could see a low-slung twin bed set against the far wall—a wall covered with gaudy, faded and peeling, wallpaper. A dresser with attached mirror leaned against the wall to the right, a *Bakelite* radio sat on a small bedside table, and a sagging door at the back of the room opened to the bathroom. Tilley took a step up the stone steps.

"Wait!" Harold grabbed Tilley beneath her knees and lifted her into his arms. "I have to carry you across the threshold."

"Dear, you'll hurt your back."

"I'll be fine."

Tilley smiled weakly, "If you must."

"It's our first night."

"And last," she mumbled.

"What?"

"The last in a dump like this I hope," she replied.

"I don't care where we stay, as long as it's with you."

"You're so sweet."

Harold put her down on the musty bed. The mattress bottomed out on the floor as dust rose into the choking air.

Harold brought in their suitcases, dropped them on the floor—hers seemed quite heavy to him—and closed the door, hopefully for the last time this night.

"Well, we're here," Harold said clumsily as he pulled his braces from his white ruffled shirt.

Tilley curled up on the bed, looking dead to the world.

Harold sat down on the bed to remove his black, patent leather shoes.

"Tilley, wake up, so you can get undressed—uh, get dressed for bed."

"Um—what?"

Harold leaned over and kissed her on the cheek. Tilley reached around him and pulled him to her. He kissed her with his dry chapped lips. Tilley pulled away and sat up on the edge of the bed. It was like kissing a corpse, a long-dead one. She pulled up her skirt and unsnapped the silk stockings from her garter belt and pulled them off carefully.

"You have beautiful legs," Harold said as he touched her thigh so delicately.

Tilley pulled back. "I'm so very tired honey."

Harold understandably felt rejected, and moved over to the dresser where he placed the contents of his pants pockets on the dresser top: a neatly-folded, monogrammed-silk handkerchief, gold fingernail clippers, a big wad of bills, some small change, and a couple of "silver" money clips. He then flipped on the radio;

it was tuned to a station with religious hymns. "Yes, it's been a long day."

"It has, darling."

"I can't wait to get to Bishop," Harold added. "I'm looking forward to some of your great cooking."

"I can't wait to see that magnificent mansion of yours."

"Oh, it's modest, only 10,000 square feet, but it has a great view of the snow-capped Sierras."

"Are there lots of pine trees?"

"Ah, well no darling, those are in the mountains; we live in the desert. We can see the—"

"A desert like this here in Nevada?"

"It's similar, but it has—"

"What? More sand?" Tilley lay back down on the bed.

"You're suitcase is darn heavy," pronounced Harold as he lifted it onto the suitcase rack by the door.

"I brought my best cutlery so I can cook you the finest of dinners."

"I have good kitchenware in my home, in *our* home."

"Yes, it is *our* home, isn't it dear?"

"Yes, yours and mine."

"Half is mine?"

"Yes, *all* if you like. I shall smother you in splender and love."

"You're so sweet."

"Now get your nighties and come quickly to bed."

"But can I keep my cutlery?" asked Tilley as she got up and came over to her suitcase and popped the latches. In a slow, meditative manner, she opened the suitcase and reached in—reaching *past* her dainty pink bras and negligee.

"Of course you can keep them, Sweetums, but,"—Harold turned serious and confronted Tilley—"you didn't just marry me for my money, did you? You *do* love me, don't you?"

"Dear, you'll never know how much I love you." And at that, she turned toward him and ran a long carving knife into his spleen. A strange, empty expression came over his contorted face. But not one of complete surprise or misunderstanding, instead he seemed kind of expecting it, to be asking, "not even one night together, Dear?"

Tilley twisted the knife viciously, pleasurably. "Not even one night," she replied softly. The radio crackled in the background with a religious hymn:

As I went down in the river to pray,
Studying about that good ol' way—

Harold went limp and fell backward onto the bed. His arms fell away from his bloody shirt. The springs squeaked, but not for the reason he had hoped—

And who shall wear the robe and crown,
Good Lord, show me the way—

Tilley grinned derisively and threw the carving knife onto the white chenille bedspread.

Oh sinners let's go down, let's go down,
Come on down, oh sinners let's go down,
Down in the river to pray—

One of Harold's arms suddenly flopped off the edge of the bed. Tilley jumped, then took a deep breath and broke in to a devilish grin. "It's all mine now, Harold T. Hempstead, not just half, you're *entire* fortune. You didn't think I was going to stay with you in that god-forsaken desert town of Bishop, did you?" Tilley, nonchalantly, sat next to her husband and removed her blouse and unzipped her skirt—

As I went down in the river to pray,
Studyin about that good ol way,
And who shall wear the robe and crown,
Good Lord show me the way—

As verse after verse of the hymn continued, Tilley rolled her husband onto the floor and dragged him into the bathroom. She carefully tore away his blood-soaked shirt and dropped it into the shiny-bright trashcan under the sink. She removed his pin-stripped wool pants, unfastened his suspenders, removed his stockings and pulled off his green calico drawers and undershirt. Harold Hempstead, who was a good deal older than Tilley, lay spread eagle on the cold tile floor.

Tilley returned to the bedroom and to her suitcase. She reached in, down to the very bottom, and retrieved a large meat cleaver. A second trip down and she came up with a bone saw. "This," she said, "is my finest cutlery."

Tilley returned to the bathroom and began to prepare her husband. The hands would go first. She scattered the fingers with one clean blow of the cleaver. She picked up the bloody ring finger as if it was a soggy French fry and kissed the gold wedding ring and then plopped the finger into the toilet bowl. She flipped the tank lever and the ring finger of her new husband circled around and around and finally disappeared. "Good riddance," she said and threw in the other fingers. She chopped off the hands as if they were veal cutlets. She began to carve up her dear departed husband's carcass like it was a Thanksgiving turkey and sawed each piece to a size sufficient to flush it easily down the toilet. Then she opened his chest, broke out the meaty ribs (if only she had a barbecue grill), ripped out the small and large intestines, cut out his stomach, his liver, bloody spleen, and finally his sweet loving heart. She flushed them all down easily. It took a lot of work with the bone saw to cut up the legs and arms into pieces small enough to go down the sewer. The knee-joints got caught in the toilet's P-trap and she had to use the plumber's helper sitting behind the toilet—*backed up toilet, must be a common problem at this flea-bag hotel*, she thought. But finally, she got them all down. *There, every last piece of his wretched body flushed away to the septic tank*, but then she noticed…his head, his big stupid ugly head with its slicked down black hair parted in the middle, his long curly handlebar mustache, his dead empty eyes, and yellow blood-stained teeth. What would she do with this dirty old goat's repulsive head? She placed both her tiny fragile white hands on his head and lifted—it was, she thought, heavier than a head of lettuce, heavier that a cantaloupe, even heavier than a watermelon; she didn't think brains weighted that much, especially Harold's. Just then, the head slipped from her fingers, bounced off the floor, and rolled over onto its nose—

A knock came at the door.

Tilley froze. Her heart missed a beat—maybe more. Her blood-smeared, half-naked body was glued to the bathroom floor, paralyzed. Who could it be? What does he want? Finally, after what seemed like minutes, she stood up in her blood-soaked panties and bra and hurried to her suitcase. She pulled out and threw on her flowery robe, tied it around her waist, and then stopped short when she saw her bloody face in the dresser mirror.

Another, more determined knock rattled the front door.

"Just a moment," she yelled and turned to the bathroom. She quickly washed the bright red blood from her face and dried her face with the ratty motel towel.

Another knock.

She eyed Harold's head still lying on the bathroom floor. She picked it up, dropped it into the metal trashcan under the sink, hurried to the door, and opened it.

The motel manager stood there embarrassed by Tilley's half-dressed appearance. He removed his hat cordially.

"Sorry ma'am, I know this is a bad time. My apologies to Mr. Hempstead but—"

"Yes?" asked Tilley looking perturbed and fearful at the same time.

"Ma'am, tell your husband he left his parking lights on—the Packard."

Tilley took a deep sigh of relief.

"The battery's probably gettin' low by now—"

"Is that it? Is that all you wanted to tell me?"

"Uh, yes ma'am, sorry, but you're the only guests we have tonight and I can't jump you—"

Tilley closed her robe tighter around her neck.

"Battery cables, ma'am, a jump start, can't do it, my pickup's at the mechanic in town."

"I see, well, thank you," replied Tilley, relieved. "I wonder if you could take the keys and turn off the lights for me—us—my husband would—"

"Sure ma'am, be happy to."

Tilley turned back into the room, closing the door behind her as the motel manager tried to peek in. Where was Mr. Hempstead, he wondered? He stepped back and tried to peer in the front window, but the heavy sheer curtains diffused the view; he could see only a shadowy figure moving inside—the door suddenly opened again and Tilley, with her outstretched arm, handed him the car keys, and closed the door again.

Tilley looked around the room. Did he see anything? There! Her bloody carving knife still lay on the bed. She quickly reached for it and threw it in her suitcase—

Came another knock on the door. She opened it, composing herself with expert acumen this time.

"Thank you, you've been very helpful."

"I'm sorry, Mrs. Hempstead, I had to…tell your husband…I'm sorry…"

"I will," interrupted Tilley and shoved on the door to close it, but the manager reached out and caught it. Terror rose a notch in Tilley's mind.

"Mrs. Hempstead, tell your husband his inspection sticker has expired; the constable is quite strict in these parts."

"As he should be. Thank you Mr.…I didn't get your…"

"Bonecutter, ma'am, Charley Bonecutter.…"

"Well, thank you," said Tilley matter-of-factly and closed the door. My God, did he know? She turned to see the metal trashcan sitting in the brightly-lit bathroom—she had failed to close the bathroom door. Puddles of blood remained on the slippery tile floor. Could he have seen them when the door was open? Could he see through the front window? She adjusted the sheer curtains as if it would do any good.

Tilley took her husband's undershirt, got back on her knees, and began to clean up the bathroom floor and the blood-splattered walls and blood-smeared frosted glass door on the shower stall. She had to repeatedly wring out the blood into the sink. There seemed to be no end to it. How could there be this much warm blood in one greedy, cold bastard, she thought. Tilley searched for every small speck of blood and scrubbed it up.

"There, I'm finished. No more Mr. Harold T. Hempstead." She was pleased with herself, a job well done. Tilley then saw that her own body was covered with dried blood: Harold, the son of a bitch was still caressing her body with his callous hands. It pained her something terrible. "You bastard, get off me!" she snapped, wildly slapping her hands across her arms and face. He wouldn't go away. The blood had dried and crusted on her lovely soft skin. She felt dirty and violated.

"The shower, I can scrub the bastard off," cursed the exhausted Tilley as she dropped her bra and panties to the floor and stepped into the pink porcelain-tiled shower stall. The shower door opened inward and she had to step around it to close it.

The slim fingers of Tilley's hand twisted the squeaky hot water valve and she waited for the rusty water to clear and get nice and hot before she added the cold water to moderate the temperature. When it was comfortable, she wet herself down, lathered up, and scrubbed and scrubbed and scrubbed. Blood dripped to the tile floor and ran into the drain. *Away, be gone Mr. Hempstead.* The refreshing water caressed her supple, white body and she felt clean again. She soaked her hair and added a sweet-smelling herbal shampoo to her disheveled auburn hair. The shower stall began to fill with a suffocating steam, but it was cold in the motel room and this felt so refreshing. She felt good again, having washed away all her sins. She lowered the water temperature a bit and enjoyed the invigorating, soothing sauna. Her mind raced and she remembered Harold's head in the trashcan. How was she going to get his head out of the motel? She strained her sweet little mind. That's it! The hatbox with her veil, it sat in the trunk of the Packard; the head just might fit. She could bury the awful thing in the desert—but then, she thought, the coyotes might dig it up, drag it around the desert floor, chew it to pieces, play with it like a soccer ball. Well, that wasn't so bad, but then the coyotes might drag it across the highway, and it might get run over by a police car, and be crushed like a watermelon and the cop would find out…oh, poor Harold, picked on by tarantulas and scorpions, and ugly vultures—dirty, nasty creatures that would pluck out his no-longer lustful eyes. The thought pleased her immensely.

Tilley suddenly noticed the water rising at her feet. She shoveled the water with her feet toward the drain but it kept rising. Was her hair plugging up the drain strainer? She looked down but couldn't see through the thick steam, and so knelt down to take a closer look. She put her hand in the murky water and raked across the drain. No hair, but something thick and slimy was oozing up through the strainer. Her feet slid on the filth, but she grabbed the soap tray to stop her fall. The strainer popped up and large chunks of something strange gushed up through the drain opening. The sewer sludge was now covering her ankles and rising toward her knees. Tilley shut off the water and reached for the glass door and pulled on the handle, but the door wouldn't come open. She pulled again harder; it only rattled in its frame: the weight of the water backed up in the stall was holding it shut. The slime was rising past her knees and she noticed it wasn't just water, it was a diluted red substance with a pinkish tissue floating on the surface. Floating on top of the sludge was Harold's ring finger, the wedding ring still on it. Tilley's usually calm demure turned to panic. She banged on the frosted glass, but only bruised her hands. She pushed with her shoulder, trying to push the door outward, but it didn't budge. The cloud of steam was clearing above her now and she could see a small glazed window high on the tiled wall. Tilley reached up and turned the catch and grabbed the handle, but the window held firm, it had been painted shut—many times over. The dark crimson protein pudding rose on her slender white legs and fear began to grip her tortured mind like fingers violently massaging her scalp—maybe they were Harold's. She scratched frantically at the putty trying to get the windowpane out. She kicked at the sewer sludge she once knew as her husband and tried to shake it off; it was like chocolate custard and it stuck to her skin. Tilley was now in abject terror, spinning around in circles, her breathing labored, her chest heaving uncontrollably. Old Harold continued to fill the shower stall, rising past Tilley's slim waist, past her youthful breasts. The very things that drew Harold to her, soon those things he would devour, and he would rise on up to cover her pretty face and her supple mouth and the cute nose she used for breathing. She would suffocate—right here in the shower. She screamed out. Her voice echoed hollow in the little shower stall that sat in a small room in a roadside motel out on a lonely highway in a desolate desert in the state of Nevada. She screamed at the top of her lungs, but no one could hear her.

Suddenly, the shower door shattered violently from the weight of putrid blood and body parts and meaty bones. The ugly mess cascaded out the door and into the bathroom and flowed into the bedroom. Along with the human waste and filth came Tilley tumbling out of the shower stall. More of Harold gurgled up through the sink drain. The toilet burped and splattered his innards on the ceiling. The bathroom trashcan fell over and poor Mr. Hempstead's head rolled out and came to a stop facing Tilley. She lay on the floor petrified. She stared into Harold's penetrating eyes and looked at his frowning old wrinkled mouth—but just then, a satisfying grin seemed to break on Harold Hemstead's face—

And a knock came at the door.

★　★　★

Where Time Stopped

By Don Kirk

THERE WAS SOMETHING about this room that was very different from any other room I had ever encountered. I had bought an old three-story Victorian with dreams of fixing it up myself. It would take time, but it could become the jewel of the neighborhood. It still had most of its original gingerbread, some original wallpaper, a grand mahogany staircase, the floors were sound, the roof in good shape. I got it for a great price. But that room, I would never have dreamed what it would do to me.

The room was near the middle of the house on the second floor and had one window that opened into an interior courtyard with a solarium. I could see across the courtyard to the windows of the other rooms on all three floors. I was going to make the room my home office and I could keep a watchful eye on the rest of the house from this room. I outfitted my office with a roll-top desk, my trusty *Underwood* typewriter and a finely crafted "Lawyer's" bookcase; you know, those with the glass doors that lift up to access the books. I hung one of those red-plastic *Coca-Cola* electric clocks on the wall in front of me, and that was where it all began. I plugged in the cord and the hands of the clock didn't move. I checked the electrical outlet with my circuit tester. There was plenty of juice—15 amps, 115 volts. I brought in my clock radio and plugged it in, the radio played just fine, but the clock's numbers never changed. The clocks worked just fine in the rest of the house so I purchased one of those battery-operated clocks and brought it into the room and as I crossed the door's threshold, the second hand stopped moving. It had to be something about this room. Some kind of magnetic field had to be interfering with the flow of electrons. But I had no high-voltage television CRT's and there were no high-tension power lines anywhere nearby. Everything else in the room seemed fine so I put my clock in the hall and positioned my desk so I could see it through the doorway—it ran just fine there. But then something else strange happened. I had brought a bowl of ice cream from the kitchen to eat while I worked. And I did, I worked, I was engrossed in a short story I was writing for *Analog Science Fiction* magazine, and I forgot about the ice cream even after the first delicious bite. An hour or so later, I noticed the ice cream, my Pistachio Almond, was still there in its glass bowl just as frozen as it had been when I removed it from the fridge—it had not melted! Further experiments using *Jell-O* and frozen custard and soft drinks yielded the same results. They stayed in the same state they had been before I brought them into the room. The drinks didn't loose their freshness or fizz. Even a hot pork chop left in the room overnight still remained hot, but when I took it out of the room, it quickly cooled down. What was going on? This little room in the middle of the house, what was so different about it? And then I noticed that when I was in that room for much of the day, my face still had no stubble; it was still smooth as Emory cloth by six p.m. I had thought my new *Gillette* twin-blade was doing a marvelous job with its close shave, but no, when I was in that room, my beard was not growing at all. It seemed to grow normally when I spend the day in the rest of the house. Was the hair on my head growing? I didn't know. I started a regiment of measuring my locks and the length of my fingernails and kept a carefully plotted chart. My hair and nails were indeed growing much slower.

Every now and again, a cockroach would scurry across the floor and even a rat would turn up from time to time. I began to think that maybe time itself had come to a halt in this strange room. Those rats and cockroaches, maybe they where actually hundreds of years old? But, was there any way of knowing how old they might be? And was I also aging in this room? Had I found immortality? Would my hair never silver, my Blood Pump never wear out? I began to spend more and more time in the room— just in case. I brought a small couch and a television set into the twelve by fifteen foot room so that I could spend my evenings there too. And then it occurred to me: we spend one third of our lives just sleeping, doing nothing but snoring loudly on a cheap foam pillow and dreaming dreams of nonsense. So I purchased a surplus military cot and moved it into the room. There, that should really lengthen my life, I thought, by another forty years at least. It got so that I didn't leave the room except to cook myself something to eat. And that seemed, logically, like an unnecessary loss of time, so I brought in a hot plate to cook on and a beverage-sized icebox to store my perishables. But, for some strange reason, that didn't work; anything I tried to cook wouldn't heat; anything I tried to refrigerate wouldn't cool, not in that room. It made sense I suppose, if time wasn't moving, how could matter change its properties?

Still, even having to leave my room to cook, I was spending most of my time in that room. I would leave the house to put my manuscripts in the mailbox, but that was about it. I had my groceries delivered to my door. I could now live, I calculated, to the ripe old age of 160, maybe more. My organs—heart, liver, lungs, eyes, bones—they wouldn't deteriorate and my epidermis would stay youthful—forever. And, well, maybe my belongings wouldn't age either.

A goodly amount of time passed, months, maybe years. I had brought my *Gillette* razor blades and other essentials into the room and sure enough the blades didn't rust, my clothes didn't succumb to dry rot, the pages of my books never browned or became brittle. I built shelves, got a TV tray for eating, and got a good quality bed with a nice headboard. Color photographs, architectural blueprints, rubberbands, nothing, I supposed, would ever age. They would last forever. Years ago, I had trapped the rats and a few roaches and numbered them with paint and I gave the rats names: Joey, Clem, and Gertrude. They returned year after year and I fed them all. They weren't aging one bit. I was sure of it. That meant I wasn't aging either. This indeed was a room where time itself had stopped.

I decided to rent out my house; I had no real use for the space. And because of the size of my Victorian, I could rent it as two or even three separate apartments. A fair amount of income. I only left my room to keep the furnace in the basement going and fix the plumbing now and again. A sweet deal. And my window in my little room became a portal to time. I watched families come and go, watched children grow up, couples get married and divorced. And every family was a different story; in fact, they became my inspiration for many of my best short stories. Many science fiction magazines had long ceased publication, but there were a few other pulps to sell stories too, and I now owned one of those new-fangled desktop computers, a *Radio Shack TRS-80 Model I* word processor. I could now get more stories out faster and money came in at a fast clip.

But time passed outside my room and the house began to crumble around me; I could no longer keep up with the repairs. People no longer wanted to rent my house anymore what with the wallpaper peeling, floorboards rotting, ceiling plaster caving in. I couldn't blame them, but I couldn't afford to spend much time outside my room; if I did, I'd advance in years along with my house, and I saw what was happening to it. I kept thinking about my room. What made it so special? Why did this room never age? The wallpaper looked as good as it did when I first moved in back in the '50's. Could I add on to the room, expand my space to capture more of this wondrous fixed-in-time space? I could sure use more space to live in. I tore out one wall and framed in some more space, covered the walls with sheetrock and pulled some of my belongings into the new part of the room. But everything I put in the new space started to show signs of ageing again and I pulled everything back into the original space. It wasn't the room that was special, I concluded, it was where this particular room had been built: some *place* in time, a warp or something between the folds of space where time did not exist. So I resided myself to the fact that this was all the bigger my world would get, this one twelve by fifteen foot room.

I now had a *Gates* computer, Apple no longer made computers, in fact no one else did, a *Gates* was my only choice, but it worked okay, crashed a lot, I couldn't get software upgrades, but I still got a story published now and again. Joey and Clem and Gertrude still scurried around my room. I could live with them here for all of eternity…and then it hit me like a ton of bricks: did I want to spend eternity in this little room with my friends and my guaranteed-to-never-rust razor blades, when my entire beautiful Victorian home had fallen down around my ears? We couldn't even grow old together. Eternity was a long time and I was running out of stories to write.

One day I cut myself, just a little paper cut, but weeks went by (I had created a sundial on my wall marking the sun's rays as they crossed my room) and the cut never healed. When I stubbed and bruised my toe years earlier it had taken almost forever to heal. I realized that every time I injured myself, I would have to spend precious time *outside* my room so that healing would take place normally. So I built a new room adjacent to mine using what old lumber still hadn't succumbed to the elements. The city's housing department had already condemned my property and was threatening to clear the lot. They said I had to leave. I told them I couldn't; that this was my home. I told them I had lived here for over a hundred and fifty years. They said I looked thirty. I said, well, that was true, but was no reason to take my property. But to make a long story short, they took me out of my room and hauled me kicking and screaming to a happy farm. The mansion some big-city folks built on my lot still had that magical place where time stood still, and my favorite rats, Joey, Clem, and Gertrude, must have gotten awfully bored because they began to reproduce, and reproduce some more, until the city was inundated with kissing cousins. Then some form of the plague took hold.

But me, I lived out the rest of my days quietly in that disinfectant-scoured sanitarium, insulated from the death happening outside. In fact, much of the population of our fair city died off, but I happily had three more nice undemanding new companions. I named them Jeffrey, Cecil and Geraldine. No, I never had a family, kids, in-laws, or friends—well, except for my editors, most of which I never met—and I never saw the world beyond my little community, in fact, not much beyond my little room, but I did live to the ripe old age of one-hundred-ninety-two and had many loyal friends—if I fed them.

100 Ways to Dispose of a Body

By Don Kirk

"LOOK WHAT YOU'VE DONE! You didn't have to kill him just 'cause he wanted last-month's rent, you buffoon!"

"He wanted *this* month's rent too," said Purvis as he held a bloody axe in his right hand.

"Stupid, stupid! What are you gonna do with him now, bird brain? You didn't have to kill him right here in our house."

"He asked for it, he got it."

"What, a splitting headache? 'Cause that's what he's got now."

"He won't be needin' no aspirin," said Purvis.

"I see that, said Quentin as he scratched his oversized head and added, "What are you gonna do now? The son-of-a-bitch weighs upwards of three-hundred pounds."

"I can't carry him outta here."

"No dummy, you can't. And I can't either. And we can't leave him here. We *live* here you hair-brained idiot! Our mail comes here, our bills come here, our neighbors know who lives here, you stupid imbecile. You coulda took him somewhere's else before you whacked him."

"He was goin' to call the cops, had his hand on the phone; I couldn't let that happen, now could I?" retorted Purvis.

"Come on grab the rug, we'll pull him over against the wall behind the couch in case somebody comes."

Quentin and the greasy-haired, undersized Purvis grabbed the rug and, with all their might, pulled on it. The big-bellied corpse lay face up on the cheap rug looking like a sleeping baby…or a baby elephant. He was dead to the world.

They got the obese corpse up against one wall and covered him with the other half of the rug. They then pushed the couch against him and sat down to take a breather.

"We mail him!" Purvis blurted out enthusiastically. "Chop him up into pieces, box 'em up, mail him."

"To where for God's sake?"

"It don't matter, all over, we just don't put no return address on him."

"Alaska maybe, where it's cold, he wouldn't stink so much," added Quentin.

"We could use quick lime to mask the odor when he got ripe, wrap the parts in big *Zip-Lock* bags, seal the box real good. Nobody'd be the wiser."

"Just might work," said Quentin as he rubbed his chin.

"Except," added Purvis, "I ain't got no friends in Alaska, or nowheres else for that matter."

"Dummy! Why would you want to send the fat man's body parts to a friend?"

"Just, I mean, we gotta have addresses don't we?"

"We just make up addresses, pick a few cities, get their zips, it don't matter if they ain't no real addresses, the poor man's body parts'll just end up in the dead letter box; they can't mail 'em, they can't return 'em 'cause they won't have a return address. I think it'll work—"

Purvis interrupted Quentin's comforting thoughts, "How much do it cost to mail three-hundred pounds?"

"What?"

Purvis stood up and turned toward the couch and leaned over the backrest. "He weighs at least three-hundred, that's for sure. What's it now, twenty-seven cents an ounce?"

"How many ounces to a pound?"

"Crap, I don't know! You're the smart one."

"It's a lot, I know that. Let's see, eight ounces to a cup, or is it sixteen…a quart is…"

"Hell, it don't matter either way, we ain't got that kind o' dough."

Just then a knock came at the door. Purvis and Quentin froze like two hens about ready to drop their eggs.

"Relax Purvis, don't say a word, *I'll* do the talkin'." Quentin stood up and calmly went to the door.

He opened it.

Quentin let the pent-up, carbon-dioxide-saturated air out of his lungs; it was just the mail carrier.

"Two letters for you Mr. Pendle, and one for your brother."

"Thanks."

"Thanks," came Purvis' voice too. He was still sitting on the couch.

"Oh hi, Purvis. I see you boys are doing a little furniture rearranging."

"Uh yeah," broke in Quentin, "we was just puttin' the couch over here sos we can see out the front window, and the TV, we'll put it over there to cut down on the glare from that there window." Purvis sat their grinning and nodding in agreement; his arms tucked up across his chest, sweat dripping down his brow. He added, "We was just takin' a break. This furniture moving is hard work."

"I know it is, my wife and I rearranged our bedroom a while back and we had a time of it, what with the dresser and blanket trunk and double bed…"

"Yeah real hard work. Well, we gotta get back to…"

"Oh sure, I understand." The mail carrier nodded and flicked his cap with his index finger and scurried off.

Quentin turned to Purvis. "What you sweatin' so damn much for?"

"Rearranging furniture's hard work."

"Oh shut up. We gotta get that body outta here, and quick."

"Yeah boss, I'm listening."

"I'm not your boss."

"You act like it sometime."

Quentin walked around to the back of the couch and took another gander at the monstrous body. "Why in God's name did you have to kill him here?"

"It couldn't wait, he was picking up the phone to call the cops.

He'd uh found out we had criminal records and kicked us out on our asses."

"Well, he was gonna do that anyways, Purvis, 'cause we ain't paid the rent."

"I think you're right."

"Well, of course, I'm right."

"Hey, I got it!"—Quentin pulled up a straight-backed chair, straddled it, and put his elbows on the back of the chair—"You can get a job at the meat packing plant; they's always needin' grave-yard workers."—Quentin reached for the telephone—"Come on, call now."

"Wait, just wait a damn minute," barked Purvis, "Watchuh up to?"

"You been in a packing plant ain't ya. They got sides of beef hanging on hooks in the freezer and they take 'em out one by one and cut 'em up into round steaks and sirloins and fill-its. Then they wrap 'em up real nice in that plastic stuff, that shrink wrap, and put 'em out in the display case..."

"And customers buy 'em and take 'em home and..."

"That's right, Purvis, and how they gonna know from sheep's leg 'o lamb and human leg o' lamb, all labeled up nice an' pretty?"

"They wouldn't."

"And they's got meat grinders at packing plants where's we could stuff him in and make him into sausages and hotdogs and hamburger," added Quentin.

"How'd we get rid of the bone?"

"Bone?"

"Nothin's worse than knockwurst with little chips of bone to break your teeth on."

"Damn, who cares Purvis, *we're* not gonna eat him! You just get the job at the plant and I'll drive ol' lard butt there in a van and..."

"Yeah, well, he's too friggin' heavy," said Purvis, "and he don't look a sight like a side of beef."

"You don't think?"

"Well, maybe he do, but it ain't gonna work and we ain't got that much time for you to work up a plan, Quentin. That corpse there is gonna be gettin' real ripe and no amount of quick lime's gonna…"

"You're right, Purvis."

Purvis leaned back on the couch, pleased with himself. He was right about something for a change.

"Fig bars!"

"What?"

"There's a plant on the southside what makes fig bars. We could put his body in the fig-mashing vat. Nobody know'd the diff, maybe even them figs would taste better."

"Now *you're* off your bean, big brother."

"Well, we could throw him into Farmer Kemp's hay bailer, shred him up real good, or maybe a big-ass wood chipper, that'd do the job just dandy. Maybe a trash incinerator…or the city dump, that's it!"

"You're still forgettin' something, big brother."

"What's that?"

"How we gettin' him outta here?"

"I'm thinkin' on it."

"And while you do, he's gettin' ripe."

"Here, I'm gettin' a *Pearl*," said Quentin. "You want one? I can think better with a beer in my hand."

"Me too."

Quentin scurried into the kitchen, the wood floor squeaking under the worn linoleum. He opened the icebox and the cold air turned to condensation.

"We gotta keep him cold," blurted out Quentin. "That's the fact of it, until I can come up with a plan."

Quentin returned to the living room with two cold beers, gave one to Purvis, and then sat down beside the phone table. He dialed up an appliance store.

"Yes. You guys got a big freezer? Yes. Your biggest? How long is it?…Seventy-three inches. How much is that in feet?…About six feet. Great! How much can it hold?…Twenty-four-point-seven cubic feet, can that hold a man, I mean some really mean-sized chickens, and a deer?…Huh, yeah, well that'll do just grand. When can you deliver? Today, great. You got a low, low down-payment plan? I can't pay…zero?…zero for six months! Oh great." Quentin hung up, elated. "Hallelujah!" We got our problem solved."

"How so?" replied Purvis taking another big icy gulp of his profusely perspiring beer.

"We freeze him 'till I can come up with a fool-proof plan."

"Quentin, can a fool come up with a fool-proof plan?"

"What?"

"Nothing."

Quentin circled the room, excited, speedily turning over ideas in his well-oiled brain—well, as nimbly as a brain of his caliber: the pace of molasses in winter. And the brew was working on him.

Then Purvis blurted out: "How wide's the freezer?"

"What?"

"How wide's the freezer?"

"Why?"

"The front door—and the back-porch door for that matter—it's pretty narrow. It ain't no three-foot wide, two-eight maybe."

"You mean you don't think the freezer'll fit?"

"No. Most front doors to houses are three feet wide, less the door-stop moulding, and this door ain't…"

"How do you know…"

"I ain't no carpenter's assistant for nothing," Said Purvis as he crossed his arms prideful like.

"You just clean up after 'em."

"I see things, I learn things, I ain't as stupid as you think—"

"All right, all right, maybe you're right. We can leave the freezer outside in the carport. People do it all the time. Won't draw no attention to itself. Right natural."

"I s'pose," said Purvis.

"See, that's why I'm the smart one here."

"Yeah, boss," replied Purvis derisively and took another big swig, and then added, "How we gonna get him *into* the freezer?"

Quentin's jaw dropped and he plopped onto the couch. He thought for a moment as he scratched his greasy mop-top head.

"I got it. We can tilt the freezer on its side, roll him in, tilt it back up. It'll work, a little leverage…tonight when it's dark."

"Fine, but that don't get it."

"Get what?" asked Quentin.

"It don't solve our little…big, problem. It just gives you time to come up with that fool-proof plan o' yours."

"Yeah well, I'm thinking on it right now."

"Take another swig 'o your beer. It'll clear your head."

Quentin did just that, a long swig, as if the answer was in the bottle.

"I got it, Lye!"

"My name ain't Lye."

"I know that, bird brain. I mean *lye* like…"—Quentin circled the room, his hand again on his chin—"Like lye soap, stupid, only we ain't gonna use it to clean nothin'.'"

"Wutch you talking about now?"

Quentin sat down again on the couch and said, "It's strong stuff, eat through anything. You see, we get us a fifty-five-gallon oil-drum…"

Purvis jumped up, warming to the idea. "I know where there's one…"

"Good…good, perfect."

Purvis sat back down confused. "But what's your idea?"

"Don't you get it? A barrel of lye will dissolve anything. We cut up the fat man, drop his body parts in the barrel, and within just a few days, gone, kaput, fini! His bones, they go first, his blubber'll take a little longer—body fat's denser than bone, you see. Three days, maybe four tops, nothing left of him, nothing, then we just dump the lye in the backyard, easy. It's perfect. Take your pickup and go get that drum."

"I'm gone as fast as fleas to a donkey's ass." Purvis grabbed his baseball cap hanging by the door and out the door he went.

Then Quentin's mind continued to churn itself over, to work out the little details: *We need a meat cleaver and a bone saw and a canvas tarp to work on. We need to let him bleed out first, not as messy that way*—Quentin began to clear the living room of furniture. He moved the coffee table aside, and the dining table he shoved to the wall along with the chairs. *There, that should be enough room.*

Soon Purvis returned from a warehouse on Sixth Street with a weathered black, rusted brown, oil drum banging around in the back of his rattle-trap of a truck. He backed up into the carport and unloaded the drum. He rolled it into the backyard and set it upright. Quentin came outside.

"That's good. The bottom ain't rusted out is it?"

"Sound as a dollar."

"Good. The neighbors'll just think we're gonna burn some trash."

Purvis then spoke up: "You got the lye?"

"Lye! Hell, I forgot."

"A perfect plan, huh?"

"I know wheres I can get it, industrial cleaning supplies, they use the stuff to clean ovens and clogged sewer lines and such. You stay here. Give me your keys. Get started on the body."

"Me! I can't cut him up. Are you flippin' kidding me! No way, Jose, I ain't…"

"All right, all right, calm down, I got it all figured out, I'll get the tarp, the bone saw, the meat cleaver…and the lye. You just stay here with the body. Don't let nobody come in the house. And open the windows, keep the place aired out."

"You're leaving me here…with that body?"

"How else? Now get in there and watch the afternoon cartoons. It's almost three-thirty, your favorite *Roadrunner* cartoons…"

"Okay, okay, but you be quick about it." Purvis tossed him the keys. "And fill her up while you're at it."

"Get in there and close the door."

Quentin hopped in Purvis' '59 Ford pickup, with it's tailpipe throwing black smoke, and left.

Purvis returned to the living room and looked behind the couch, checking to see if the body—the big three-hundred-pounds of blubber—was still there. It was. He then went into the kitchen and cooked himself a hamburger, then placed it between two pieces of stale bread and added a river of soupy red catsup. Returning to the living room, he sat down on the couch and turned on the television set. The roadrunner streaked across the screen; the coyote lay in wait on the side of the road ready to dynamite a mountainside on top of the poor little roadrunner. *Beep, Beep,* the roadrunner streaked by and the fuse went out. Purvis laughed, he knew the coyote would get his. Purvis took a big sloppy bite from his burger. Suddenly there was a knock at the door. Purvis jumped to his feet. *Who could that be? The mail carrier has already been here.* He slicked back his hair and tried to act calm. He opened the door very slowly as if some evil monster was out there, worse, maybe the men in blue.

"Pendle?"

"Yes?"

"Sign here."

"What?"

"Your freezer, where do you want it?"

"Freezer? Oh yes, we did order that, you bet, sure…just put it in the carport."

"Just sign here."

"Be happy to."

Purvis scribbled his Hancock, and the delivery boy went away. *Thank goodness*, Purvis thought. Purvis looked at the freezer. *We ain't gonna need this now, well maybe, it might take a long time to cut up that bastard, maybe…*Purvis uncoiled the power cord and plugged it in. The compressor started to hum. Purvis smiled, *we got a place for a hefty stash o' Pearl! I think I'm gonna like this freezer.* Purvis returned to the living room. The body was beginning to smell something fierce; it would make even a coroner's nose turn a trick. Purvis opened the windows and returned to his *Roadrunner* cartoons.

It wasn't long before Quentin returned in Purvis' truck with a bed full of gallon jugs of drain cleaner, a white canvas tarp, and the tools of a butcher. One by one, he and Purvis poured the yellowish alkaline mix into the oil drum. It bubbled and looked downright scary, like something from the bowels of the Earth, like those gurgling mud pots in Yellowstone.

"Don't get it on ya if you don't wanna see your skin boil," warned Quentin.

Purvis cringed. "Is it acid?"

"No, actually it's not, it neutralizes acid."

"I don't get it."

"You'll see."

Purvis and Quentin pulled the couch out and rolled the fatman's carcass onto the canvas tarp. "Now for the hard part." Quentin handed Purvis a big meat cleaver.

Purvis stared at the cleaver and then the body. "Couldn't we just dump the body in a ditch or something?"

"No, we couldn't. Somebody'd find him in a day or two, identify him, then trace him back to us. No, we've got to get rid of him good. No body, no crime. They can't prosecute without a *corpus delicti*."

"A what? Sounds tasty, I'm getting hungry," said Purvis.

"You just start cuttin' and you can fry yourself a T-bone…or shall I say leg-bone."

Purvis started to upchuck.

"You ain't no good for nothin', Purvis. Here, give me that cleaver, I'll show you how it's done." Quentin took the meat cleaver and raised it high over his head. Purvis looked away and closed his eyes. Down came the cleaver. Blood splat in Purvis's face.

"Eeeuh!" Purvis lost it.

"Get over there and close the blinds," said Quentin coolly, "this is gonna take a while."

The sun was beginning to set, the horizon turning orange, the sky turning a deep blue as the warm temperatures of the day began to drop. Purvis made repeated trips to the oil drum with pieces of the fat man wrapped in a towel, and dropped them into the lye. The lye bubbled violently; it was doing more than just cleaning.

The living room now looked like a slaughterhouse: spatters of blood on everything in the room and on the walls and the television set. But the job was finally done; the fat man was no more. Purvis and Quentin worked through the night cleaning up the mess. They put the bloody canvas, tools, and axe back in the pickup truck with plans to burn them in a trash incinerator down the street.

Three days passed and the bubbling had ceased. No one had

bothered them, no one had come to the door except the mail carrier and the living room furniture was all back in place, well except for a new afghan throw draped over the couch to cover some fresh stains.

"Okay," said Quentin, "I think we can dump the lye now. It's done its job."

They hurried out to the backyard and pushed on the fifty-gallon oil drum.

"Be careful, don't get it on you," said Quentin.

But the drum wouldn't turn over. It was too heavy.

"I got it. We'll, hook your tow rope to the truck's bumper, pull it over."

And they did, and it worked, and the fat man washed over the lawn. They put the oil drum back in the pickup truck, rubbed their hands together, and smiled.

"We've done it. The perfect crime," said Purvis gleefully.

"As soon as you get that drum back to where you got it, dump them bloody tools in the trash incinerator, *then* we'll be free and clear."

"Right boss, we done it!" Purvis drove off.

It wasn't long before a shiny black cop car, with white door panels and a red bubble-gum machine, stopped in the street in front of the Pendle's home. Two men in blue came to the door with Purvis in tow, his hands in cuffs behind his back.

"This here's Officer Rand, I'm McGregor, San Mateo Police Department."

"Yes," replied Quentin, scared out of his ever-loving mind.

"Your brother?" asked McGregor.

"Might be. Did he do something, officer?"

"He stole an oil drum from *Strong's Mill Works* on South Sixth Street."

"You're kidding, that feller? You got him cuffed just for that? He was just returning it."

"Then he *is* your brother?"

"He didn't mean no harm, just wanted to burn a little trash."

"You don't mind if we take a look around, do you?"

"Uh, why no, officer, the backyard's right through there."

"We was just thinking, you don't have some other things that don't belong to you by any chance? This here freezer, maybe? It's still got a sale tag on it. Where'd you get that big thing? It's just you two boys live here?"

"Why yes sir."

"You cook a lot do you?" asked the cop as he lifted the lid. There was nothing inside but a couple of six-packs of beer. "I see."

Purvis broke in: "We got the receipt, just bought it." Purvis pulled the receipt from a drawer. "See?"

"Okay…Officer Rand, you check the backyard, while me and the boys have a talk inside."

McGregor led Purvis up the steps and into the living room.

"Nice place you got here; you keep it clean," said McGregor as he ran his fingers over the top of the television cabinet. "Not a speck of dust anywhere."

"No sir," replied Quentin as he sat down on the couch and crossed his legs. "We keep it right clean."

"I see. This your television set?"

"Yes sir, had it for years."

Just then Officer Rand opened the screen door and entered the room. Quentin leaned over to Purvis and whispered into his ears, "Did you get rid of the bloody tools?" Purvis smiled and nodded.

"Clem, you better look at this." Officer Rand opened the white handkerchief he had in the palm of his hand. McGregor stepped over to him. Rand carefully unfolded the handkerchief.

"Look here, Jack, teeth, human teeth; they ain't animal, that's for sure, they got silver fillings in 'em."

"You boys know anything about this?"

Quentin stood up. "No sir."

"No sir, we don't know nothin'," parroted Purvis.

"Do you boys know there's been lye in this oil drum?"

"No sir."

"How you boys suppose it got lye in it, in an oil drum?"

"I don't know," said Quentin. "Oil drums is used for lotsa…"

"And no soot, no sign anything was burned in it."

"Uh, well, we…"

"Cleaned it up," butt in Pruvis, "right good we did, with drain cleaner after we burned our…"

"I see," said McGregor as he rolled a couple of human canines and molars over in the palm of his hand. "You boys know these teeth can be matched with dental records."

"No sir."

"Well they can. Lye, my boys, will dissolve bone and skin tissue and body innards like nothing flat."

"Yes sir, we know…" blurted Purvis, and then quickly cut himself off.

"You do, do you? Well, I'm sure you didn't know lye won't dissolve enamel…like on animal's teeth, or a man's—"

"A man's? No sir, we didn't know—"

"You ain't got a body," added Quentin, standing tall and over-confident.

"What's that you say about we ain't got a body?"

"I uh, nothing, officer, I read about them corpus delicti's. Without a corpse, they ain't no proof of a crime."

"No, Mr. Pendle, you're wrong on that score. A *corpus delicti* don't mean the *body* of the victim. Corpse and corpus ain't the same thing ya' see. It's the facts that prove a crime. You know what I'm saying? The fact that a death *has* occurred, and these teeth show us that. We just have to prove that the death is the *result* of a murder. You see, we don't need the body."

"I see."

Officer McGregor shuffled over to the couch. "Mind if I look under that afghan?"

Quentin tensed up and said, "It's an awfully dirty couch."

"But the rest of your living room is so clean," said Officer McGregor as he lifted up the afghan. "What are these brown spots?"—He touched one with his index finger and then brought his finger to his face—"Looks like blood, dried blood."—McGregor sniffed at the dried goo—"Hum, no, it's just catsup. You boys eat in the living room a lot?"

"Yes, sir!" came their reply in unison.

"A murder probably happened around here and we'll prove it. You can count your chickens on that."

"If we had any," replied Quentin, "But we ain't been rentin' here mor'n three months, maybe someone before us…that's it officer, someone else done it before we got here."

"Could be boys. In the meantime, you should stock up that freezer with some suds, so when I come back, you can treat me."

"Why yes sir, we'd be happy to."

"I'll leave you boys to attend to business, but don't leave town until we clear up this matter."

And that was it. Officer McGregor and his partner apologized for the interruption and then left, taking a pair of *Pearls* from the freezer on their way out.

The next day, the Pendle boys filled their freezer to the brim with beer to make sure the officers stayed happy, then packed up their belongings and left town without leaving a forwarding address. The grass died in the back yard that summer and the appliance store eventually repossessed the freezer for non-payment.

Night Flight

By Don Kirk

THE PLANE BEGAN TO BUCK. The pilot fought the yoke and pulled and pushed on the throttle. The left wingtip would suddenly drop and then the right would follow suit. We could see a lightning show off to the Northwest embedded in huge white puffy clouds that resembled Chinese lanterns glowing from within. The sun had set, but the sky was still a deep Dresden blue and the twinkling of city lights appeared ever so often through the silky transparency of the thin wispy clouds moving by below. The lighting would set the thunderheads flashing like the nightglows of a hot air balloon celebration. One cumulonimbus lit up and then another and then a frightening, jagged ray of light energy pierced the air and hit the earth. Something or someone on the earth below was being taken out at every strike, like the attack of alien space ships in the War of the Worlds. The storms were coming closer now; new ones were forming all around us.

"Looks like I picked a bad time to get us up here," I said as I tightened my seat belt and braced my arms against the dash to keep my head from being slammed into the body of our single-engine Cessna 210.

"It didn't look like it was gonna be this bad when I filed my flight plan to Grand Rapids," grunted Sidney. "I'm trying to circle around this cold front, but a warm front is pushing in from the South and setting off new storm clouds…all ahead of us."

"I'm glad I didn't eat before we left."

Sidney Bertram didn't laugh at that. He was too busy manhandling his plane. The gusting side winds kept us off balance and headwinds were slowing our progress and gobbling up precious fuel. I had flown with Sidney before and trusted him with my life because of his many years and millions of uneventful flying hours as a commuter pilot—because simply, he was the kind of guy you knew you could trust with your life. He was now graying around the temples and showed some deep ravines in his face. We had left St. Lewis two hours ago and were flying northeast.

"Irwin, I'm afraid I'm going to have to turn her about and find us another airport," said Sidney. "Could you grab my sectionals and airport directory?"

I pulled the books out with one hand as I braced myself with the other.

"Northern Illinois, Chicago area," said Sidney.

Suddenly the plane took a nosedive and the engine raced. Sidney pulled up on the yoke and nursed the throttle. The plane yawed and pitched and rolled, but after a heroic battle by Sidney— and relentless praying on my part—the plane leveled off again and we both let out a sigh of relief. Sidney rubbed his left arm as if it was bothering him. I thought he just had a muscle cramp from working the yoke, but I'd soon find out that wasn't the case.

"Irwin, give me the A-T-I-S, the radio frequency for Chicago-Midway. You'll find it in the directory."

"Here it is, Sidney, one-two-eight-point-zero-five."

Sidney turned the dial on the radio and took the mike from its hook on the instrument panel and pressed the COM button. "Chicago-Midway, this is Cessna Nancy-seven-eight-Zebra. We're having trouble with this storm front. Our destination: Grand Rapids. Request clearance back to Chicago-Midway at a lower altitude."

"Roger Cessna Nancy-seven-eight-Zebra, turn right to heading two-two-zero. Descend and maintain altitude at six thousand feet. Are you declaring an emergency?"

"Not at this time."

A burst of lightning lit up the clouds next to us, and a spectacular streak of blue lightning flashed past our left wing. I had never seen thunder and lightning from this vantage point before, and it would have been a terrific light show if I hadn't been so concerned that we were becoming part of that show.

"Cessna Nancy-seven-eight-Zebra, we have you on our scope. Be careful out there."

Irwin reached over and dialed in 2-2-0 on a button labeled "HEADING" and pushed it in. He did the same with the "ALT" lock, and then started to make his turn. He seemed starved for air, sucking deeply, and sweat was surging across his forehead like Niagara Falls.

"You okay, Sidney?" I asked.

"I need...I need to roll down the window."

"What? You're kidding right?"

His hands began to shake on the yoke—the yoke wasn't doing the shaking; it was the other way around.

"Irwin, I..."

Sidney groped for something in his shirt pocket and pulled out an orange prescription bottle and fumbled with the childproof lid—childproof even to us adults. The cap finally popped off, but as it did, he dropped the entire bottle and small pills scattered wildly to the floor like flower pollen in the wind.

"Irwin, I...I need those."

I grabbed for them, but my seat belt held me too distant. Sidney leveled the plane out and reached to the left of his control column and flipped the autopilot's master switch. It was next to the two buttons that he'd already pushed. A red light went on. I don't normally like to see red lights, but this one would turn out to be a good thing.

I popped my seat belt and dropped to the floor and scraped up a few of the tiny pills on the deck around Sidney's feet and then returned to my seat. I looked over at the pilot and saw that Sidney was slumping forward. He let go of the yoke with his right hand and grabbed his chest, digging in with his fingers as if he was trying to rip out his heart. I reached over and pushed him back in his seat and stuck one of the pills under his tongue—it was Nitroglycerin, that's what the label on the bottle glaringly said. Sidney should have told me and not let me talk him into this trip. He should have been grounded. What was he doing up here flying? I told him I had to get to Cleveland and I had to get there fast. It couldn't wait until tomorrow, I had said. I couldn't just take a scheduled flight; it had to be now I told him with all the fervor of an escaped convict—

Sidney's face suddenly shuttered and contorted in strange wrenching shapes; the nitro wasn't helping. Suddenly the facial gyrations disappeared like the waves on a pond when the wind suddenly stops. He went limp. I tried to take his pulse, first looking for his juggler, then the artery in his wrist, and felt nothing, but then again, I was no good at this sort of thing. I shook him violently and pounded on his chest. Sidney—my pilot—didn't respond—

He was dead. A heart attack I supposed. I had heard of things like this happening, but not here in this plane. Not to me. I looked out the window, just blackness broken by bright flashes. I couldn't see very well out the window—there was nothing to orient me to the world below. I saw in the window glass, only my worried and perplexed face. I felt completely alone—horrifing solitude. The engine drone was soothing and yet frightening. It reminded me that I wasn't home in bed. I would've been if I hadn't got that call—a call that came at two in the morning. A call that required me to get out from under my warm security blanket and call Sidney and beg him for one last favor. Just one last favor. The plane's drone reminded me of the Hindenburg as it hovered over the Lakehurst airport. And why couldn't someone else have been with us—there were two more seats in the back—I'd feel more courageous, more willing to work my way out of this predicament. I would have felt especially good if one of those passengers had been a pilot. At least the plane was on autopilot and headed in the right direction—away from the storm.

The plane bucked. Rain smashed against the windshield. I couldn't see Mother Earth anymore. It was getting blacker outside if anything can get blacker. That had to mean I was moving away from those lightening storm clouds. I hoped. I looked at the instrument panel all lit up in front of me. I saw the dial with the horizontal line I knew told us our orientation; like a wing, lower on the left we would be turning left, lower on the right, we'd be turning right. That's how a plane turned isn't it? And if the whole wing were below the center of the gauge, it would mean we were nosing downward. And then this large gauge, right in front of me, with glowing white numbers, it had to be the altimeter; 6,000 feet it read—and was holding there. I knew nothing about flying, God no, nothing, only what you see in the movies, and that surly wasn't going to help me get to the safety of Mother Earth. I once bought one of those computer flight simulator games, but never got around to playing it. Oh God, I wish I had. I wanted my two feet firmly on the ground. I didn't play games much, thought they were a waste of time. "Was it too late to reconsider," I asked myself as I looked over at Sidney, his face beginning to look peaceful and relaxed again. I figured he'd flown on up to heaven—thirty thousand feet, fifty thousand, a hundred. I realized Sidney lay crumpled in front of the plane's only controls, none were duplicated on my side. If I was going to try to get down out of this—I looked for the fuel gauge, and I had to do it quickly—I would have to get Sidney out of the pilot's seat and get myself strapped in for a fun ride to Heaven, or more likely Hell. It was time to take action.

I unsnapped Sidney's belt, and pulled him toward me. My heart pounded horribly in my chest. I struggled to get Sidney between the two seats, and there, his torso fell backward. I wrestled with his legs to get them clear of the throttle. Sidney was gone to this world and the burden was left on me—he had taken the easy route—it was I who had to fly this friggin' plane. Every muscle in my body tensed up as I fumbled to put on the pilot's safety belt. The yoke moved around in front of me as if an invisible force was flying the plane; I knew it was the computer—or maybe the hand of God giving me time to take control of my life.

I could fly this machine—maybe—just a machine that anyone could master, but could I really land it? No way, I thought, no way in God's blue sky—which there wasn't one—could I land this little Cessna. I tried to calm down, slow my heartbeat. Whiffs of clouds rushed at me. The engine hummed, the plane running comfortably now. Call ground control, that's it! They can talk me down—maybe. I carefully put on the radio headset and took the microphone and pressed the button.

"S-O-S! S-O-S!" I screamed in the mike, but it didn't sound right. "Uh, Mayday! Mayday!" I released the button. I figured it would operate like a trucker's CB radio. But it only responded with static. I pressed the button again. "Mayday! Mayday! Anyone out there."

Just static.

I looked for the radio controls. I turned the frequency selector one notch and tried again. "Mayday! Mayday!"

No answer.

This wasn't going to be so easy. Time, time, how much time did I have? Where was I flying? I looked at the fuel gauge. The needle vibrated around the fifteen-gallon mark. How far would that get me? I had no bonehead idea. Just then I noticed a red mark on the radio frequency selector at 121.5. I turned the knob to it and pressed the mike button.

"Anybody out there?"

"Who is this?"

I screamed in excitement, "Mayday! Mayday!" Then there was silence—until I realized I was still holding down the COM button. "…ight designation. Is this an emergency?"

"Yes, damn it! The pilot's had a friggin' heart attack."

"Are you flying the plane?"

"Are you kidding me? I can barely drive a car."

"So the autopilot's on?"

"I think so. There's a red light on beside the switch. I think the pilot set it before he…he expired."

"He's dead?"

"Yes, he's friggin' dead!"

"Okay, okay, I just thought he might be…is the plane flying straight and level?"

"More or less. I see the dial with the big wing, it looks level."

"Are you Cessna Nancy-seven-eight-Zebra?"

"What? Come back," I said.

"The plane's call numbers are printed near the top of the instrument panel."

I looked for the numbers and found them.

"Cessna N-seven-eight-Z. That's it," I said triumphantly.

"Okay. What is your heading and altitude? Look for an instrument with an image of a plane in the center and give me the reading where the nose is pointing. It's like a compass; north's at the top."

"I see it. The nose is facing southwest."

"Okay, good. And the three numbers at the top of the gauge, what are they?"

"Two-one-eight."

"Good. There's a magnetic compass on the top right side of the instrument panel. Read those for me."

"I see it, two-two-zero."

"Okay, good. That's the more accurate heading. Use that from now on when you change course."

Change course, to hell you say! A crash course in flying, no simulator, no test flight with an instructor, no one with me qualified to take over the controls—no, no such luck. This was just great. I looked at the fuel gauge: fourteen gallons—

The Com cracked, "Now look at the altimeter." It's in the middle of the instrument panel at the top, a dial with a black face and white numerals and a zero at the top. The small hand indicates thousands of feet and the large hand indicates hundreds of feet above sea level. So read me your altitude?"

"We're sitting at 6,000, I think."

"Be sure. You're about to fly a plane."

"I'm sure, damn it! But I can't fly this thing. Are you out of your ever-lovin' mind?"

"Calm down. You can do it. You can take all the time you need. I can talk you down. I know that aircraft well. I've flown it many times. You just have to do everything I say when I say it. Get yourself familiar with the instrument panel and the controls. Oh, how about an introduction, I'm Norwalk, and I'm gonna get you down. What's your name, pilot?"

I pressed the COM button, "Irwin, Irwin Coleman."

"Irwin, pleased to meet you. Do you know how to use the yoke?"

"The steering wheel, the…the stick?" I said, just to make sure we were talking about the same thing.

"That's right. It turns the plane and controls the pitch. Pull back to bring the nose up, push forward to point it down. Turn it right to bank right, left to bank left. Just like driving a car. Do you understand?"

I pressed the mike button. "Yes, yes. I've seen *Airport* and all the sequels."

"And did you see *Airplane*? I'm sure you learned a lot from that movie."

"This autopilot doesn't look at all like the one on that seven-forty-seven, over."

"Not as well endowed, but it'll have to do. Now remember this, before you take over the plane…"

"What? I thought you guys would bring somebody up here. I can't fly this contraption."

"Yes you can, now listen. The yoke is very sensitive. You need only move it an inch or two to turn the plane. Now I need to know one more thing. Find the fuel gauge…"

Oh damn, I thought. I'm probably running on fumes. This is not going to work.

"I'll assume the pilot had enough fuel to reach his destination, Grand Rapids. Is that where you were going?"

"Yes."

"Then you should still have plenty to get you down. You were about three-quarters of the way to Grand Rapids before you turned back and there's a lot less distance back to Chicago."

"The needle is riding on thirteen gallons, my lucky number."

"That's plenty if you don't stop off somewhere for dinner. You should be in good shape."

I wasn't in good shape. The needle was a lot lower than when I first looked at it. The storm had taken a toll on our fuel supply. How many gallons does this airplane consume in a mile, anyway? I had no idea. Did I have a headwind to slow my progress? And how could I determine that? A tailwind would be nice, I knew that would help my bottom line. I looked out the window. The red navigation light flashed on my left wing, a green light flashed on my right. I knew they were colored that way to tell the direction the plane was moving. But I couldn't tell my direction, no sir. Just blackness and dark clouds. I could sure use someone in this cockpit with me. If they didn't know how to fly, well, we could at least make decisions by committee. Someone to go down with me at least. Someone to talk to. Direction, my direction? Oh, the little airplane instrument, the compass! I looked at it. Still heading southwest. That was comforting: I could actually read one of the instruments.

"Irwin? Are you still there?"

I pressed the button. "I'm here, feeling a little tired though; I'm not a night person…and I haven't had dinner."

"We'll buy you a T-bone if you get down here."

"I feel better already."

"It's time, Irwin, to make a course correction. We're going to direct you to Meigs Field. It's on a peninsula in Lake Michigan."

"Are you kidding me; in the ocean?"

"It's a small commuter airport outside of Chicago. It's safer for you to land there."

"Safer for who? Me or the citizens of Chicago?" I asked.

"That's right, Irwin. Hundreds of lives are worth more than one; you've got to admit that." I guess he really didn't want to buy me a steak.

"We'll get you down Irwin, I'm sure you're worth something."

"Something, maybe."

"Okay, Irwin, we have just one runway here so we won't have to divert a lot of traffic. So Irwin, we need you to change your heading to three-one-five."

"I just flip these three numbers and the plane turns—"

"No Irwin, to do this you'll have to disengage the autopilot."

"I need to take a leak."

"What?"

"I need to relieve the pressure before we start this. I'm already wetting my pants."

"Irwin, to the left of your seat, there's a rubber tube with a funnel on it—goes straight to the outside."

"Okay, just hold on a minute." I figured this to be my last piss; I was gonna make it a good one." I laid down the mike and relieved myself. It was the best I'd felt all night.

"Irwin, we have to bring you up from the South so you can land into the wind. First set your "HEADING" lock to three-one-five in case you have to switch back to autopilot. Now put your hands on the yoke and flip the switch, the plane will be all yours."

I didn't respond; I was distracted by a presence; I sensed a life other than my own. It tugged at me; pulled at my internal organs, at my brain thoughts. I saw a blurred gray image reflected in the windshield. I twisted my head toward the co-pilot's seat and recoiled. There was an entity looking at me and nodding his head. I could see right through it, to the far door, but it was there all the same. One side of its mouth rose slightly and it nodded again as if it was trying to assure me. But no, I wasn't assured—a ghost in the cockpit with me! That's all I needed. It was coming to take me…to the netherworld; the Grim Reaper waiting for me to fail, watch me dive helplessly into Mother earth. I could tell—I knew—it didn't think I was up to it, up to taking the yoke by the horns. That's everybody's fear, isn't it? If they got into a situation like this, would they have the courage to fight back? Did I have to show this specter I could get out of this mess? Was he testing me? He was evil incarnate, I was sure of it, come to take me with him. No, I wasn't going to let him take me now, not me, not now.

"Irwin? You there?"

I grabbed hold of the yoke and flipped off the autopilot.

"I'm here Norwalk. I've got the stick."

"Okay, then, make a slow, easy turn to the right and watch the Heading Indicator."

"The what?"

"The dial with the plane on it. Roll out of the turn about ten degrees before you reach your new heading."

"Okay, then, here we go." I began my turn; the right wing began to drop—but the nose was falling too! I might be spiraling down, into a tailspin, unable to pull out. I looked out of the corner of my eye to see if the apparition was still there. It was. And it appeared concerned as it shook its head, slower this time.

"Watch your altimeter and airspeed gauge," declared the voice over the headset. "It's normal to loose a little altitude, but you may have to pull back a bit on the yoke. You should keep the airspeed at about one-hundred-twenty knots."

"Knots? Christ! I thought ships used knots."

"Irwin, you don't have to translate them to miles, just watch the gauge. But for your information, a knot is about one and a quarter miles per hour. At one-hundred-twenty knots, you'd be moving 150 miles per hour if you were on the ground."

"But I'm not on the water! I'm up here where even the eagles don't fly."

"Stay calm. Have you reached a heading of 3-1-5? When you do, straighten your plane back up. Watch your airspeed."

"I'm there," I yelled. "It's leveling off."

The entity in the co-pilot's seat cracked a grin and stared at me with prideful eyes. Maybe it wasn't against me.

"Great Irwin, see, it's not so hard. I need you to make a slow descent to four thousand feet and level off there. You'll use the throttle on your right."

"Okay, I know that lever, used in many a movie. Pulling them back toward me will cut back on power…and I will plummet."

"No Irwin, I don't want you to plummet. Just ease it back a little bit. Keep your wings level. Your airspeed will increase a bit and you can compensate by pulling back a little on the yoke, just don't push on it. Watch the altimeter, let that needle drop ever so slowly; we don't need you in an uncontrollable dive.

"No one in control here."

"You'd better be."

The apparition in the co-pilot's seat cracked a strained grin at me; his lips split as if dry as the Arizona desert in summer; his coloring: heavy on the pale blue side. Then I took a second look, the ghost looked eerily familiar to me, overweight, slovenly dressed, a sign that his hair follicles had been dying out for a long time on his head…It was Sidney! No it couldn't…I looked on the floor behind me: there was Sidney, his body…dead. I looked back at the ghostly image of him in the right seat, translucent, not there, but definitely there…and he looked at me with an upturned mouth.

"Sidney? Is that you?"

There was a slow measured nod.

"I'm going down now," I said into the mike, with the apprehension of a stray mutt who's just seen a dogcatcher. I wanted to go hide too. "The engine is much quieter now."

"Good Irwin. Put the nose about four inches below the horizon."

"Horizon? You're kidding me! I can't see a friggin' thing."

Sidney's hopeful grin disappeared.

"Fly by your instruments, Irwin, not by the seat of your pants. Watch the Artificial Horizon, that big wing. To stop descending, pull back on the yoke and push forward on the throttle; that'll raise your nose back up without loosing too much speed. Level out at about four thousand feet. Got it Irwin?"

"I got it. I'm pulling. My descent is slowing, but I'm falling below four-thousand feet!"

"Pull the yoke toward you—slowly."

That's what I was trying to do. I was trying extremely hard. The engine was screaming at me. Wind noise, a little shaking, and billowing blankets of clouds obscured my view. I looked over at Sidney; he appeared concerned. What would he be concerned about? He was just a ghost, already dead to this world. It was me that had a lot to—

"Pull up Irwin," cracked the COM.

I broke through the clouds and a clear evening sky became visible with colorful, green, red and blue lights twinkling on the ground—on Mother Earth—racing off to the horizon. It was beautiful. I felt like an eagle descending on the earth, racing down to catch it's pray.

"Irwin!"

"I'm here boss, I'm leveling off at three-thousand-six-hundred feet."

"Okay, maintain your altitude. Check your airspeed; keep it at one-twenty for now. You'll need to make another course correction to line up with the runway. It will be the longest turn you've made so far."

"Just tell me what to do. I think I got a handle on this barnstormer."

"Don't get too cocky, Irwin. It's not a seven forty seven; you're in a Cessna; she can't fly by herself. It's up to you."

Up to me! Up to me to kill myself. I was in the mercy of…of white-haired Sidney's ghost. I looked at his image in the windshield. His eyes, they looked deep into mine, and mine into his; he was scared too.

"Irwin, you're leaving my area. I'm going to have to hand you off to Meigs. You'll have to change your radio frequency to one-twenty-one-point-three, got that? Switch over now and good luck buddy."

What? Was that it? He was leaving me! "Norwalk. Norwalk!" The radio had gone silent. What was that number? I was ascending to the pinnacle of terror. His voice had been so comforting. "Norwalk?" There was just the hum of the aircraft—trying desperately to hum me to sleep. That number, it was 1-2-1.3. I dialed it in and pressed the COM button and spoke in a panicky shaken voice.

"This…this is Cessna Nancy-seven-eight-Zebra. Come in. COME IN!"

"We've got you Cessna Nancy-seven-eight-Zebra. Irwin, I'm Barry. I'm bringing you in."

"How'd you know my name?"

"Irwin, you're our star attraction tonight."

"I bet."

"I can see lots of lights now."

"What is your altitude, airspeed and heading?"

"Three-thousand-six-hundred and uh, one-twenty knots and a heading of three-one-two."

"Okay Irwin, turn right heading three-five-niner. Descend and hold at two-thousand."

"Hold on, slow down. Didn't Norwalk tell you, I'm not a pilot. Over—shit!"

"Sorry, Irwin. Make your turn now. Right to three-five-niner."

"Okay-okay, easy." I pulled the Cessna to 3-5-9 and congratulated myself.

"Okay boss, I'm there."

"We know; we have you on radar. Now drop down to two-thousand feet!"

Drop! Did he have to use that word? I could make slow turns in this huge vast empty space, anybody could, but these dives, they were much too scary. Christ! My pants weren't getting a chance to dry out. I didn't know if I could pull out again: I was closer to the ground this time. If I couldn't, I'd become one with the sheet metal of this plane. I'd be mincemeat, and the plane, just so much scrap metal. I wondered where the Black Box was located—it was all that would be left of me, my hysterical words as I screamed in the ear of a plane jockey who sat safely on the ground—

I bucked up and pushed on the yoke. Easy now, 3,500—3,000—2,500. Okay, now pull back up. And then, the worst happened. Sidney's ghost grabbed the throttle lever and pushed on it as I tried to pull back on it. There was anxiety revealed in his eyes…and abject fear in mine. I couldn't move the throttle; the terror-crazed phantom was stopping me. The flickering lights were looming large among the blackness of the earth. I tugged hard on the throttle and Sidney pushed as if his life depended on it, and I pulled as if my life depended on it, but I couldn't get the nose up. My muscles, strained to their limits, ached with wrenching pain. Pull back on the throttle; that's what I was supposed to do to get the nose up; reduce the power to the engine. Sidney shook his head "no" as if he had heard my thoughts. And then, no, wait! Norwalk said I had to give the plane more thrust to pull up! Push on the throttle he said, don't pull. I stopped pulling and began to push—

Sidney let go of the throttle. He seemed happy with my decision. But was he trying to help me or hurt me? Get me safely to the ground—or take me with him? Pushing on the throttle gave the Cessna more power. I pulled on the yoke—

The plane began to level off. The apparition was right. I would be okay.

I looked at the altimeter. It read 1,500. Oh Jesus! I'd gone too far down.

"That'll have to do Irwin," uttered the disappointed voice over the COM. "Come left to zero-zero-one. This is your final approach."

"But all I see is water up ahead! I see lights on my left."

"That's beautiful South Chicago. You're almost home."

"That's not my home, I wouldn't live in Chicago if my ass were frosted over."

"Okay buddy, I take that personnel."

"I take it back. I take it back. Just get me down."

"You're gonna be fine. The airport's on a peninsula east of Chicago. The runway's nearly 4,000 feet long; plenty of room for you to land your puddle jumper."

"Now I take that personnel."

"Fair enough. Do you see the runway lights yet? Are you lined up with them?

"Yes, I think so, white chase lights."

"Pull back on your throttle until the airspeed reaches one hundred knots and pull on the yoke as necessary to keep it there."

"Are we going down?"

"Yes, Irwin. And since I know you'll never be ready, we're just going to do it. Okay?"

"Okay, Hell!"

"The levers for the landing gear are just to the right of the throttle. Pull them all the way back. Make sure they're locked in place."

"How do I know that?"

"You pray."

"*You* pray for me, my hands are busy, besides, it looks bad for a pilot to have his hands together."

"Who said you were a pilot, Irwin?"

"Norwalk, did."

"Never been in a plane in his life; he's just a radar jockey?"

What?" I said befuddled and frightened.

"He play's that *Microsoft Flight Simulator* computer game."

"You're kidding? Tell me your kidding."

"He got you this far, didn't he?"

"Yeah, I suppose."

"You suppose! Damn, son, you're life is on the line. You need to wake up and smell the roses."

"Roses, hell! How in God's name am I gonna—"

"Just be quiet and listen. It's my turn and I'm gonna get you down and if you listen to me, carefully, you won't get me fired. You see, I'll get fired if you mess up this runway and my wife wouldn't like that. So listen, we've cleared the runway for you and the emergency equipment is standing by. We've got skin divers suited up."

"Skin divers?"

"We loose a plane in the drink about once a year."

"You what? You lose a plane once a year? That's just great! And if I smash into the runway, do they have snow shovels to push me aside?"

"Big snow shovels, Irwin. We'd have to clear the runway fast to make room for the next stray Cessna."

"Thanks. I feel better."

"You better put on your life jacket. It's behind the seat."

"How in blazes am I gonna do that now?"

"I guess you're not."

There was silence for a moment. All I could see were two rows of white lights in the middle of the lake. I'm landing in a freezing lake! Who they kidding? They just want to get rid of me. That must be how the Bermuda Triangle works. Chase lights appear in the distance, the pilot approaches and attempts to land—attempts to land in the friggin' ocean. It's an alien's sarcastic way of taking us out plane by plane—

"Cessna Nancy-seven-eight-Zebra, we've got you on approach. You need to come down to one thousand feet, but easy does it. Remember, the altimeter gives your distance from sea level, not to the runway! Our runway is at five-nine-two feet. At one thousand feet you're four-hundred-eight feet above the runway. You follow?"

"I get it—*if* there's a runway there, but maybe there's just fish."

"What? Come back."

"Nothing."

"You could take out a lot of people, Irwin, if you don't get it right."

"I got it."

"Just put the plane at the altitude I tell you. Are you aligned with the runway?"

"Yes. It's an amazing sight. Wish I'd practiced on those computer games."

"Me too. Have you found the brake pedals? They're the upper pedals on the floor; the lower ones are for steering while on the ground. Brake when you hit the pavement, but do it easy, very easy; you don't want to flip the plane. Now cut your speed to seventy knots with the throttle."

"Cutting to seventy knots."

"Irwin, I have to tell you this now; you won't have time later to listen. The plane stalls out around fifty knots and you want to be low over the runway when that happens. You should be about one hundred feet above the runway when you first reach it. The rear wheels must hit first so keep your nose up. Remember rear wheels first; pull back on the yoke to get the nose up. Got it Irwin?"

"Got it. The altitude gauge reads nine-five-zero."

"You're coming in good Irwin. Okay, now listen, when the plane comes to a stop, get out as soon as you can and get away from the aircraft—and if you can, bring the pilot with you."

The pilot! Sidney! I had forgotten about him. I looked over to the co-pilot's seat: the ghostly image of Sidney was gone. I looked back at Sidney's body laying between the seats. He looked peaceful, his eyes closed. He got me up here; I hoped I could get him down. I'd known him for years. I couldn't believe he didn't tell me about his heart problem. I knew he needed money, living in an old shack at the end of the St. Lewis runway. I guess flying was the only thing he ever loved or cared about. He was married once and that was enough for him. Living at the end of the airport was just fine with him; dishes rattling hundreds of times a day—

The plane shook—I came out of my daydreaming and read the altimeter: "The altitude reads seven-hundred, and now six-hundred."

"You're coming in too steep, Irwin. You're still a half a mile from the runway! You're going to…pull up Irwin! Pull up now! Push on the throttle. You'll have to come around again."

"What? To Hell you say!" My heart banged against my rib cage, my muscles as tight as trampoline springs. I pulled on the yoke as hard as I could. My airspeed dropped. The netherworld image of Sidney appeared again. He reached over with his left hand and grabbed the yoke and pulled with me. He nodded.

"PUSH on the throttle, Irwin, you'll stall out. Give her the gas! She needs power." I pushed.

I could see the end of the peninsula. It was like the approach to England over the Cliffs of Dover. *Up. Up. Get her up!* Sidney pulled on the yoke—he was helping me! I looked in his eyes, I could see confidence, I could see hope. The concrete landing strip passed just below me. I could see a row of aircraft buildings on my left; tin buildings full of airplanes I could have hit. I could see a Yacht club on my right. The debonair men in their white suits and ascots would be pissed. There, an office building at the very end of the runway—it looked me square in the eyes. Barry's words repeated themselves in my head: *You could take out a lot of people if you don't get it right.* My plane was gaining altitude. I peeked into the windows of a nearby high-rise and turned the yoke to the right and skirted the building. I swear I could see rows of people at the windows looking at me and I think I had a good look at every last one of them: a beautiful blond with rose-red lips to match her dress, a young wannabe executive with the sleeves of his silk shirt rolled up, a white-haired gentleman in a gray three-piece suit, the top button of his waistcoat unbuttoned—

Suddenly, an alarm bell went off in the cabin. I think it burst the blood vessels in my ears.

"What's this?" I screamed into the mike, "An alarm is going off."

"It can't be the stall alarm, check your fuel gauge."

I looked for it. Damn! The needle was on empty. "I'm outta friggin' gas!"

"Shit!" said Barry. It was the first time I heard him curse.

"Level off, hold your course. Irwin, listen to me, you're going to have to ditch; you're going to have to crash land into Lake Michigan. The lake's calm now. You can do it.

"I don't have any choice, do I?"

"Change course by just a few degrees to heading zero-two-five, and hold at eight-hundred feet. Do it now Irwin. Don't drop any lower until you clear the city."

I followed his directions; I was getting good at this turning stuff now—like riding on one of those merry-go-rounds in an amusement park. It was the landing I was worried about, and I hoped it wasn't going to be my last.

"The lake is just ahead—a lot of open water—can you see it?"

"Yes, I think so, but it's dark down there. I can see the North Shore lights to my left."

"That's good. Now don't aim for any lights out in the water: they might be boats."

"Oh great! Any whales I should know about?"

"They don't have navigation lights so don't concern yourself—now listen carefully, Irwin, you must not fly into the face of the waves. And that's the way you're going now. If you hit a swell, the waves would submerge you. That means you'll need to turn back downwind and approach the waves from their backside. You got that, Irwin?"

"Yes, yes, cut the chatter, my engines are cutting out."

"Turn now and level off. Heading two-nine-zero."

"Okay, okay, then what? I'm loosing altitude."

"That's good. You'll need to pull back on the throttle and bring the plane to an altitude of seven hundred feet. That's one hundred feet above the water. Just watch the water from now on. You'll want to stall the plane before you hit. And put your landing gear backup—now! And make sure it's up. The red light will go on."

Another friggin' red light, always bad news, I thought.

"Okay, tower, I'm at two-nine-zero."

"Irwin, reduce power until the tachometer reads fifteen-hundred rpm. Then move the nose of the plane up five to ten degrees above the horizon."

"Okay, doing it now, but my engine is quitting."

"That's okay, you're gliding, just keep the nose up. You must keep the propellers out of the water. Keep the nose high enough so you can't see the horizon."

"I'm pulling."

"When you're ten feet above the water, pull the throttle all the way back toward you, cutting the power. Then pull the red fuel mixture control knobs all the way out to cut fuel to the engines and lay her down like you're laying a newborn in her crib."

"Yeah right."

"But keep the nose up! You hear?"

"Roger."

"My name's not Roger, its Barry. Listen, as soon as you hit, open the cabin door and get to Hell out, break out the window if you have to. Can you swim?"

"Why in Hell are you asking me that now?"

"We've got helicopters and boats—and some of the finest yachts—headed to your landing site. We got you on radar, and the plane's ELT will be transmitting your location. The lake is calm. Good luck."

That was all I heard from the ground—from Barry. If I made it, I wanted to meet him—and Norwalk too. Did Norwalk have a pilot's license or just a *Microsoft Simulator* license? The landing gear was up. I was down to twenty feet—ten feet—hold the nose up, up, pull, let her ass hit the water first. Oh God! Hold the plane level. Keep the wings out of the water. I could just see myself cartwheeling. Oh hell, this is gonna hurt. Throttle back. Fuel off. Airspeed dropping. Five feet—four feet—three—two—BANG! A bellyflop to beat all belly-flops. The plane's belly pounded down into the water and the tail came up. My head and arms banged on everything in the cabin—

But I was still conscious.

Get out, I screamed at myself. The plane was still floating; *I'm alive! I'm alive!* I could see the shoreline lights flickering in the crisp air. I released my seat belt and reached for the life vest behind the seat—and that's when I saw Sidney still on the floor. Suddenly a big breath of air burst forth from him and he moved his head. Shit! Sidney was still alive!

"Irwin," he murmured.

"Holy Christ! Sidney, get up, we're going down! We're friggin' sinking!" I grabbed his arms and pulled hard. "Jesus, I can't believe you're alive. Get up!" I was able to open the cabin door and water sloshed in and the sea began to flood in like a glacier had suddenly melted up river in Canada. Sidney got to his knees.

"Did I do good?" he asked.

"What?" I grabbed the other vest. "Hold on to this. Come on jump. I was in the water—we were in the water, ice-cold water.

I had Sidney around the torso as I tried to swim away from the sinking Cessna. I looked back into the cockpit for a moment; I thought I saw Sidney's apparition again—the lovely graying around his temples, the deep wisdom-filled ravines in his face. I then looked into the face of the man I had under my arm—he was still alive. I looked back into the cockpit—the apparition was fading slowly away—

Thanks Sidney.

I Carried It
in My Pocket
By Don Kirk

I ALWAYS CARRIED IT WITH ME. No matter what I wore, I kept it in my pocket. At night, I put it on my bedside table. I assumed it was safe there, that it wouldn't walk off on it's own. And year after year, it was always there the next morning. I was attached to it and I guess it was attached to me.

I walked the streets with it, took it to work, and I always had it when I needed it. It was comforting to know I had it. I could depend on it. It was always right, and as long as I took care of it, it took care of me. I was partnered with it, but I knew I could never take it into the shower with me. It wouldn't like that. Water would hurt it, and then I could never depend on it again.

One day a little girl asked me what it was I had in my pocket and I said it was a secret. "Ungh-uh," she said, "it isn't." I said, "Yes it is. It wants to stay in my pocket and stay warm and cozy and safe." She replied, "I want to see it."

"Are you sure?"

"Uh-huh."

"Okay then, I'll get it out, but are you absolutely sure you want to see it?"

"Uh-huh."

"Okay, here goes." And I reached slowly into my vest pocket and carefully cradled it in the palm of my hand. "My daddy gave it to me. He used to carry it."

"Really? Let me see."

I kneeled down so the little girl could get a good look at it. The chain attached to it—the chain that kept it from getting lost—wouldn't reach all the way down to the little girl so I had to kneel down so she could see it up close.

The girl pulled my hand down in excitement and looked at it. She asked, "Does it tell time?"

"Most certainly little girl, it's a pocket watch."

The Visitors

By Don Kirk

WE WERE SITTING AROUND our dining room table, my family and I—my wife Caroline, and daughters Kristin and Keri— when I thought I saw something in front of me. A streak of light came out of the wall to my left—up near the ceiling—and raced across the room and went into the wall on the right. I quickly turned to look out the front windows; I figured it was the glare from the headlights of a car, but I saw no car on the street.

"What is it, honey?" asked Caroline.

"Oh nothing. I thought I saw a flash of light behind you—just car headlights or something."

"Is that all? You looked so surprised."

"Just headlights."

Well, that was the 15th of March, the day my life began to take a turn, the day I was introduced to another world.

Over the next few days I saw some more of those streaks of light, not just in the dining room, but in our den where the television sits, and in our bedroom appearing late at night. The light was like a wide fuzzy bolt of lightning, but it moved slowly across the room, and always high on a back wall, like about six feet off the floor. One day it seemed to me to be moving even slower, and the ray of light was wider still. It appeared to me like a lot of grayish-colored pixie-dust floating in the air, kind of like the dust you see in a room when rays of sunlight streak through venetian blinds, except the particles were moving from one side of the room to the other, not twisting and turning in the air currents.

I asked my wife if she had seen anything and I described it to her and she hadn't seen it, except she saw light coming through venetian blinds and dust floating in the air and all; what we've all seen. I was beginning to lie awake at night waiting to see if the weird ray of light would return. And it would take me a long time to eat dinner when I came home in the evening: I would find myself sitting there holding a tablespoon of soup in front of my face as I stared at the wall behind me.

"Daddy," asked Keri, "are you all right?"

"Uh, yes dear, I'm fine."

"You don't look like you're fine, Daddy?"

"I am dear, just a little tired, I had a long day."

Just then I saw the streak of light come out of the wall, even slower this time and it seemed to have a shape to it. I dropped the spoon into my chicken-noodle soup and the hot sustenance splashed all over the table.

"Look, look! Did you see that! Behind you," I screamed.

"What Daddy?"

"Honey, are you okay?" asked my wife Caroline.

I stood up with a thrilled expression of awe, like seeing the space shuttle leave its launch tower and climb majestically into the blue heavens. "Did you see it?"

"What dear?"

"Daddy, you're scaring me."

"It's okay Keri, I just thought I saw something behind you. A vehicle I think, it had two small wheels and…and it was like a big rectangular bucket, like, like an ore car, like they use in gold mines on tracks to take miners in and bring the ore out."

Carry turned around to look, "Daddy, I don't see anything."

"It's gone now."

"Shucks," Keri blurted, convinced she had missed something very neat and exciting.

"It was nothing dear," I replied, "just lights from a car's headlights, that's all. You know. You've seen them in your bedroom at night, streaking slowly and mysteriously across the walls of your room, making strange patterns as they crawl around the corners of the room…and then they're gone and it's dark again."

"I've seen them, Daddy."

"Me too," said Kristin, not wanting to be left out.

"Well that's what they were, what I saw."

"But Daddy, you spilled soup all over the table. I don't do that when I see headlights on the walls."

"No dear, thank goodness, you don't."

Caroline entered the conversation and took the soup bowl from in front of me. "Honey, you're tired. Why don't you get ready for bed? I'll take care of the dishes; the girls can help."

"I think I will. This tie is too tight on my neck, I need to loosen it up, get the blasted thing off."

"Yes, dear."

I yanked on the greenish-blue tie with the boring falling-off-the-tie white stripes and loosened my top button. There, that was better. I would sure like to know who invented this monkey suit; it had caused a lot of men a lot of discomfort for a lot of years and I figured I would never put one on again, not even for funerals—or weddings—or even for the boss. My customers didn't care what I wore, just cared about the quality of my merchandise. No, never again shall I wear a monkey suit. I went up to our bedroom and started to unbutton my vest, eleven buttons, that also kept me from breathing naturally—maybe I had gained some more weight? I figured it was like a woman's corset and I figured it must have been a woman who designed the monkey suit for men—to get even for all the years women had to wear corsets and hoop dresses—

The ore car came through the wall. I stopped breathing and stared. The image was semi-transparent like a reflection in water. I could see the back wall, but I could see a form, a shape to it—it wasn't the streak of headlights from a passing car. The image stopped high on the wall in front of me. I blinked my eyes and rubbed them. I looked around the bedroom to see if the room was still there. It was. I looked back at the ore car and the four people staring at me.

With fixed pupils, they stared back at me, and then the car slowly moved off and slipped through the very solid, wood and plaster wall. I grabbed a chair and stood on it and rubbed my hands on the wall where the ore car had merged with the wall's surface. I tapped on it. Solid as a rock—Caroline entered the room.

"Honey! What are you doing up there?"

"I…uh, nothing. I think we need to repaint this room?"

"Why, Francis?"

"Uh, a crack in the wall, see it dear, it's getting bigger, see it?"

"No dear, I don't. It looks fine to me."

"It's the light. Come here; from this angle you can see it."

"Dear, I'm worried about you."

"I won't fall off the chair."

"That's not what I'm talking about, but you should get down from there, anyway."

I got down and put the chair back in its place by the window, lining up the legs in the indentations in the white carpet. The chair had been in that very spot for many years and I had just pulled it out of its assigned place in the universe. I wondered if I had changed something, upset nature's balance, messed with Einstein's space-time continuum. I stared at the inert chair and wondered if it had a life of its own. Just because it didn't have a means of locomotion didn't mean it wasn't living, plants don't move and yet—

"Honey, get yourself into bed, I'm tired."

"I haven't said goodnight to the girls."

"Well, go do it now."

"Yes, dear."

I crossed the hall and entered the girl's room. It was like walking into what I imagined would be the room of a circus clown, all colorful with deep red and green walls with white trim, and the room all bright and cheery with toys strewn about the floor— enough toys to play with for the rest of their lives.

"Are you okay, Daddy?" asked Keri, my youngest daughter, five or maybe six years old I think.

"I'm fine, just tired, Honey. Don't you ever get tired?"

"No, Daddy."

"Yes, you do. When we spend the day at Sea World, you get very tired and fall asleep in the car coming home."

"Yeah, Daddy."

"And when I try to get you to help me do something, you're always tired."

"Nooooo."

"Yesss."

"Nooo."

"Then, you could help me downstairs, I have some dishes to put away?"

"No, Daddy, I'm tired now." Keri pulled the covers over her face. Kristin quickly did the same thing.

"I thought so."

At that, I sensed something behind me. I turned around and looked up above my shoulder and strained my neck. Several people were leaning out of the ore car and staring done at me. One of them smiled and said, "How sweet." Another nodded and said, "Very nice, Mr. Keck."

I dropped back on the bed. Keri screamed and sat up.

"Daddy, you're sitting on my feet!"

I stood back up, shaken.

"Daddy, I'm trying to sleep," said Kristin.

"It's okay, darling—" I stared at the people, they stared back— "Who are you?" I blasted.

"Oh, we're so sorry to disturb you. I didn't think you people could..."

"Get out of here, you're scaring my daughters!"

"We didn't mean to...so sorry...," and the car moved forward and melted into the plaster wall.

"Don't you come back!" I screamed.

"Honey, what is it?" Caroline had entered the room, her raggedy pink terry-cloth robe trailing behind her, her age-old nightgown hanging loosely over her tired body.

"Mommy, mommy, Daddy's gone crazy!"

"What's happening?"

"Daddy's talking to the wall."

"Go to bed girls. I'll take care of him."

Caroline pulled me back into my bedroom and sat me down on the bed.

"What's wrong with you dear? I'm worried about you."

"I…I'm seeing things, people in the house, riding around looking at us, they smile and stare…and say they're sorry."

"They're sorry? For what?"

"For scaring the kids."

"Honey, you were scaring the kids."

"No," I said, shaking my head, "It was *them*."

"Who?"

I cradled my head in my hands, "I'm going nuts. You need to take me to see a doctor."

"You're okay dear, just a hard day."

"No, no, I can see them." I looked up at her with the look of a child trying to understand the curiosities of the Universe. "Do you see them?"

"No dear."

"See there, I'm going to la-la land."

Caroline sat down beside me. "Tell me what you saw?"

"People, ordinary people, just like you and me. Nice people, I think. They have these nice sweet smiles and a fascinating look in their eyes, a gleam in them, like they're thrilled at what they're seeing."

"What are they seeing, dear?"

"Us, they see us. They're watching us, all the time, all the damn time."

"Calm down dear, you had a bad day…"

"NO! I didn't. Not until I came home, these people…"

"Tomorrow we'll take you to a doctor, not a psychiatrist, just to a doctor. Maybe you have a brain tumor."

"I don't have a damn brain tumor; I feel fine." I stood up, hands shaking. "They're watching us, even when we're making love."

Caroline straightened up and looked at the wall in front of us, actually at the empty space between us and the wall. "They watch us?" she asked as she closed her robe tightly up to her neck.

"Yes, from up there."

Caroline's eyes traced the corners of the wall and ceiling, looking for something, a telltale sign…of something, anything to confirm my story.

"They're not there now, dear," I said.

"Why can you see them and I can't?"

"I don't know."

I pulled off my shoes and my slacks and crawled into bed.

"I won't be coming in today, Ralph. I'm feeling a little under the weather. Going to see the doc. Yeah, I'm fine. Just the sniffles, want to nip it in the bud. Sure. Okay, tomorrow." I returned the handset to the phone and took a bite of my buttered-with-margarine burnt toast. What would I tell the doctor, that I was seeing things? He would run a CAT scan, find nothing. He'd send me to a psychiatrist and the psychiatrist would send me to the loony bin. No, I couldn't tell him I was seeing people floating around in my house. No, I was just having a few little headaches. Just then, the ore car slipped through the kitchen wall cabinets and stopped in front of me. Only one ghostly gentleman was sitting in the floating vehicle. He spoke to me:

"We're so sorry, Mr. Keck. We didn't mean to upset you. We didn't think you could see us."

"I *can* see you."

"Yes, you can. You're very special, Mr. Keck. We have a lot of people like that in the future but…"

"In the future! What, here on earth?"

"Yes, here on earth, we're here with you, but in a different time. We're from your future."

"How can that be?"

"Time is just a dimension of space. We learned how to travel through time, like you travel through space in a train or spaceship or on foot. It's just as easy to move through time when you know how."

"I don't get it, what are you doing here, in my house?"

"We travel through many people's homes and businesses and places of entertainment; we travel through their everyday lives. You see, Mr. Keck, we operate a living historical museum. Guests hop a ride on our time train and visit the past. They can see the architecture and furnishings and behavioral patterns of people who are a part of our history. A lot better than reading about it in books don't you think?"

"You've got to be kidding?"

"I am not, sir."

"Why my house?"

"You're a typical American family of the early twenty-first century, the 2-1-C-0-5 tour."

"Jesus! You watch everything we do?"

"Everything. Oh, it's okay, it's how we learn, appreciate what has gone before and avoid repeating the mistakes we've made in our past. And it keeps our government from rewriting history to meet its political agendas. And well, it's fun—watching you. You're funny and charming and do some of the darndest things, as Art Linkletter once said."

"I'm sure." I took a bite out of my heavily-buttered toast leaving a greasy glob of it on my upper lip.

"Well, you won't be seeing us again..."

"I won't, why?..."

"We've removed you from our tour schedule. We don't want you to go crazy, Mr. Keck."

"No?"

"Bye, Mr. Keck. Enjoy the twenty first." At that, the ghostly gentleman nodded his head and the time-traveling tour vehicle slipped away.

I buttered another piece of toast.

Marberger's Syndrome

By Don Kirk

"YES, DOCTOR, when I watch something, it changes the outcome."

"You mean—if you watch something—things happen differently than if you hadn't watched it?"

"That's right, Doctor. The other day I looked out the front window at a girl playing hopscotch on the sidewalk and she fell and bruised her knee."

"So?"

"I caused it."

"I don't quite understand. Why do you think the girl wouldn't have fallen if you hadn't watched her playing?"

"I just know it, Doctor. She wouldn't have fallen."

"You don't know that."

"But I do."

"Give me another example."

"Well, last Friday, I was sitting in my recliner in front of the television set and turned to see my cat Suzy tip over a bowl of milk."

"But...well, is it always something disastrous that you witness?"

"No, not at all, it's just different than what would have happened."

"Again, how do you know that?"

"The rain, it stopped. It was raining one evening and I looked out the window and it stopped."

"What stopped?"

"The rain stopped. It wasn't going to stop until I looked at it."

"Again, how do you know?"

"I guess what I see just doesn't feel right, not right with the world, not as it was meant to happen."

"I see, Mr. Fleabody. Well, I think we're going to need you come in again. I must get a better handle on this if I'm going to be able to help you."

"I understand. It doesn't make any sense to me either."

"No, I don't suppose it would. Thursday at three then?"

"Sure."

"Okay then."

Francis Fitzgerald Fleabody, a spindly little man with jet black, well-oiled hair brushed straight back on his head, rose from his chair, and left the room, and closed the door quietly behind him.

Thursday came quickly and Mr. Fleabody had a new observation to tell the doctor—an observation that was tearing him apart, challenging his very sanity.

"Doctor, I was looking out of my living room window again when I saw the same girl that had fallen earlier and bruised her knee."

"And why was that so unusual, Mr. Fleabody? She had a bruised knee; you saw her fall."

"I did. But it wasn't the girl with the bruised knee that bothered me."

"No, then what?"

"The other girl, her twin, I mean she's not her twin, I know her mother and she has only one daughter."

"I don't under…"

"She was identical to the girl with the bruised knee, same sandy-blonde hair, same blue-print outfit, identical in every way, even for the bruised knee."

"You're saying you saw a second girl that looked like the first, and she too had a bruised knee?"

"That's right, Doctor, a bruised knee. And she laughs the same and her mannerisms are the same. Cute as a button if I dare say so myself."

"So this second girl, how does she interact with the first?"

"She doesn't."

"She doesn't?"

"No. It's as if the two girls are totally unaware of each other, as if they're in two different universes. They come and go and never speak to each other. They jump the hopscotch pattern on the sidewalk and never run into each other."

"Are you sure of what you've seen."

"I am, and as I said, I know the girls…the girl well, I know one of them, I know their…her mother, and she has only one daughter."

"You're talking in riddles now, Mr. Fleabody."

"I didn't create the riddle, I just saw it."

"Well, would it be okay if I came over to see these two identical girls?"

"Yes, you're welcome, sir. I'd be most appreciative if you did."

"Tomorrow afternoon?"

"Sure. The girls play after school, about three thirty."

"Then we have a date."

The psychiatrist, Dr. Norman Marberger, showed up promptly at 3:30. He was dressed immaculately and his black patent leather shoes reflected a fisheye view of the entire apartment.

"Thank you for coming, doctor."

"My pleasure, Fleabody. Now show me this girl…these girls."

Fleabody directed the psychiatrist to the front window in the living room and sat him down on a couch where he could see all the activity outside.

"Care for anything to drink, doctor?"

"No, thank you, Mr. Fleabody. Just show me the two girls."

"Why there, doctor, don't you see them?"

"I just see a pretty girl in a blue dress skipping a rope."

"You don't see two of them, one skipping and the other playing hopscotch?"

"I do not."

"They're there, right in front of our eyes. I see them as well as I know my name."

"And your name is?"

"What?"

"What is your name?"

"Why, you know it's Francis Fitzgerald Fleabody."

"Are you sure?"

"I am."

"As sure as there's two girls out there?"

"Two girls? No Doctor, there's three girls out there now."

"What!" The psychiatrist looked back out the window. "I see only one."

"There's three, I swear it. You see, I just looked out the window and changed the outcome."

Dr. Norman Marberger felt helpless. He wanted to help his new patient, but these symptoms—afflictions—were quite new to him. A hallucination about multiplying girls was indeed unusual. He had seen patients who had deluded themselves into believing hundreds of spiders were crawling over them, and he counseled woman who pulled out all their hair because they thought it was some alien growth taking over their bodies. But Fleabody, with his multiplying girls—

"Fleabody, I need to see you back in my office at your earliest convenience."

"You don't believe me?"

"It's not that, I think I can help you. Maybe even give you a medication that'll make the girls go away."

"Just two of them I hope."

"Just two of them, I promise."

The following week, Francis Fleabody lay on a fine leather couch in the doctor's well-appointed office. He had a wall of fine books and several pieces of elegant sculpture carefully placed around the room, each with its own little spotlight on it. The door opened and his new psychiatrist came in with a notepad and sat in a tall winged-back leather chair next to Fleabody. He got straight down to business.

"Did you have a good childhood, Francis?"

"I suppose."

"No problems?"

"Like?"

"Problems. Things that made you unhappy."

"Where you ever mistreated by your parents?"

"No, they were great."

"Great, huh. Sex, how about sex?"

"Huh? I've had my share."

"No problems then?"

"In what way?"

"I have to do the asking," retorted the doctor.

"I see, well, Doctor, I had a normal childhood. No child abuse, no sexual dysfunction and I had good grades in school. I'm fine doctor, except that there's three identical girls out there now… and they're not triplets."

"I saw just one girl."

"I can't help that, Doctor Marberger. I think I have the ability to see more than one universe at the same time."

"Isn't that confusing?"

"To say the least. It blurs my reality, if you know what I mean, Doctor."

"I think I do, but maybe I can help you. I'm giving you a prescription for *Clonapen*. It should calm you down…"

"I don't need calming down, Doctor. I just don't want to keep changing things when I look at them."

"How about I write you a prescription for a dark pair of sun glasses. Maybe then you'd have a hard time seeing and thus not disturb the universe."

"That might work, Doctor."

"I think it will, you'll see. Here's the script for *Clonapen*. It'll help."

"Okay, Doctor."

"And you need to come and see me again every week. Okay?"

"Won't that cost me a bundle, Doctor?"

"Not at all. You have insurance?"

"I doubt that it covers psychiatry."

"Oh, don't worry, I have ways of making it work."

"I'm sure you do."

"Then you'll be here."

"Okay, sure."

A few days later, Francis Fleabody called the doctor's office and insisted Marberger come to his aid at his home—the *Clonapen* wasn't working and neither were the dark glasses. The doctor cancelled his afternoon appointments and rushed to Fleabody's side. The doctor had a policy of not seeing his patients outside of his office—outside of his sanctuary, an environment where he was in control—but in this case, well, it was indeed unusual and very tandelizing to the doctor. Fleabody was surely bipolar with a borderline personality, but maybe it was an entirely new permutation and he could write a paper on it and name the disease after himself. He'd call it Marberger's Syndrome.

The doctor sat down beside Francis in his living room and again looked out the front window. They waited until the girl—or girls—showed up.

"There, there! There they come," exclaimed Francis.

The good doctor stood up and approached the window, "I...I, I can't make out..."

"See them!"

"Why, why yes, Mr. Fleabody, I wouldn't have believed it if I hadn't seen it myself. Three girls hopping along happy as a lark, playing games, smiling and dancing like the characters in the Wizard of OZ."

"You see them then?"

"I do, Francis, I do! I can't believe it."

"Here, maybe you should take these dark glasses. Maybe they'll help you."

"No. I don't need them."

"Take them, they'll cure what ails you."

"Well, okay, Francis." And Dr. Marberger appeased him and put them on.

"Do they work, Norman? Do they work?"

"Why...no, Francis."

"I didn't think they would. They didn't work for me."

The doctor lowered the glasses and turned to Fleabody, "No, I suppose not."

"You saw the three girls, didn't you Doc?"

The Doc looked back out the window to confirm his vision.

"Oh, my! Francis look, four girls! There are *four* girls now."

"See there doctor, you changed the world. Do you actually see four girls? You're not just trying to appease me?"

"I must say, Francis, that I do. I don't believe it, but there it is."

"You and I both can see four identical girls when there's only one."

"Like looking through a prism," exclaimed the Doctor. "We must be looking at parallel universes, created when you—and I—observed the girls and disturbed the natural order of things."

"We both see them, Doctor, don't we. It means I'm not hallucinating doesn't it Doctor?"

"Well, I suppose your right."

The next day, Dr. Marberger had to tell his office partner, Dr. Nelson, what he had seen. He explained the phenomenon in exacting detail, everything that had happened, especially the multiplying girls and how he and Francis Fleabody were seeing into another universe, three other universes in fact.

"It was remarkable seeing those four little girls playing, each from a different universe, wearing different clothes now, and their hair done up in different ways, and yet they weren't interacting with each other; they were each in a different universe…"

"Norman, you're looking a little beat, you've had a heavy schedule the last few months; maybe you should take a few days off. Get some of that energy back, get back to running in the park."

"I'm fine Clifford…"

"You'll only short change your patients."

"I suppose you're right."

"See you next week, Norman."

So Dr. Marberger took a few days off, not because he felt tired, but because he wanted to explore this multiple-universe thing. He had stumbled onto something that might win him the Nobel Prize in physics. Can you imagine, the Nobel Prize, and he was just a psychiatrist. But first he had to prove it, and write about it in the trade journals. Yes, the Nobel Prize would be his.

The good doctor called Francis Fleabody to see if he could help him devise an experiment. Fleabody, indeed, had a plan that might just prove his theory. He said they could use the prescription dark glasses he was given. Fleabody instructed Dr. Marberger to make another dozen of these glasses and invite twelve of his most distinguished colleagues to his house where they would demonstrate how events could be changed just by looking at them and how it was actually other universes they were looking at. How, every time something caused the universe to split, a whole new universe was created. How it had the same history, but now was heading off in a new direction with a new future, how each girl would grow up with totally different lives.

Well, twelve doctors of psychiatry showed up at Fleabody's house at 3:00 one afternoon and knocked on the door and no one answered. Marberger found the door unlocked and entered. He walked down the hall and the others followed him like cattle to the trough and he entered the living room and found it to be devoid of furniture. The walls were bare, the strip-wood floor covered with a fine layer of dust. It looked like no one had occupied the space in a long time.

"I don't understand, gentleman. Fleabody was one of my patients. I saw him here on several occasions, right here."

Several of the psychiatrists looked at each other and one spoke up.

"It's against psychiatric ethics, and it's not safe to see patients at their homes, Dr. Marberger, you know that. Why would you..."

"He was here, right here!"

"Calm down Norman, it's okay, we understand," said Dr. Clifford Nelson, Marberger's office partner.

"What, what are you talking about?"

"We talked to your secretary this morning. She says she doesn't have anyone on her appointment calendar by the name of Francis Fitzgerald Fleabody."

"What? I had several appointments with him?"

"Here at his home?"

"No, well yes, no not exactly, I saw him in my office several times, just ask my secretary…"

"Funny name, an unusual moniker, this Francis Fitzgerald Fleabody."

"That was his name…"

"He's not in your appointment calendar."

The good doctor stopped talking and looked at each of the twelve men—looked deeply into their eyes. What he saw wasn't good: disdain, sadness, disillusionment. Just then, there was the sound of a little girl laughing outside on the sidewalk and Marberger hurried to the big picture window. His demeanor brightened.

"There gentleman, there she is, by god, the little girl!"

The twelve men shuffled to the window and peered out. Clifford Nelson spoke:

"Norman, I see only *one* girl."

"One girl, yes, yes, one girl, turn away, no wait, I'll turn away and then look back and there'll be two girls."

The doctor turned away and back again, but there was still just one girl. He glanced at the distinguished gentleman in their elegant Park Avenue threads. "I know, here, put on these dark glasses, it'll allow you to see into the other universes—"

He handed them each a pair, and a couple of the gentleman slowly, obligingly put on the glasses. The others would wait. One of the gentlemen in the back flipped open his cell phone and entered a few numbers.

"Now watch gentleman, watch closely," directed Marberger.

They watched, and watched, as the little girl played hopscotch.

An ambulance pulled up to the curb behind the girl and two men in white jackets jumped out. They entered the house and came into the living room.

"Is there a Dr. Norman Marberger here?"

"Here." Norman raised his hand and then slowly lowered it. The two men came forward.

"Put your arms at your sides, Doctor."

"What?"

The men quickly buckled a leather strap lined with soft lamb's wool around Norman's arms and waist, and another strap was placed around his legs as he screamed, "What are you doing? What in God's heaven is this all about?"

"Sedate him with a shot of *Ativan*," ordered Dr. Nelson.

A third EMT came into the room rolling a gurney and the three lay Norman down and tied his arms and feet securely to the gurney.

"Take him to Sun Valley Mental Health Institute, please," said Dr. Nelson, "and give him 400 milligrams twice a day of *Seroquel* to help with the hallucinations and two milligrams of *Perhenzazine*, one tablet taken three times a day, that'll help him sleep. I'll be his doctor of record. I'll look in on him tomorrow."

"Yes, Doctor. We'll take good care of him."

"Clifford, Clifford, what's happening?"

"You really need that rest Norman. Sun Valley's got a swimming pool and a bowling alley and lots of books about the universe…you'll like it."

"Clifford?"

And with that they took Norman to the ambulance and the other doctors just shook their heads in disquieted disbelief.

"He seemed so normal," said one of the twelve Apostles. "I didn't believe it when you told me. Not Norman. Multiplying kids and multiple universes. I guess he's been at it too long."

"If we don't take life easier, we'll *all* be hauled off one of these days," said one.

"I'm taking the whole week off," said another.

"You got that right."

And meanwhile, on the other side of town, a spindly little man with shiny black hair rang the doorbell of a modest single-family home. A tall nice-looking sandy-haired woman came to the door.

"Ah, Mr. Franks, how did it go? Did you accomplish what you wanted?"

"I did. I did indeed."

"Will you be needing the quadruplets anymore?"

"No, I think now everything's right with the world."

Printer's Ink

By Don Kirk

I RETURNED THE COUPONS to my billfold and took the paper and sat down in the hoverport waiting room for a commuter flight to Houston. I had a few minutes to get my daily fix of the *Wall Street Journal* and checked my stocks on the American Stock Exchange. *Endrun* down twenty dollars, *WorldCon* up ten, *Bank of China* up twenty-five, *DigitalDesign* up sixty points, no eighty, ninety points; there, the numbers stopped changing. These instant updates were fantastic of course, but it was a little disconcerting to see numbers changing on a printed page as you tried to read them. Many of the papers around the country now had this inking technology. Stock prices were constantly updated, almost in real time, just as tickertapes had done, except it was happening in a newspaper you might have bought weeks before. Wireless technology, satellites, and a special printer's ink that could shift the look of a number on a page anytime a new signal was sent to it, made it possible. One second you read "23.26" and in a blink of an eye, it might read "26.12."

We had come to demand information NOW, not an hour from now, not ten minutes from now, but NOW, this second, this very moment in our lives. We wanted information instantaneously and many things in our society had reached a breakneck pace. Newspapers had finally found a way to compete with the Internet.

I remember the first generation of cell phones that allowed us to conduct business anywhere, anytime—and not just when there was someone at the other end of the line. If the party wasn't there, I just connected directly to a service, an electronic mailbox as it were, and talked to it, left a message. The humanoid voice would record everything I had to say and then responded to my comments with suggestions of it's own. We sometimes made some important business decisions, the humanoid and I, and if I thought it was good, the humanoid made it happen. We even had board meetings online with the electronic mailboxes of the other board members, and that left us real humans more time to transact other important business. It even allowed us to be on other corporate boards.

I flipped to the financials as a casually dressed young man sat down next to me and opened a magazine, *AmCor's Field & Stream*. I ventured to guess that he dreamed of someday fishing in a real, living river. He probably had a Video Effects Generator where he could simulate fishing in any river he chose around the world, one of those rivers of the nineteenth or twentieth centuries. That was the only place he could fish; there were no more rivers, at least not ones with fish.

I glanced at his *Field & Stream*. I knew there was a tiny microchip on the cover of every magazine—and daily newspaper—that received a satellite signal and then sent the changes to all electronic printer inks in the magazine everywhere the stock prices were quoted. And now, if I wanted to buy or sell some stock with this new information, all I had to do was think it, add a personal identification number, and whamo, it was done, just that simple. It was just one of many benefits of the imbedded chip under my skin at the back of my neck. It had been put there when I was a young child as a way to track me if I ever got lost or heaven forbid, kidnapped. My parents had volunteered me for the implant. They saw that it was important, that maybe someday it could save my life, that maybe they could feel more secure in knowing there was less chance they might loose me. This new technology was also used to find Alzheimer's patients that had walked off and not found their way back home. Of course, it soon became useful for tracking criminals. All prisoners now had them, and since most crimes were committed by repeat offenders, they were now easy to find. A bank robber running out the front door of a bank could be scanned and thus instantly identified—name, social security number, last known place of residence. And the Global Positioning System—this tracking technology would keep tabs on him until a SWAT team could pick him up. The criminals always tried to beat the system, wearing clothes with aluminum threads to disrupt the signal, or hired sophisticated underground hackers who would try to reprogram the embedded chips. And then there'd be the back alley sawbones who would actually try to cut it out, the result being death to the patient. The chip was wired directly to the brain and would create an overload signal that would short circuit brain function and quickly kill the host. Criminals are stupid; I guess that's why they're criminals. In this society, you were either a Loafer or a TechnoFinancier. The Technos sat in glass-shrouded towers overlooking the Loafer class. If you couldn't make lots of Shekels for the corporation, you stayed in the consumer class, not that we weren't consumers, but we chose what we wanted. To get into the Elite class, you could make money for the Corp anyway you liked, and you got to choose what luxuries you desired. If you could make it as a celebrity on one of the corporate sports venues or High Deaf Transfer Video subsidiaries, or you acquired a managerial position in production or distribution, moving merchandise around the globe and to subsidiary planets, then you were in high cotton. You didn't have to be born into the Elite class, just have what they needed at that particular time. I was in P&D, had a plush 78th floor corner office. When some of the products we manufactured still required some hand-making operations where people were needed, then those most backward, the Third Worlders—some still living in thatched huts—got the job. It took a savvy man to manage people like that and then get their menial work to market, and for that I was paid well.

I took my *AmCor* laptop from my black *Plasto* briefcase and opened it. I tapped the power button, the screen lit up. *AmCor's* homepage came up. I'll send a few memos, post a few economic reports. There was no down time for a Techno.

I worked for *AmCor*—all company names were anagrams now—no chance of offending someone speaking another language, and no way to tell what kind of business the Corp was into, in fact, most Corps were involved in everything—including pornography, a very high-profit market. That way they could protect the stockholders. Businesses were always coming and going, and as long as each was just a small part of the Corps' revenue—and each was—the loss of a few companies didn't matter so much. The nineties of the last century had brought the first wave of major mergers, and the philosophy that led to those mergers, continues until this day. I expect it won't quit until there is one universal corporation—simply labeled UC. If we're lucky, it'll be ours, *UniCor*. The idea of competition was never much liked by Big Business, it prevented the control of prices, and that was not a good way of doing business. If you couldn't stay competitive with lower prices and cheaply made merchandise, you went out of business, and corporations didn't want to do that; their stockholders would be unhappy.

The Loafer sitting next to me decided to talk to me. I didn't mind. It was an opportunity to learn their nature.

"That's a nice laptop. Is it the latest model?" he asked.

"It is. Fifteen Gigahertz, G12 processor, twenty-one sixty interlaced, 3D interface, eighty hours of battery life, E-mail flagging, direct satellite communication, FailSafe Protocol, and Loafer Virus Protection."

"That's crackerjack! Can you use it to crap in?" He snickered. I didn't think it was funny.

There weren't many jobs for the Loafers anymore: computers, automation, and a world choked with poor people—over seven billion—made that inevitable. Who wanted to work anyway? Loafers like watching television, taking their family to picnics, guzzling *AmCor* beer. We Elites take pride in working sixteen hours a day. Of course, having no jobs for the Loafers created a new problem—I don't know how the corporations of the twentieth century missed it. No jobs, no income, we had successfully created a consumer society that did what we wanted them to do: buy, buy, buy. They'd buy gifts if they didn't need anything for themselves, and more often than not, it was useless, unwanted junk. They'd use credit cards and rack up huge debts and pay huge interest rates they could never pay off. They even mortgaged their homes, and lost them. Fifty percent of sales had become gift purchases. Back in the nineties it was around twenty-five percent of sales and most of that was during the Thanksgiving and Christmas holidays—so we created more holidays. And fifty percent of book sales had long been for gifts, but book sales gradually dropped off—fewer and fewer of the Loafers could read—but if they had been able to, they wouldn't have cared to learn anything new anyway. Voting had fallen to four percent of eligible voters. Why? Politicians weren't saying anything the Loafer wanted to hear, and they no longer believed anything they had to say anyway. That was fine by us. If they could read, they could think, and if they could think, they could raise protests and maybe even rebel, so the corporation started in the 1970's to "dumb down" the proletariat. It eventually worked. We now have to give the Loafers "PCs"—not the old Personal Computer, but Purchasing Coupons—so they can go out and buy things, and if they don't use up their month's allotment, they're fined or jailed or both. It worked, it kept them in line, kept them buying and buying and buying.

My illustrious neighbor, a might malodorous, was jawing on a chunk of tobacco and spitting in an empty cigarette pack. Rubbing shoulders with a Loafer wasn't all it was cracked up to be. Maybe we could make a shirt-pocket spittoon for his market type.

He looked up at me and suddenly pushed something cold into my neck. It was a *Tazer*, one of those antique devices for disabling a person with an electrical shock—a shock that stunned the victim with thousands of volts, temporarily allowing the attacker to gain complete control over him. It was an antique, but I'm sure it still worked. He had my attention. The Loafer put his face in mine.

"You know what this is?" he asked.

"Yes," I replied with a strained voice.

"It don't feel so good, and I promise you, you'll pee in your pants, mess up them nice *Haggers*."

"I'm listening," I said.

"I want your laptop."

"You won't get away with this. The laptop has a *SmartTag*."

"A what?"

"I'd be glad to explain it to you if you'd just ease off a bit so I can elaborate. Just pull it away a few millimeters."

"I don't trust you."

"No reason you should, but I can't get away; what's a few millimeters?"

The Loafer slowly pulled the Tazer back, giving my juggler a chance to circulate some blood again.

"So what's these *SmartTags*?"

"There probably isn't one in your Tazer, too old for that, but my laptop has one."

"So?"

"It'll track the laptop. Wherever it goes, the police will know where you take it and where you sell it."

"That doesn't scare me. I'll rip the friggin' thing out."

"It's very tiny, embedded somewhere where you can't find it: in the plastic cover, in the plasma screen, in fact, there's a *SmartTag* on every major component."

"Ah, come on now, you're messin' with my brain."

"I'm not. You can't even sell the parts; and you can't take it home to use it yourself. The police will be on your doorstep before curfew."

The Loafer stared at the laptop still sitting open on my knees.

"You kin play games on it?"

"I haven't installed any, don't have time for games, my man."

Today's *GetSmarts* were developed years after the *SmartTags*, those micro-sized UPS barcodes that were placed on all merchandise. *SmartTags* had two little tiny antennae and reminded me of the little anchovies, though *SmartTags* never swam off. It was much better than the old UPC codes that required large scanners and a large barcode of black vertical lines on the outside of the product. The readers for the *SmartTags* could be as far away as thirty feet and could read multiple products in a single pass. All the products in your shopping bag could be read at once. It eliminated the need for a clerk, and the cost of the items was billed directly to you. The system became so popular that tag readers were put in refrigerators and even medicine cabinets. They kept track of what food you had and needed, and warned you if something like milk and cheese or hamburger meat had exceeded its expiration date. And the medicine cabinet readers made sure you were taking your medicines, taking the right ones, and not using BMMs (Black Market Merchandise), one of the biggest headaches of our Corps. The *SmartTags* were also placed at strategic places around the city so they could read all the tags you were carrying or wearing. The readers could even read the size and color of your underwear. Why? Simple: market research—and targeting. Every *SmartTag* had a unique number with ninety-six bits, thus billions of number combinations—enough numbers for every product we could produce in the foreseeable future. When a Loafer purchased a product, the number was tied to his name. How he used that product, who he sold it to, or gave it to, or where it went when discarded was tracked. The IRS had always hated bartering; in fact they made it illegal, but the practice still went on. They wanted to tax every sale, every transaction, over and over again, and the *SmartTags* made it easy. Even if the purchaser bought a can of *AmCoke* and then threw the can out the window into a ditch, it could be, and was, tracked and you were billed for highway littering. Many people early on called them the "Spy Chips" because they allowed the Corps to know everything about you. It was necessary, the Corps said, so they could get you what you wanted; they could market directly to you, not waste time and money trying to sell you something you didn't want—or didn't *think* you didn't want. Grocery stores first saw the benefit of keeping a computer record of all your purchases and they would print out coupons at the bottom of your receipt, and you didn't know it, but they were different for each and every customer. Even mailings to your home became unique. It had become too costly to send out general mailings to the masses when less than one percent would respond, but now this way, the return rate was much higher. Why? Because they knew all about you, your nationality, income, debt, your family unit and it's members, their ages, hobbies, hair color, school friends, any illnesses (the national medical database made that possible), and well, you name it, they knew all about you. I once worked for a company, *Privacy Anonymous*, who's job it was to combine databases from different sources—like licensing, taxing, banking, entertainment, credit cards, and purchasing—so that a complete profile of every Loafer could be created and then sold and resold. In fact, a client could request any kind of unique information—all Orientals, Italians, clergymen, child molester's, auto speeders, lemon pie eaters, and those under five years old with a toothache—all cross-matched to meet the specific needs of a client.

The invention of the EPIs (Electronic Printer's Inks) was a marketing coup because it didn't just allow the *Wall Street Journal* to dominate the market. The technology was leased, not sold outright to other corporations (like Billy Gates did in the 80's to eventually dominate the world market) and its use expanded exponentially. The entire text and images of a magazine could be changed after the magazine had already been purchased, though changes were usually only done late at night so as not to confound the reader. A man at a keyboard somewhere on the planet could type in changes, hit send, and all the targeted magazines would change. Of course, this wasn't initially to revise entire articles, only to correct errors, photo credits, wrongly placed photos, and wrongly accredited quotations or simply wrong ideas. It was as easy as changing a page on the old twentieth-century World Wide Web. In fact, you no longer had to be connected to the Web, it was connected to you; Big Brother was connected to you—directly—thanks to the embedded chip in all of us.

Not only did newspapers like the *Wall Street Journal* have *Smart-Tags*, so did magazines, of course, and Loafers bought them, we all bought them, and that allowed the information read by each of us to be unique. The article I read in this month's issue of *AmCar & Driver* might be different than what the guy sitting next to me was reading. Same basic article—review of a class of cars for example—but the recommendations of each model was tailored to the reader, a potential buyer. Features, body colors, personality of the vehicle, all tailored to the reader's personal profile culled from our databases. It was an exciting time. We could sell everything and anything, well, until the Loafers started to rebel. They didn't know at first that the magazines they were buying were unique to them, changes were subtle, just like the regionalized magazines of the late twentieth century. Different ads for different regions they knew about, but different words within articles, different photos—*AmCor Pictureshop Image Doctoring* software made that possible—too much gore for this particular reader, no problem, it's gone. A reader's celebrity idle gets jailed for drug possession or drunk driving could be bad for his psyche—no problem, we just revise the story. The first incident of this technology was the death of Beetles star John Lennon, but only some people saw those articles, others were informed of the death of Zoey Widlow.If you haven't heard of her, you got the Lennon stories. Corporate CEO's statements to the public were tweaked for the individual reader; if you were liberal, you got rhetoric about environmental issues, if you leaned to the Waconites, you were told that the FBI was being dismantled. You wouldn't know the difference—unless they came to your door, and then it didn't matter. But the people had had enough. They couldn't believe what they read anymore, not that it really mattered, and it didn't. You see, we were rewriting history with our electronic printer's inks. Why? Because it was so easy, and because we could justify whatever the Corporation's current political positions, ideologies, and new tax structures with what had happened in the past or actually what we said had happened. We could get away with it because the public seemed to have a short memory and seemed to not have any cares in the world about anything that happened beyond their immediate sphere of influence—and that didn't usually go much beyond their own home. Food on the table, an SUV in the driveway, and an *AmCor WidePlasma* screen in the living room, that's all they cared about.

The Loafer snapped the cover of my laptop back down, took it, and laid it on his lap.

"You sure about this?" I asked. "*SmartTags*, remember."

"I got a friend kin help me. He's Techno savvy."

"Won't work."

"I'll take my chances."

"But you don't need the money."

"I do, I can't buy anything I want with my PCs. Only what they want to sell."

"What do you want to buy? Maybe I can help you?"

The Loafer unrest was increasing and not everyone had a *GetSmart* planted in his brain—it was done without their knowledge, during a routine medical checkup. No, *SmartTags* weren't enough anymore. Tracking the Loafer's behavior wasn't getting the job done. The instantly changeable Printers Inks weren't enough either: we had to feed the populous information *directly* to them, I mean very directly, so they couldn't subvert our intention and throw it away or ignore it (like they did with the junk mail and spam in the late 20th century), and this was accomplished with the *GetSmart*. We could now download doctrine directly into their brains. No more ads on gas pumps, no banner ads or product pop-ups on the Internet, no billing envelope inserts, no, ads were just sent directly and economically into their brains while they slept. The next morning—and to him the ad was the "honest-gods truth"—the car he now dearly wanted, he just *had* to purchase it this very day. Sure, reality was blurred for them, sure we had circumvented their right to choose, their privacy rights, and their own hopes and desires, but the important thing was that they didn't know it. A few did, but that didn't matter either, they didn't have a soapbox to speak from—we controlled the media—and we made sure they *believed* they were individuals with wills of their own in a country where freedom reigned. They never knew that all the many brands of soap on the supermarket shelves were made by the same company, all priced to sell to specific target markets. I looked at my wristwatch.

"My hoverjet is ready now," I said, "passengers are embarking. What are you going to do?"

"It's what *you're* going to do, get on the jet without your laptop."

"I don't think so." I pushed a button on my wristwatch.

The Loafer pulled his Tazer away from my neck and started to blubber:

"I…I'm so sorry, sir. I had no idea you had done that much for me, the pension fund increase, the hospital payments for my daughter's surgery, I had no idea. And the fact that you're related to me, a second cousin, one I had heard of, but never had the pleasure of meeting. I wouldn't want to steal from you, blood relative and all, even if you *are* an Elite. I'm indebted to you John. Here, I didn't need your laptop, I'm so sorry. Please forgive me. I hope you can come to dinner sometime. My wife makes great pasta."

"I promise, I'll do that."

The Loafer smiled and backed away and scurried along the gray carpet of the hoverport corridor like a little mouse: he had a *GetSmart* implant.

I think I'll purchase some more shares of *DigitalDesign*, the company that makes *GetSmart. Two thousand shares DigitalDesign please, pin two-six-seven-zero-one. Thank you.* Yes, these days I had only to think it.

Hello Goes the Fizz

By Don Kirk

"WHAT ARE YOU DOING?"
"I'm listening."
"To the fizz?"
"No, I'm listening to my brother."
"He's not here at the party is he?"
"No, he's home, he didn't come."
"But you've got your ear close to your *Coca-Cola*."
"Yeah cool, isn't it? I can hear everything he says, well, almost everything."
"What's he saying?"
"He wants to know if Darlene came to the party…No, she's not here, John…Why don't you come on over anyway?—"
"You can talk to him?"
"Sure, here, speak to him, Peter. Just talk into the glass, don't spill the *Coca-Cola* and don't poke the spoon in your eye, a few inches away will do."
"You're an idiot, Larry. Who drinks *Coca-Cola* with a spoon in his glass? And why don't you just drink out of the can?"
"You'll see. Here, just listen."
"This is crazy, you're off your rocker, Larry."
"Look who's got his ear in my *Coca-Cola*."
"I think I hear something! A little voice…it's John!"
"I told you," said Larry Edwards.
"The fizz is popping in my face. I hear him…"
"Talk back to him."
"Hello, John, this is Peter. I'm talking into your brother's *Coca-Cola*."

"I know; I can hear you. I can hear the kids around you. You're at the party," replied John through the *CocaCola* phone.

"Ah, this is some kind of joke. Where is he, Larry? In another room?"

"No he's at home across town," replied Larry.

"No, he's here," insisted Peter as he handed the glass back to Larry and then ran out of the room to look for John.

Larry spoke into his cup of *Coca-Cola*, the freshly poured soda still popping in his face. "He doesn't believe it John, he thinks you're in another room."

"When he comes back, have him call me at home. That'll prove it to him."

"He'll never believe it, it's too simple…here he comes now…did you find him, Peter?"

"No. This is a good trick. I even looked outside."

"Did you look in the attic?" asked Larry.

"No, I'll go…"

"Now hold on just a minute. Why don't you call John at home and see if he's there? Use a real phone."

"Yeah, that's it. He won't be there."

"Sure he will, Peter. I just talked to him."

Peter ran out of the room and into the kitchen where the phone hung on the wall by the knick-knack shelf that divided the kitchen from the dining area. He dialed John Edwards's number. It rang once, and then again and again.

"He's not there…"

"Hello?"

"Is this Mrs. Edwards?"

"Yes."

"Is John there?"

"Yes, he's in his room. Who shall I say is calling?"

He's there! "It's Peter Langford, fourth grade."

"Okay, I'll go get him." *He's not in his room, can't be.*

"Hello?"

"This is Peter."

"Hello Peter. Larry said you'd be calling."

"I don't believe this. You talked to him through your soda?"

"Yes, it's true. You can use freshly poured *Coca-Cola* or even *Seven-Up* sometimes. As the fizz bubbles up you can hear my voice. It's something about the acidic chemicals in the drink that transmit and receive the sound, that secret formula, you know. The spoon works as an antennae…"

"Like a crystal radio?"

"I guess. And the container has something to do with it: it has to be made of glass; a paper cup won't work. The carbonation in the soda—when the bubbles pop—releases my voice so you can hear it."

"This is ridiculous! It's impossible," blasted Peter, a short, pudgy little kid who was hard to convince of anything, even that Buck Rogers was not a real person.

"Go open a can of *Coca-Cola* yourself and try it. It only works for a few minutes, until the fizz stops."

At that, Peter hung up the phone and opened the Fridge. Plenty of soft drinks stocked the icebox; after all, it was a party. In fact, it was Peter's ninth Birthday party and this would be the most unusual party he had ever had up to this day.

Larry came into the room.

"Was John there, Peter?"

"Yes, I think so, but it's still a trick."

"You gonna try it yourself?"

"John said to call him, well, wait, he didn't say 'call', he just said try it. But how, how do I contact him?"

"He'll be there, not many other people out there at the same time with freshly poured *Coca-Cola* in a glass with a spoon in it."

Peter poured a bright red can of *Coca-Cola* into a glass. It fizzed with excitement and popped with a fresh thrilling sound. Peter stared down at the soda.

"You better hurry, you haven't much time," said Larry.

Peter held the *Coke* up to his mouth.

"Hello, John, you there? John?"

"Hello, this is Mary Martha."

"Is John there?"

"I don't know any John."

"John Edwards. One-Sixteen Telephone Road."

"No, this is Thirty-eight, 127th Street, twenty-sixth floor."

"What? There's no building that tall in Edisonville."

"Edison what? I'm in New York City."

"New York City! That's thousands of miles from here. I'm in Edisonville, Texas."

"Who's that?" interrupted Larry. "Who you talking too?"

"New York, I think…who did you say you were?"

"My name's Mary Martha."

"You're fading out, pour another *Coca-Cola*."

"Okaaaaaaay…"

"That was Mary Martha from New York, here take my drink, I've got to pour another one."

Peter hurried to the Fridge, opened the door, grabbed another *Coca-Cola* and the can opener and forced a little triangular hole in the top and then rotated the can and made a second hole in the can to let air in. He poured the drink into another glass. It fizzed with abandon. Larry stood there holding two fizzed-out *Cokes*, one in each hand, taking a sip from each one now and then.

"Hello, Mary Martha, you there?"

There was no response. Peter put his ear closer to the glass. Fizz droplets popped in his ear. Nothing happened, just the sparkling sound of fizzing carbonation as it was released into the air.

"This is crazy. You got me doing it, Larry. I look like a jerk."—Peter glanced around the room—"This is a practical joke and everybody's in on it."

"You heard a little voice in the drink didn't you?" asked Larry.

"Yeah, I heard John and I heard Mary Martha in New York City!"

"See."

"I'm just dreaming; that's got to be it. This is not my birthday party. It's still night time and I'm still asleep. Pinch me, Larry. See if I'm real."

Larry pinched Peter.

"Owe, easy, that hurt."

"You're real. Try again, maybe you took too long to get another soda and hers had already fizzed out."

"Yeah, that's it."

Peter took another glass from the kitchen cabinet, poured another *Coca-Cola* and put the spoon in it. It crackled.

"Hello, anybody out there?"

"Hello? Who is this?..."

"I heard a voice, Larry! I heard a voice!"

"Great. Who is it?"

"This is Peter Langford calling from Edisonville. Over."

"Hello. Is this K-21?"

"No, this is Peter."

"Are you a new member?"

"What...member?"

"CCI, Coke Communications Incorporated. We're having a conference call. Take your..."

"George here."

"Kevin here."

"Icky here."

"It's three-oh-three. Where's Henry?"

"I don't know K-3. Let's get on with today's business."

"Larry, listen, do you here this, open another *Coke*, we're on a party line."

"Is that a joke?" asked Larry.

"No, like in the olden days. Several farmhouses might be on the same phone line. If you wanted to talk to someone, you'd have to tell the other person to get off the line—nicely of course."

"I hear them. It's a business meeting."

"They're talking about how the *Coca-Cola* business is picking up, a lot more sales, but they, they need more kids talking to sodas..." Larry looked at the kitchen table with empty *Coke* cans strewn about and several glasses full of fizzed-out coke.

"Who's that on the line? Is that you K-21?"

"NO! This is Peter Langford in Edisonville..."

"And Larry Edwards at your service. Who are you guys?"

"Please get off the line, we're having a business meeting."

"How to sell more *Coke*?"

"Yes, now hang up, or not as you wish, because your fizz will stop soon, anyway."

Peter lowered the glass away from his ears. "I think I'll *drink* my *Coca-Cola*."

"Sounds good to me," said Larry as he took a big swig of his flat soda.

A hard knock came at the front door.

"Peter! There's someone at your door."

"Let him in."

A few moments later two tall, lean men in dark blue suits and hats walked into the kitchen. With them was John Edwards, Larry's brother.

"Are you Larry?" asked one of the suits.

"Uh, no, I'm Peter Langford, this here's Larry Edwards."

"I know who you both are. We just heard you over the airways." He reached behind his back and pulled out a pair of shiny handcuffs. "Both of you are under arrest."

"What for?" Larry and Peter piped in unison.

"The FTC has not approved this method of transmitting radio signals."

"You're with the Federal Trade Commission?" asked John.

"You don't have a license do you?" asked a suit.

"We're too young to drive," replied Peter.

"No, I mean a license to broadcast electromagnetic waves over the airways?"

"What, electro what?"

"You've got a transmitter there."

"Huh? It's just *Coke*."

"Doesn't it require a strong signal to be regulated by you guys?" asked John.

"You transmitted across state lines…to New York."

"You heard us?"

"That's right. We can listen in on your conversations."

"What! That's not fair," yelped Peter.

"Do you use drinking glasses filled with *Coca-Cola* to listen to us?"

"That's right."

Peter and Larry looked at each other. They could imagine thousands of empty, and not so empty, cans of *Coke* strewn around FTC headquarters, on the tables, on the windowsills, on the floors, tons of tin cans piled to the ceiling.

"Then it must be you FTC guys that are making Coke Company sales go up! You got stock in the company?"

"Hum."

Top Secret

By Don Kirk

WE SPED DOWN a dusty dirt road along one side of which ran a ten-foot concertina-topped chain-link fence. We slid to a stop and turned into the last checkpoint and came to a stop. The sergeant at the guard shack held his hand out to indicate to us exactly where we should stop.

"Security passes please, for everyone."

The driver pulled his electronic pass from his shirt pocket and handed it to the guard wearing camouflaged army fatigues, the creases pressed perfectly, his "gig line" straight. Creases always looked sharp on a Class-A dress uniform, but on fatigues designed to work in, that seemed pointless.

"He'll need your ID too," said the Colonel to me as he removed his identification card from the plastic sleeve clipped to his coat pocket.

I pulled out my billfold and flipped it open. Among a short stack of credit cards, my driver's license, voter registration card, and pilot's license, was my private dick's license.

"Will this do?" I inquired as apprehensive as a kid might be who had just stolen a pack of chewing gun from a convenience store.

"It will."

I handed my ID over the seat to the driver. He reached around to grab both of our cards and handed them to the guard.

"Three people?"

"Yes."

"Roll down your back window."

The driver complied and the guard bent down and peered in

at us. He wore dark glasses; I couldn't see his eyes and yet I felt them burning into me like a predator ready to pounce. He wore a sidearm in a black leather holster with the flap snapped over the butt of the gun. He looked at the photo on my ID and back again at me.

"You look a lot different in this photo: dark complexion, disheveled black hair, glassy stoned eyes—"

"It was taken a long time ago," I replied with a crack in my throat, "and you know those driver ID photos."

"I do, look at 'em all day."

He handed our ID cards back to us. "Have a nice day," he said as he motioned the driver to move on. The colonel rolled up his window. I watched through the front window as the tall chain-link gate was opened up.

"I hope that's the last checkpoint," I said, "but it still doesn't seem like adequate security. A thousand square miles to protect and nothing more than ten-foot-tall chain link."

"We have numerous monitoring stations with video cameras, infrared sensors, motion detectors, and listening devices, and we can get a security team to a breach in less than a minute. Besides, it's what you don't see that'll catch you. When our window was open, a camera snapped a shot of us from the guard shack and it was run through a face recognition database, comparing us to millions of other known terrorists and other Enemies of the State. An X-ray device on your right and another above us took beautiful skeletal photos of the limousine's interior, and a chemical sensor in the pavement checked the car for explosives. There's also a camera to observe the underbelly of the car."

Just then, a security helicopter flew low overhead, stirring up the dust and scarring the bejeepers out of me.

"Is that all?" I asked calmly.

"No. The greasy fingerprint you put on your ID card when you handed it to the sergeant was electronically compared to the embossed one already on your card."

"Amazing, I didn't even—"

"They got your DNA too."

"How in the world?"

"From your breath."
"Do tell."

We drove onto the apron of a dull-gray concrete runway blackened with tire marks. Low-rise living quarters of World War II vintage and large airplane hangers hugged the perimeter of the airfield. A black & white checkered water tower stood tall in the distance and an air traffic control tower stood sentry behind us. I heard a strange low-frequency drone behind me and turned to look out the rear window. I was taken back as if hit with a blow to the belly. My breath taken away, I was overwhelmed with wonderment. I was sure I was in a drive-in theatre watching a *Star Wars* movie. There, flying, or shall I say suspended in the air not far above the runway, were two planes, no, I couldn't call them that, they were oddly-shaped, dark, earth-toned metallic things resembling iron crosses. Raised rectangular panels covered their entire surface. The two objects hovered around each other like two dogs that were meeting for the first time. Suddenly one of the floating objects began to change shape, morph into something different, something more like an airplane with fins that looked somewhat like traditional wings. The top and bottom of the craft telescoped out like a series of nested boxes. The craft was like one of those "Transformer" toys sold in the 80's to children. It then pulled away from the other airborne craft, a thing that looked a bit like a huge hex-head machine bolt. Looking quite heavy, it had no business floating above the earth. The Transformer began to spin slowly on an axis about its geometric center. The wings, like knife blades now, cut through the charged air of the desert and sent huge dust devils scurrying about. Heat waves rising from the pavement made the image seem so surreal. I opened my window to make sure I was really seeing them, but a blast of hot air and choking dust engulfed the car and I quickly rolled the window back up.

"Not the most comfortable place to do research," said the Colonel, "but it's secure from prying eyes and well off the public's radar.

"But satellites can get good close-ups these days, read a license plate," I said.

"Where'd you hear that? How could a camera flying overhead get a shot of a vertically-placed plate on a bumper?"

"Well—"

"Thermal Imagery *can* see the heat signatures of our bodies sitting in this car, and satellites *can* hear what we are saying, but they can't read our plates—not from outer space anyway."

"Oh." I looked straight ahead and then back out the window. "But then how do you keep these flying things out of the newspapers?"

"It's true that our government has been unable to completely control the release of satellite imagery through its shutter control policy because of the competitive nature of the private sector, so we've come up with a technological breakthrough in visual stealth with DVDS, our Dynamic Visual Distortion System. No satellite circling now or in development can photograph the true nature of this area. We're still one step ahead of the new half-meter satellite imaging."

"Why is that?"

"With *Viacom*, a dynamic image of the area is projected onto a dome-shaped transparent grid that's electrically produced over the airfield making the area appear to be abandoned, all the while activity is taking place beneath it."

"Amazing, but exactly how is that accomplished?"

"Top secret."

"That's a cop out, Colonel. I have a top-secret level-3 clearance. Give me a hint. I've seen the unusual, very unusual, aircraft you have flying, or shall I say floating, around here."

"Have you?"

"Have I what?"

"Have you *actually* seen them?

"Well I, they were very real to me, I choked on dirt that was stirred up by them, no virtual reality there."

"Are you sure?"

"Sure, I'm sure, and I can speak of them when I leave here."

"Will you?"

"No, of course not."

"Let's hope not."

At that my stomach tightened a bit.

One of the big flying Transformers—at least six car lengths in diameter—began to hover directly over us, keeping pace with our limousine doing about thirty. A huge ominous shadow fell over our car. The Colonel just looked ahead as I squirmed in my seat and tried to look up at the underbelly of the craft.

"What's the UFO doing, Colonel?"

"Don't call it a UFO, Donner. We know exactly what it is."

"You maybe."

The Transformer came closer to our roof and suddenly the ground outside fell away from us. I could see the runway; I could see the whole damn airfield, and lurking beyond, the soft blue Nevada mountain ranges: the Papoose and Freedom Ridge. In fact, I could see Groom Lake. We were in Area 51.

Our car was given a little turn high in the air as I white-knuckled the armrest and then we were returned softly to Mother Earth, dust swirling around the car.

"Do you have a car wash out here?"

"For what purpose? Clean for maybe five minutes so what's the use, besides the sun would reflect a glint of light for miles. We want to be low-key around here you understand. Dirt makes for great camouflage."

"I wouldn't call those huge *Star Wars* vehicles low key…"

"You didn't see them."

"No, no sir, just a desert mirage. Like the Marfa Lights of West Texas."

"You know about those?"

"Yeah, some kind of visual illusion caused by swamp gasses or atmospheric reflections."

"Is that right." The Colonel responded half-heartedly, as if I was some uninformed buffoon from the cow pastures of Texas and should know better. Well, I was from Texas, but hadn't been back there since my college days at Sul Ross in west Texas, a small green oasis in the middle of an arid nothingless—an arid nothingness like this place. I had left the Lone Star state for a graduate degree at the University of Maryland and after an obligatory tour of duty in the Middle East, a stint as a personal security guard for the rich and famous, and two uneventful years as an agent at the White House, I was now just a private dick with some useful security credentials—

I turned to Colonel Wayne Edward Conrad, a plethora of colorful ribbons plastered to his chest. "This demonstration is most fascinating, Colonel, but why did you bring *me* here?"

Before my host could tell me, the car pulled up to a long nondescript shiplap barracks-like building with a corrugated tin roof. It had been painted a dull sand color, but the gray-silvered wood underneath had been marred by the battering of sand-carrying winds. A faded sign painted on the side of the building could barely be discerned. It read: ARMY AIR CORPS. It reminded me that this site was first used as a gunnery range during World War II. And in the 1950's, it was used by Lockheed to test its new U-2 spy plane, a long-kept secret of the Cold War. In the 60's, it was the A-12 and SR-71 Blackbird. This was the place of military secrets, of R & D beyond our wildest imaginations.

The driver got out first and opened the Colonel's door. I opened my own and climbed out, fighting to close the door against the muscle-laden wind. We entered a five-paneled door—the word "SUPPLY" stenciled on it in faded black paint. The wind forced the door closed behind us, and we found ourselves in an empty building: you could see from one end to the other, the vacant building broken only by wood posts that supported lightweight roof trusses. A few birds nestled comfortably in the rafters.

"What are we—"

"Come with me."

The Colonel's driver pulled up a lone olive-drab, wooden folding chair of obvious military vintage and took a seat. He pulled a thick trade-paper-sized military manual in a sand-colored cover from his coat pocket and flipped it open to a page he had marked with a sheet of toilet paper. I followed the Colonel as I watched dust curl across the bare concrete floor in this drafty structure disguised as a building. The creaking of tired timber in this arthritic old building made my own bones ache.

"Stand right here next to me," said the Colonel. He was a full bird; his polished gold wings shining brightly in an otherwise muted environment. I brushed the sand off my jacket.

The silver-haired Colonel rotated a white porcelain light switch, but no light came on, instead, the floor beneath us dropped. I think I left my eyeballs and innards behind. We were being lowered through the floor like an elevator. I looked up to see a second "concrete" floor spring up on hinges to replace the first.

"Keep your elbows in if you don't want them scrapped."

I pulled them to my sides. We were lowered by jerks down a small concrete chase. A line of red, wire-covered light bulbs gave the Colonel's face an eerie glow that looked as if the light was emanating from *within* him, and he stared at me as if he was sizing me up, take a measure of the man, his eyes dark and piercing.

The elevator came to a stop and a steel door opened in front of us. We stepped into another world: a huge control room full of video monitors,and men sitting in front of consoles with rows of buttons, knobs, and meters. The men all wore audio headsets. On the screens were images of the UFO's—correction, the aircrafts—we had just seen on the surface. The room was lit with a soft bluish-green hue of radiant energy without an apparent source; the light seeming to radiate from below, with shadows softly painted on the ceilings, not the usual overhead light I'm accustomed to. The Colonel walked me across the room, my eyes trying to pick up as many details as I could before I was brought to a large double-door. The door swung open. Effulgence greeted us and I had to shed my eyes. I squinted, trying to peer into the blinding white light. As my pupils adjusted, I could just make out a shadowy object—and then I saw movement on its surface and a crawling sensation ran over the surface of my body as if some small creatures were moving under my skin. What was I looking at? Highly reflective, a shimmering surface one moment and clear as a mirror the next, like the skin was molting every few seconds, the surface completely renewed. It was shaped like an egg as viewed from my angle, but more like a donut if seen from the side. It certainly didn't look like anything that could fly. Workers scurried over the mysterious craft as if thoroughly examining it or maybe making miniscule, but critical repairs. This was the stuff of science fiction, of late-night talk radio. I had the urge to walk toward this thing, and I did, powerless to stop myself; curiosity and wonderment had pulled me in. I could see an extremely wide-angle view of the massive room reflected in the curvature of the craft—I could see myself, a tiny strange creature with four long appendages and a small head. I reached up to the underbelly of this thing and touched the surface ever so softly with my fingertips, no pressure, just enough to tingle the nervous system. It looked metallic, but was not cool to the touch as I had expected. It was soft like clay. I pushed in on it to see if it was malleable, but it didn't deform. How could it feel so soft and still be steel or aluminum. It was some high-tech alloy with something other than just metals in the mix, aluminum and *Silly Putty* maybe?

I turned to the Colonel who was now standing at my side apparently waiting for me to get over my euphoria. "Why am I here, Colonel? I'm not a scientist or engineer—"

"We've got a spy in our mist and you're here to ferret him out."

I looked at him with dashed expectations; this wonderful, awesome machine lurking in front of me and he wants me to find a thief. Somehow it seemed unimportant in the grand scheme of things. And this machine was somehow grand—something for all of mankind to benefit from, not just the U.S. government.

"We must protect our investment. This *is* important," the Colonel replied as if he had heard what I had just *thought*. "To lose this secret is to lose all we know as America. It could be used to destroy us, to destroy freedom. I'm told you're the best man outside of Central Intelligence for this job; one of a very few that my people say can be trusted."

"Who are these people? I'm sure they're not the top military brass. My military career was not so illustrious and my secret service work quite uneventful, no near assissina—"

"It's the sum total of your career, your experiences, your relationships with the community of people you've worked with. Also, it's the fact that you're single."

"Single? You're not suggesting…"

"That, Mr. Donner, depends on you…and whether or not you catch this guy. Your credentials are on the line."

"Okay, I'll do it." I said, ready to prove my superior skills; I *was* the best man for the job and I knew it. I love to outsmart guys who think they are smarter than anyone else—smarter than myself.

"It's done then." His mouth turned up ever so slightly. He had me.

"Get me the jackets of everyone working here," I said, "including yourself. And I need a cover; I can't be a civilian private investigator and blend in with this bunch. I wouldn't get the time of day."

"You're from an Air Force study group headed by a congressional committee to do a time & motion study of our procedures. It'll give you ample reasons to ask questions and poke around. Tell them they're talking about budget cuts and you're defending our position. That'll get them on your side."

"Get me a Lieutenant's uniform with very few ribbons, so they won't feel intimidated by me."

"Good."

This should be fun, I thought, a good adversary in a top-secret environment of intrigue and subterfuge, fun for the best sleuth in the country.

Colonel Wayne Conrad gave me an office deep in the bowels of the Nevada desert where I was completely secluded from the outside world. There could have been a nuclear war and I wouldn't have known it. Maybe that was part of the idea, to build something for the future of Earth after everything on the planet had been destroyed. Or maybe these experimental aircraft were built to travel to other worlds. Maybe it was a new weapon to annihilate our enemies? *Annihilate our enemies?* I couldn't keep that last thought out of my mind as I tried to construct a plan to "ferret out the guy" as the Colonel put it. He gave me the names of four scientists that his security team felt were possible leaks; two of them were women, that's where I would start. He told me his security team would get me any information I needed and their trustworthiness could be counted on. We would see, because I knew the leak could also be there.

I carried a small black satchel, walked tall in my pressed, blue officer's uniform and patent leather shoes, and wore a disarming smile. I also wore a pair of military-issue black-rimmed glasses with a nearsighted prescription to disguise my intelligence. I felt like I was a Pentagon investigator in a fifties science-fiction movie, there to examine a flying saucer half-buried at a canted angle in a pile of sand on a Hollywood sound stage. Yes, my disguise was a bit over the top, but that's what might make it work. Who would take *me* seriously?

I passed cloesd doors labeled "Chief, Propellants Division" and "Technical Advisor, Space Propulson" and passed through an open door into the well-ordered office of Dr. Millicent Snodgrass and to my welcome surprise she was a very attractive young woman with only a last name she needed to change. I surmised it had to be a married name. I looked for a diamond and indeed, found one on her ring finger. She looked up from her work.

"I'm Lieutenant Singleton, Air Force Special Projects, assigned here to do a time & motion study of operations."

"I see." She looked back down at her work.

I continued, "I'll be hanging around looking for ways to improve efficiency."

"I can't be disturbed."

"No, ma'am, I understand that. I'll just be a fly on the wall so to speak, maybe a question to you now and again, that's all."

"As you wish." She got up from her desk without looking at me and crossed the room to a filing cabinet and opened it. I stood there looking at this tall, slender, ash-blond bombshell and wondered how she managed not to get knocked up in high school. Spent all her time in the chemistry lab, that had to be the reason.

"Is that all?" She looked up at me for the first time.

"Yes ma'am, thank you for your cooperation."

"I haven't helped you yet."

"You've already made my day."

She *really* looked at me this time.

"Well, I'll be going for now, other team members to meet."

"What did you say your name was?"

"Bradford Singleton."

"Ah, I see. *Plus tard* then. She turned away and I left the room closing the door quietly behind me. She was of French ancestry with blond hair—and *did* give me a second glance even with my bottle glasses.

Maybe Chin Lee, my other female suspect would be more attentive to me. She was petite and cute and not as business-like as Millicent—and she was single. Metallurgy was her specialty and I had found her in a chemistry lab at the end of a long, cold concrete hallway.

"Hello. I'm Brad Singleton, efficiency expert."

"We could use some efficiency."

"How's that?"

"Someone took my box of Herbal teas. *Celestial Seasonings,* green box. I can't do my work without a regular fix. If you find the double-dealing, treasonous rogue, I want his head."

I took a step backward. She wasn't to be crossed; I wasn't going to touch a thing in that lab.

Chin Lee lay down a pair of metal tongs next to a dish with a smoking, mercury-like substance, and flipped a rocker switch on a battery charger-like box. It stopped humming. She then removed a pair of gray welding gloves and sat down on a stool. She was clearly of Asian ancestry with her narrow eyes, tight white skin, and small body frame.

"So, Lieutenant Singleton, what do you want to know?"

"I'd like a peek at your procedural records for the past month. You keep a log of your research activities?"

"I do."

"Good."

The attractive Asian was warm and open and tried to be as helpful as she could, well, short of revealing the real purpose of the hovering aircraft I had seen. That subject was not discussed.

That afternoon, I came upon a large set of double doors with a red light above them. A guard stood at ease in front of it. He came to attention. I handed him my security pass. He looked at it and returned it to me.

"You're not authorized entry."

"I need to go in there to complete my efficiency study."

"You don't have the proper pass."

"Colonel Wayne Conrad has authorized me complete access."

"Who did you say you were?"

"Lieutenant Singleton. I look for ways to improve work efficiency. I use covert observational technology and spectrum analysis to examine hot zones."

"Hot zones?"

"Ways to track slackers by using real-time finger and voice print analysis. And then there's the trace evidence like the condensation ring on a table from a water glass or coffee cup—"

He tried to process the information.

I continued: "The mean of the sample should be reasonably close to the mean of the population. With sufficient readings and a dispersion characteristic constant, the movement of the glass *or* coffee cup can be determined. In other words, we can follow the movements of all employees around here."

He looked down at the coffee cup in his hands, "I see."

"Yes. Statistical methods are used as an aid to determine the number of trips you make to the john." It was twaddle, and the worse the better, I figured. Sufficiently confused by it, the less chance he might challenge me but—

"You cannot pass."

"But I've got you on spectral observation."

The guard looked around apprehensively, then repeated, "You cannot pass."

"Sorry, but I must report you," I replied and quickly turned away.

"Now hold on, wait just a minute."

I turned back to him.

"Where did you say the rectal camera was?"

"Spectral, spectral observation. If I tell you..." The double doors began to open slowly.

"Thank you. And it's not a camera, it's a sensor, and it's in the bottom of your coffee cup."

The guard peered into his coffee as I slipped through the doors. My spy could be anyone, not just the four suspects I was given—maybe even the Colonel himself. The fact that I was barred from this room made me all the more curious. Here was the mysterious aircraft that I had seen defy gravity. It sat there quietly, glinting in the dimmed overhead lights that left much of the room in darkness. It was three in the morning and operations had been shut down for the night. Even research scientists needed sleep. For me, the night was when I got things done, the best time to poke around, when the rest of the world slept and dreamed nightmares.

I looked at the computer workstations; the monitors were left on. I was hoping that an application had been left open that might clue me in on something, but what I saw was all gobbledygook. Charts and diagrams were all coded in something other than English and standard mathematics symbols, more like Chinese characters, all Greek to me. I walked around to the backside of the aircraft looking for a way in. I found what appeared to be the rectangular outline of a flush panel, like the typical aircraft door that opens to the inside, but it was larger—both taller and wider—than I would expect. Maybe it was a cargo door. I looked for ways to open it, touching the surface and waving my hand to block a laser, but nothing happened. I had gotten through the high-security double door with some fast talk, but there was no human here to bamboozle. Talk? I said a few open-sez-me passwords and—and nothing.

Next to the panel, I could see an image behind the surface of the metal, like a television monitor behind smoked glass, only it wasn't a television and it wasn't glass. But I did recognize the image. It was a greenish DNA double helix slowly revolving on its lengthwise axis. Decode it and I could get in—right. I then saw some glowing colored LED's and touched the cherry-colored one. I heard a musical tone. I touched the other seven delicious colors—lemon, lime, raspberry—and each sounded a note of music. That was it, to open it, I had to know the password tune—not a chance. The only tune I knew was "Happy Birthday." So I played it, nothing happened. Then that mesmerizing tune from "Close Encounters of the Third Kind" reverberated in my head. I punched it out on the colored buttons and wah-la, the door opened sweetly. Somebody around here had a sense of humor—but poor security procedures.

I cautiously, apprehensively, entered the craft and looked around the cockpit and found that I could see through the heavily tinted windshield—it hadn't been visible from the outside. I sat down in what appeared to be the pilot's seat though it was quite large. I stared at the console. The controls were very strange, not switches, not knobs, and no levers or joysticks, not like anything I'd ever flown in. Then it hit me—as it often does, like a sledgehammer—this was an *alien* spacecraft, and I don't mean from south of the border—it had to be from another world, another solar system. My mind was really blown now, a real UFO. Since I was a kid, I was fascinated by the possibility of aliens visiting earth. I wasn't fearful, but intrigued, hopeful of meeting one someday. And now, our military's best was trying to reverse engineer this contraption. If they succeeded, and it appeared they'd made great progress, America would be a formidable foe again. We could use the technology peacefully to get all the other nations to lay down their weapons like Gort did in *The Day the Earth Stood Still*. Just then, the lights came up to full brightness. How long had I been sitting here? What time was it? My goose was cooked.

Colonel Conrad climbed in behind me. "Bypassing security protocols is a serious matter, Mr. Donner."

"It is."

"Pretty nifty, huh?" His demeanor changed dramatically. I followed suit.

"A kids dream."

"We didn't want to tell you. This is a hard thing to keep from the public."

"We always suspected Roswell…"

"Who?"

"Not Roswell?"

"I don't know the man."

"Ah, come on Colonel, more misinformation?"

"It's still on a need-to-know. Your clearance, level-3 isn't…"

"Isn't sufficient. I understand."

"You need to get back to the task at hand: the spy in our midst. If you don't find him, this is all for naught."

"Yes sir, I understand."

And so, after a not-so-good-morning's sleep, I was back to my task. I had long talks with the two male suspects the Colonel had given me, and then I returned to the metallurgy lab to see the dazzling Chin Lee—

But I found her questioning *me* instead of me her—not good.

"I use techniques developed by Lowry, Maynard, and Steinman," she said. "Do you like their work?"

"Their techniques are very effective in identifying weak protocols."

"Lieutenant Singleton, Steinman was a physicist."

Uh-oh, I'd been caught. I had taken just a basic course in time & motion studies and that's all I could muster, but I tried to recover, "Steinman also had a profound influence on efficiency testing."

"Then the four factors that influence a worker's performance still apply?"

"Well yes, of course, but mathematical derivative applications have made the process so much easier to analyze."

"Get off it, Lieutenant, you're no motion-study expert. What's with that black satchel? I haven't seen you open it yet."

My cover was blown. "You're right, Ms. Chin Lee, I'm not an expert at this, I got the job because of a little white lie on my job application…"

"I'm calling security!" She reached for her cell.

"I am security, the highest kind. Special Investigations, appointed by the White House."

I pulled out a faked Department of Homeland Security identification card to show her, but it was too late—

She pushed a button.

"Yes, Ms. Lee?" came the intercom.

"I've got an intruder. Says he's Lieutenant Brad Singleton, time and motion expert, or is it Special Investigations…"

"Yes, he's cleared, Ms. Lee. He's whoever he says he is."

Lee looked at me strangely.

I grinned.

For several days, I observed Chin Lee and the other three scientists, taking notes and logging their every move with the help of a couple of guys from base security. I initially could not find any pattern that revealed a way that anyone of them might be passing information to the outside until finally I hit on it.

After my charade with Lee, she had now become concerned that we might be on to her—my intention, of course—and her behavior and movements changed ever so slightly as we watched. She was now "looking over her shoulder," being extra careful, and that's what I wanted. I figured she'd delay in sending out any more classified documents and that alone would change her schedule. Our security team scoured the surveillance video, comparing her activities before my charade and after she suspected me. We were trying to determine what she was *not* now doing. We clocked her and she was spending less time at her computer and we noticed she didn't make trips to the blueprint archives as she had done almost everyday previous. She also had been routinely scanning drawings at her desk, but wasn't doing so now. Then I noticed something else missing on the most recent videos.

"There, see that?"

"See what?"

"She didn't throw anything in her trash can."

"Huh?"

"Look at last week's video."

The operator punched in a few numbers and ran the video forward at double speed until—

"There, stop, cue time mark, step back five frames a second— there, after she did some scanning in of documents, she opened the side of her CPU and removed a DRAM DIMM from a memory slot and then she threw it in the trash can. Threw it in the trash!"

"That *is* strange."

"It leaves her computer with less memory."

"Yes, or—"

The next morning, I returned to the Operations Building and approached the Colonel with my findings.

"Sit down Mr. Donner. Tell me what you've found."

"Ms. Chin Lee is your spy."

"Ms. Chin?"

"She's been passing information to the outside via coded data chips."

"How so?"

"Your waste paper—shredded documents, notes, Kleenex—all go to your land fill at Groom Lake, right?"

"Yes."

"Chin Lee throws her chips away so they end up in that land fill."

"How does that help her?"

"Each chip has an embedded low-frequency transmitter so that it can be found again."

"How in the hell…?"

"A remotely controlled model airplane of sorts, disguised as a vulture, retrieves it."

"Oh really!"

"Really."

"Whom do you think you're kidding. That's ludicrous!"

"You monitor the vultures, do you?"

"Well, no. I suppose…can you actually prove this?"

"I can, I have one of the vultures."

"Brought down with a shotgun, I suppose."

"It worked."

"Okay then, who do you think Lee's passing the data to?"

"That I don't know."

Well, Mr. Donner, your job is done, you can gather your things. A nice deposit will arrive at the bank of your choice—"

A soft knock came at the door.

"Come in Ms. Lee, we were just talking about you."

"You were?"

"Yes. Mr. Donner has just told me what you've been up to."

"Mr. Donner? I thought he was Brad Singleton."

"No Lee, he's a private detective under my employ. A very capable one I might add."

I spoke, probably out of turn, "Ms. Lee, I found the culprit who's been taking your *Celestial* tea."

"You have?"

"I'll give you a full report—"

I was rudely interrupted by Colonel Conrad, "Who have you been sending our secrets to, Chin?"

"Whatever do you mean?"

The Colonel turned to his desk and opened the top drawer and removed a pistol-like device and zapped her with it. A ray of reddish light hit her and she writhed like a caught fish and then vaporized.

"Thank you, Mr. Donner, that'll be all."

I stood up. "But—"

At that, the Colonel began to morph into something, something inhuman. His clothing dissolved into a wavy image like that of water hit with a stone, and as it leveled back out, there was something else—not of this world—standing in front of me. It was about a foot taller and more massive than Conrad and had a single eye on its face, if you can call the appendage dangling from his shoulder a face…or even a head. It spoke, but I saw no mouth moving.

"Well, Mr. Donner, welcome to Alpha Base on Planet Earth."

I dropped back into my chair like a rag doll with the stuffing gone out.

"Then who was Chin Lee?" I asked.

"A human. Infiltrated our post. CIA, I surmise, gathering data for your government before they try to eliminate us. They like our weapons I think."—at that he paused to reflect—"I hated to see her go. I liked her herbal tea."

"You're an Alien?"

"If that means I'm not from you're planet, it is so. None of us are. Lee was the only homosapien, and you found her for us. Congratulations."

"There's another human here," I added quite frankly.

"Yes, Mr. Donner, and we have plans for you too."

I eyed his laser weapon and then stared into his fully dilated green eye.

"Would you like to take a trip to see our solar system?" the creature asked.

"I'm not leaving this place am I?"

"Not by the front gate."

Prime Beef

By Don Kirk

THE COUNTRYSIDE WAS COVERED with tall green corn stalks swaying and rustling in the breeze. Diesel railroad engines could be heard racing across the landscape and behind the chain of droning engines were hundreds of black tank cars, rocking and rolling at over 40 miles an hour. Stenciled in large white letters on the side of each tank car were the words, "HIGH FRUCTOSE CORN SYRUP."

And that's how it all began—with corn syrup. Cheaper than sugar, it was used in processed foods to add sweetness, depress freezing to prevent crystal formation in ice cream, improve the viscosity of salads and dressings, improve color and texture, and provide the suspension necessary to keep other ingredients evenly mixed. The government, to the tune of 20 billion dollars a year, had subsidized agribusiness—80% of it going to large producers over 500 acres—and 10 billion of it went to the corporate farms that planted corn. Yes, corn. And less than one percent went to farmers who wanted to raise fruits and vegetables, the healthy way to eat, everyone agreed. This went on for years and the price of corn was kept so very low, that it was very profitable to use corn syrup in all of North America's processed foods. Nearly 300 million people began to gain weight. No matter what they did—expensive, time consuming weight loss programs, workout gyms, and low-fat, low-carb foods—they continued to gain weight. It wasn't long before they had become the fattest nation on Earth, with over seventy percent of the population, not just overweight, but seriously obese. Clothes had to be made in China specifically for Americans; no one else in the world needed two, three, and four-X sizes. In fact, their used clothing—going to other third-world countries—had to be re-cut to be used. The government had long since stopped trying to educate the masses, in fact, they were aggressively working to "deprogram" them about freedom and independence and graduate them from high school with no more than a third-grade education. But the taxpayer kept pouring more money into the federal school system hoping the trend could be reversed. But the billions of dollars invested in public education didn't help, and the taxpayer didn't know that was the intent, for it *not* to help. Very few meat products were found on the grocery store shelves those days, and what there were, they were made primarily of soy and cornmeal. The Mad Cow Disease scare at the beginning of the new millennium had frightened the world—they had believed in the FDA, that they were doing their job and American beef was the safest in the world—but now American's, and the rest of the world, would no longer buy American beef. The cowboy, as we had known him for 200 years, had finally ceased to exist. If there had been at least one cow left, there would still have been at least one cowboy, but it was not to be. The economy was devastated and the United States sorely needed a new product to export.

There were no manufacturing jobs left in the U.S. and most of America's jobs had been exported by 2015, including most white-collar jobs. Only a few executives of one large Corporation had a paying job. But the American people were happy. They were given all the food they wanted—made mostly of corn syrup—with free government food stamp programs, and all they had to do was sit at home and watch television and eat and eat and eat.

Finally, the United States had their export. The world now reveled in the finest cuts of meat from America: sirloin, T-bones, ribs, filet mignon. Not any part of the animal had been wasted: the stomach, lower intestine—tripe and menudo were popular—and of course the brain (considered a fine delicacy) kept the world fed. No longer were there any starving nations. And the United States no longer had to encourage birth control; in fact, they gave tax breaks to those who procreated profusely. Cornmeal had efficiently—profitably—fattened cattle, hogs, and poultry and now America had become one big feedlot because the American people, fattened up for the kill, had made *North American Meats*, the largest Corporation in the world.

Last Stop

By Don Kirk

IT WAS GETTING LATE, very late. In the misty fog, my headlights caught a flickering neon sign up ahead; it read "ROOMS." I wasn't going any further. I hoped they were open. I was lost in an inky blackness in a state I had never been in before. I had been driving north on Highway 43 for hours now and should have reached my destination. From Mobile to Gadsden had been the plan, but leaving in the evening had not been my idea; they said I had to report for work the next day. I had just seen the lights of a large city down in a valley below on my left, but no such town was on my map, at least not based on where I thought I should be. I could be anywhere in the state for all I knew. I was a good navigator, but without the sun to help me with my compass directions, I was not so good.

And now I was driving off the black pavement onto a gravel parking lot covered with bottle caps. I pulled up to the front door and shut off my engine. Climbing out of a '69 white Ford sedan—with the words "U.S. GOVERNMENT MOTOR POOL" printed in black on the door panels—I could see I was standing in front of a large rectangular two-story clapboard building of 1917 vintage—at least that was the number painted high up on the gable. The wood siding, without so much as a chip of paint left, was almost as black as this moonless night. I climbed the wooden steps, pulled open a torn screen door and entered a large hall with tables of various sizes and shapes scattered about. Several men were laughing and growling and smoking and cussing around a long table at the back. As I approached the men, I could see a row of framed black & white 8x10 photos of men in military dress aligned horizontally along the walls at eye level. All of the men seemed to have very heavy eyelids, their eyes squinting—maybe when they were photographed a bright light was used. Above the photos hung a large hand-painted wood placard of an American eagle and the words VFW POST 666.

"Are there rooms for rent for the night?" I asked.

"Sure son," see Miss Lilly," said one and pointed to a crude saloon bar in the corner. Four streetlight posts surrounded the bar each with capitals of grotesque animal gargoyles. Hung high along the walls, in several rows like a collection of sorts, were humanoid looking masks with distorted, devilish-looking, rubbery faces that would give anyone under the age of seventy nightmares. Who would want to collect such things, I wondered?

Another slovenly man sat at the bar gulping down a beer, and a bony, wasted-looking lady with long, frazzled black hair and a drawn, washboard-like face that had obviously seen many decades pass by, wiped down the bar.

"I need a room," I said.

"Weekly?"

"Just one night."

"Sure honey. sixteen bucks."

From my hip pocket, I pulled the hand-stamped leather billfold my mother had made for me, and gave the barkeep a crumpled ten and six ones.

She handed me an old skeleton key. "Upstairs, turn right, at the end of the hall on the left, room seven. The only bathroom is out back. There's a fresh roll of toilet paper in your room."

"Thank you ma'am."

"Don't let the bed bugs bite," she replied.

"No ma'am…oh, could you tell me where I am, what town?"

"Oh, dear, there hasn't been a town here in a very long time—ain't that right boys?"

"That's right, Miss Lilly." The boisterous men in the back had been listening to us.

The slouching man drinking at the bar spoke up. "Sheol. This here's Sheol, a place in the depths of the earth where the dead are supposed to go. It's still on the map. You can find it there."

I nodded and said thanks to the both of them and returned to my car and got my simulated leather, box-shaped old suitcase and tattered Alabama State map and climbed the narrow, steep stairs that creaked all the way to the second floor. I turned right and walked down a long, dimly lit hall with doors on each side, all painted a deep, dark red. I passed an open door and peeked in. On the worn pine floor was an old Persian rug and over the window, cream-colored sheer curtains. The walls were plastered with yellowed, 1940's newspaper headlines and the room contained an iron clothes rack with several military uniforms, all with a spattering of ribbons and metals. The beginning of a historical museum, I figured. I reached the window at the end of the hall and on the left was my own red door, room number "7." I put the skeleton key in the lock and began to turn the worn brass knob. I hoped the room was halfway presentable, with clean sheets on the bed and a not-to-musty smell. The door creaked open and I felt for the light switch. My fingers found one of those push-button type switches—push the button on top and the light would go on— I pushed it, but the light didn't go on. I stepped into the room, hoping my eyes would adjust and I could at least see something, see the bed, see a nightstand lamp—there, I grabbed the base of the lamp and turned the knurled knob on the light socket. A dim, twenty-five-watt bulb came on and I could see that my hand was around a plaster sculpture of a slender naked lady, the paint chipped and faded, a nipple missing. I eyed a single bed with a steel-pipe headboard and a tattered crazy quilt on a mattress that sagged in the middle as if a two hundred-pound invisible man was currently sleeping there. The corners of the high-ceilinged room were dark, but I could just make out peeling wallpaper over shiplap walls. I could see the cheesecloth tacked to the horizontal boards on which the wallpaper was once glued. I was in a corner room with double-hung windows on two sides. They still had some flakes of paint on them and they were each open several inches at the top and bottom. A whistling breeze of chilly night air and orphaned dust particles meandered over the bed. I lowered my suitcase to the floor and sat slowly on the bed. I was a long way—from nowhere.

I opened my map on the bed and began looking for the town of Sheol, Alabama. It was to be my first real job, a summer job after my second year of college. I was to be a fallout shelter analyst in Gadsden, Alabama, my job to crawl into musty basements in schools and churches and the like and take measurements of all the windows and doors and ceiling heights. I had to determine the materials and thickness of the walls and ceiling and the rest of the building around it. I had to fill out forms that a computer keypunch operator could use to punch the data on IBM cards. The deeper in the ground and the more material around you, the better chance you had to survive a nuclear blast, or so they said, but I didn't believe it, and this job seemed like a big waste of tax-payers hard-earned money, but hey, it was a job.

I pulled the blanket down on the bed to see if the sheets had been slept in—they were clean, technically, but they smelled as if it had been years since they were washed. I raised the top sheet up to make sure there were no spiders or scorpions beneath it looking for a meal. As a child I had been stung by a scorpion in my bed, its long, segmented tail curled over itself, and I was sure I was going to die, the burning sting, the hot poison surging through my body as it headed for my brain soon to send me to unconsciousness—and to the netherworld.

The terrifying death masks I had seen on the walls downstairs danced in my head. These masks were not of horrific fantasy creatures, but instead were large grotesque, life-size human faces with tiny bodies and hands with extra-long fingers and spindly arms and legs—and they were all naked as jaybirds. I didn't need these images floating in my head while I sat in a large drafty, musty room on a second-floor in the back of an old building that sat at the side of a dark country road in the middle of a state I had never been to before. I lay down on the bed, on top of the blanket, and stared at the decorative plaster casting on the ceiling from which a bare light bulb hung. I lay there afraid to take my clothes off and get into bed. Someone might come to the door or I might have to get up and leave in a hurry—so, on this night, I'd keep my clothes on. I took off my shoes and got into bed and snapped off the pornographic table light. The glare from an alley light on a telephone pole shone into my eyes and muffled, drunken laughter filtered up from the room below. I wished I had gotten a room at the front where I could see my car, watch it in case anyone tried to steal it. But no, it was a government vehicle; no one would dare steal that, would they? My eyes got heavy—

Bang, bang! Sure enough, a loud knock on my door. I didn't know how long the unwelcome guest had been knocking. I jumped up and shuffled my stocking feet on the dirty floor and as I grabbed the door knob, I delayed opening it and asked:

"Who's there?"

"Are you a vet?" came a deep disembodied voice.

"No, I'm in college."

"Don't matter none," the voice said. "You're welcome to join us for a beer. We'd like to have you."

"I'm awfully tired."

"Ah, come on now son, humor poor old Matthew Hadean will you. We'll tell you some good World War II stories."

"No, I don' think…"

"Come on now!" His voice was more insistent now. I figured he was half-drunk or more so. I tried to quietly hook the chain on the door.

"I have to get up early," I said.

"Too late for a good nights sleep, no sense in going to bed now, it makes the morn' even harder to rise."

"No thank you. I appreciate it though."

Suddenly the paneled door splintered inward and the chain broke from the doorjamb. I reared back and stared at a short, scruffy, gray-haired man who glared back at me with glassy eyes like cats-eye marbles and nothing behind them except beer.

"I won't hurt you kid. We just want you to join our little get together. We're all from the same platoon and we meet here each week to talk old times and we're organizing our own political party. Both the republicans and the democrats ain't a-doing us no good, and we'd like you to join."

"I'm not a vet."

"You don't need to be for this party son. We need your help. The vets ain't gettin' a square deal. The government keeps cuttin' our benefits."

"I'm sorry, but I—"

"Get you're butt down stairs or we'll all come up to your room."

"Well, okay, just for a minute."

"That's all I'm askin'. Here us out about this new political party we're forming. The republicans and democrats ain't a-doing us no…"

"I'm coming, be right there."

The resolute man walked back down the hall and I put on my shoes and pulled the broken door shut and tried to lock it without success.

"Sit down son. Have a beer."

"No thanks…"

A thin, lankly old man with sunk-in cheeks and thinning hair glared his disproportionately large eyeballs at me. He wore an olive drab baseball cap with the VFW 666 logo sewn on it along with some military ribbons, U.S. flags, and assorted fly hooks. He pushed his beer bottle toward me and it slid passed an old *Roloflex* twin-lens camera. I looked at the other men. They all had their eyes on me. I was way out of my element. I couldn't get away if I tried. I wrapped my fingers around the dark glass bottle, raised it to my lips, and let a small amount of the bitter beer dribble into my mouth.

"Good," I said. "Sometimes there's a right time for a beer, when it really, truly tastes good…"

"Unless it's warm as panther piss," one of them added. They all laughed a gut-deep, drunken laugh as if they would all throw up at any moment.

"So what is this veteran's political party all about?" I asked, trying to get their attention off me.

"We already done got eleven states signed up with their own organization and we're trying to decide who's going to represent the national chapter so's all decisions'll funnel through one organization. That way's we can find one candidate to support."

"You're going to run your own third-party candidate?"

"We will eventually, but right now we support any candidate who says he will support House Bill seventy eight."

I took another swig of the hot beer. "What's this House Bill seventy eight?"

"Guarantees all vets get a fair shake at the VA hospital as long as they live. We done fought for America, and a lot of us gave our lives to guarantee America's freedom. Don't you think the government should take care of us?"

"I do, sure I do."

The lanky man turned to the bar and yelled out, "another round Lil', and one for the boy too."

"Why sure, Jud."

"Anyone can join, you see, you don't have to be a vet. You don't like your presidential choices now do you?"

"No, not particularly," I said. "I voted independent in the last election."

"There, you see, our kind of man…"

"You don't have to pay no dues or nothin', just sign our ledger here, show your support for our cause." The vet plopped a large leather-bound ledger on the table and opened it; dust rose from its brittle pages. "Just sign right there, just below John G. Houseman, right there."

He handed me a metal quill-nibbed pen and I scratched my name, Jeremy Clifford Warner.

"That's good son, now you're an official vet supporter. Your freedom is assured. You're safe with us, son."

"If you can just get that beer down," said another.

"He's nursing it like a baby," added the short stocky Matthew.

I took a big swig. My head felt light and airy. The human gargoyles on the wall seemed to move and grin at me. I felt my chair falling backward and I fell sideways, hitting the floor, and saw a fan turning slowly above me. I felt a burning sting and a hot poison streaming through my body.

A car's headlights blasted through the front windows and streaked across the walls of the hall. A tall man in a well-appointed gray suit came in the screen door, letting it close softly behind him.He walked to the back of the room and asked the rough-looking men sitting around the long table, drinking and talking and cussing, "Are there rooms for rent?"

The new visitor looked at the strange human, mask-like gargoyles on the walls. The old vets noticed him eyeing them.

"Nice ain't they," one vet said.

"I suppose. Who'd want to collect such a…"

"We got us a new one," another blurted out, and he pointed at the wall of pictures of fallen comrades, all in their military uniforms.

"Our latest tragedy; he died so young."

"I'm sorry," replied the tall gentleman.

"He was a nice boy."

"You said you had a new gargoyle?"

"Oh yes, there behind you, over the front door."

The tall gentleman turned around to see a pristine, human-faced gargoyle with tiny legs and arms. It looked eerily like the young stranger in the photo, eerily like the one who had lost his way just a week before and had rented a room upstairs for the night—for just one night—in a room numbered "seven."

A Frame In Time

By Don Kirk

HE HAD INVITED Marion SIMMONS, a colleague at MIT and noted researcher in molecular biology, to witness an astounding experiment that would redefine our view of the universe. Einstein had opened up our thinking and demonstrated to us that the universe was much more complex than we believed and he made clear that there are so many more mysteries yet to be explained. Professor John Granger was about to show Mr. Simmons the next breakthrough in science. Granger fit the typical profile of a college professor, engrossed in his own research in the field of mathematics, oblivious to the needs of his students, only teaching to pay the bills. Tenure kept him comfortable and protected. With a haggard look and dressed haphazardly, necktie always loose, it appeared as if he wore and slept—if he slept—in the same suit for the entire semester.

Marion Simmons met the professor in his third-floor office of the old science building. The cramped office, squeezed into a once unused space next to a mechanical room, had an open ceiling occupied by asbestos-covered ductwork and steam pipes that radiated out from the adjacent room. It was lined with rickety, teetering, overloaded bookshelves and a metal WWII desk piled high with papers on the verge of collapsing. A trashcan in the form of a cut-in-half brass bomb was overflowing with crumpled papers, and a whiteboard on an easel was marked up with equations, or chicken scratchings, depending on who was trying to read them. The dark and marred old pine floor creaked as Marion Simmons entered.

"Come on in Mr. Simmons, I want to show you something."

The professor quickly tried to remove the pile of papers on the only other chair in the room, a heavily padded armchair of dark-green cloth punctuated with numerous cigarette burns. Marion carefully took the seat as Professor Granger approached his easel—a burning cigarette squeezed between the yellow-stained fingers of his left hand—and erased what was inscribed and began to explain the new project he was engrossed in.

"Our world," said Professor Granger, "is made up of frames of time, like the frames on motion picture film. Each frame of film has no motion, just a still image, but each frame is a record of events at any given moment in time, and the frames, projected in sequence creates the illusion of motion made possible by the way our brain interprets and overlaps the still images on our retina—a persistence of vision phenomena."

"I don't quite follow you John, what do the movies have to do with our universe?"

The professor scribbled a diagram on the whiteboard that looked like a bunch of crisscrossing lines of doodling. He put his cigarette stub out on a glass ashtray overflowing with butts and smutty ashes.

"Time is not continuous, Mr. Simmons, but made up of moments in time strung together, and those strings of time, those paths we traverse through the universe are not at all like strings, but more like a stack of still photographs organized by a program to retrieve them in a sequential order. Apparently the universe is finite, having limited space to store the events of time. As Einstein professed, the universe has a fixed amount of energy-mass, limited resources you see, but which can be used and reused by converting mass to energy and, in some cases, back again."

"You're confusing me, Professor?" Mr. Simmons fidgeted, shifting in his chair, not sure why he was here, not sure if the Professor, a colleague yes, but only an acquaintance, was a tad off his rocker, spending, he assumed, much too much time in this secluded office.

"Our universe is like a computer hard drive," the Professor continued.

"A hard drive?"

"Yes, the events in our universe are not necessarily laid down in a sequence on a single track like the undulations of a groove on a vinyl record if you will, but are bits of information that can be fragmented, parts of it placed in different areas of a digital recording disk, that is, in different places in the universe. Your lifeline may just be segments of your life laid out in many sectors of the universe. This means that individual events—the frames—in your life are parts of a bigger file, your life-line, and they can exist right next to the events of another person's life and—this is important—those might have occurred much earlier in space-time. Do you follow me Marion?"

"Well, I think I'm getting some of it."

Professor Granger reached for a soft pack of *Marlboro's*, pulled a fresh stick, and raised it to his nostrils to sample the fresh tobacco aroma.

"Then I'll continue if I may. Parts of *your* life are scattered throughout this magnificent universe. In other words, and here's the kicker, not only can your lifeline be located right next to the life of some medieval knight living four hundred years before, but it suggests that many different sub-universes—program apps—can exist side by side. But we, you and me existing right here now together, in one file or segment of time, cannot know what might exist directly next to us in space, nor directly ahead of us, or directly behind us, or here, beside us"—Simmons glanced around the room thinking about what was beyond the four walls—"Remember, our lives are made up of single frames, or groups of frames, distributed in many parts of the universe, wherever your program, your lifeline, can find unused space to inhabit. We know that the universe operates on limited resources and a universe made up of billions of 'strings' of individual lifelines would result in a tangled mass satiated with empty space—'ether' as it were—that could not be accessed, and would be a waste of the universe's finite resources."

The professor finally took time to light his cigarette and then inhaled deeply with blissful satisfaction. The smoke quickly replaced the 'ether' in the room, and in his lungs.

"You mean John, that when a person dies that maybe, like a

hard drive, the universe overwrites the life-line of that person in order to provide more space for a new life, resulting in a fragmented universe, like a fragmented hard drive, possibly quite different from what Einstein ever envisioned?"

Professor Granger turned away for a moment and you could see that his mind was clicking away processing information and analyzing data to come up with the proper response. He took another puff and picked at his stubble of a beard.

"Well, I don't know if overwriting ever actually takes place, I haven't pursued that aspect of my research, I only believe that, because of these physically adjacent frames of different lifelines, that it may explain how some people have reported seeing into other universes, even crossing over into them, a failure, if you will, of the universe's software to keep track of all frames and keep them in line and separate from all other timelines."

"A software glitch, I think I get it, professor," said Mr. Simmons as he stood up with a tingling thrill of excitement running through his veins and forgetting for a moment that this might be just so much hokum. "If your theory is true, looking into the past might be possible, and time travel might also be, well maybe, at least to time periods and lives that haven't yet been overwritten."

"That's right, and in addition, Marion, many distinctly different 'sub-universes' might exist side by side in our universe."

"Different movies?" Mr. Simmons asked.

"In a way. But why and how are these different sub-universes brought into existence? That's what fascinates me the most. That's what I'm studying and what I intend to discover with my *RotoGen Embalizer*. I can now break through a frame of our lives here in the present and see into an adjacent frame, either beside, behind, or in front of us."

"How, can . . ."

"How can I break through?"

"With the *RotoGen*! I establish a force field of electromagnetic radiation that can breakdown the wall of energy that separates us from other frames. That energy is the negative mass of the universe. As soon as I get the generator up to speed and transfer an electrical current to the *RotoGen*, it will be ready to positively charge a frame wall of my choosing and thus eliminate it. Are you ready for a demonstration?"

"A demonstration? I uh, yes, of coarse, you kidding, on with it professor."

"Then let's adjourn and reconvene in an hour at my lab in Building 16." The Professor snuffed out his cigarette on the edge of the ashtray. Marion Simmons looked at the dirty, overflowing ashtray of crumpled butts and thought that it might represent how the universe actually looked.

Mr. Simmons arrived at Professor Granger's lab on schedule. He had been there twice before about a year ago when the professor had proposed a project requiring several disciplines, but which fell through the cracks because of a lack of federal funding. The lab was roomy and organized, not like the Professor's office. Neatly arranged tables with black granite counter tops were covered with various pieces of testing devices, glass flasks and crucibles. I'm sure it remained uncluttered and emmaculate only because other professors and graduate students also used it.

"I must warn you, that I am still experimenting and nothing is perfected yet so I can't guarantee results every time. And, I must warn you, there could be as yet unseen side effects."

"You've done this before?"

"Oh yes, with good results."

"Only *good* results?"

"As opposed to a negative result, yes."

"I'm not going to send you anywhere, not yet anyway. You're just going to observe. Here watch."

The professor sat down at his Linux computer workstation, dragged the mouse to open a window, selected several variables and clicked "SEND." A progress bar appeared and the *RotoGen Embalizer* sitting inertly across the room, began to hum. The *RotoGen* was a room-high black vessel wrapped in a superconducting coil of wire obviously designed to produce a strong magnetic field. It had a small window cut in one side with a very thick piece of glass inserted into it.

"Mr. Simmons, you'll have to stand on that platform and look into the glass window and soon you'll be able to see a frame, or frames, of another's lifeline."

"Okay, I just stand on this platform here, professor?"

"Yes, right there."

Simmons climbed onto the platform, stepped slowly toward the small window and peeked in, blocking reflected light hitting the glass with his cupped hands.

"I don't see anything professor except a shiny silver surface."

The professor replied, "Contained within this vessel is a dense spinning cylinder made of an aluminum alloy that appears opaque when at rest, but almost transparent when rotating at a high speed due to some narrow vertical slits in the cylinder."

"I see the fluting, but they're not actually slits, professor."

"Just observe. I'll try a video capture of the space in time so that we can study it later. Ready?"

"Ready."

The area around the cylinder began to fill with a gaseous white substance and Simmons stared at its meandering, curling motion, slowly enveloping the space, reminding him warmly, and apprehensively, of the mysterious low-lying fog in one of his favorite 1950's horror movies, the creepy *Thing from Another World*. The fear and trepidation he remembered, surged with his thoughts.

Cheeuuooooh. A warbling, shrieking sound so strange it wasn't of this world, emanated from the shiny black vessel that Professor Granger had called the *RotoGen*. Mr. Simmons cried out in a glee of wildly frightening wonderment as he saw what appeared to be a look at another part of the universe.

"Whough, Professor! It's like nothing I've ever seen. Huge, strange twisted trees wrapping themselves in grey-colored leaves, a soft, thick atmosphere with no apparent light source, architecture of the sharpest angles with glinting and weirdly textured materials that could be imagined only by science fiction writers…wow, professor, I saw it! I actually saw it."

"Here, come here Mr. Simmons." An image was forming very slowly, line by line, on a large rectangular, high-definition, plasma screen above the computer console.

"That's it, that's what I saw! Look at those vivid colors and angular shapes of the structures surrounded by a forest of grotesquely twisted trees. But I can't get a handle on the scale of the buildings. Are they a hundred feet tall or a thousand?"

"Look here, Mr. Simmons, forming near the bottom of the frame, something, dark, tall, and slender, here, I'll magnify those pixels and interpolate to fill the screen with the shadow and . . . look! A life form! It has appendages, it's a creature with a potential for mobility."

"Nothing like I've ever seen, even in the insect world. Was this in *our* past?"

"It's nothing from our known universe."

"You've done it, Professor! You've captured a frame of time in another world."

"I have, haven't I? The Nobel Prize in physics will be mine. I'll publish a collection of my captured frames, revealing the true nature of our universe, and it's no telling what I can do with my *RotoGen*. Maybe, if I could just reverse engineer the universe's system language that links the frames of a single lifeline together, I could capture it and play it back as a life recreated, one that we could interact with. We could talk with Wilhelm Roentgen, Sir Joseph Thompson, Albert Einstein, King Arthur, the possibilities are endless—"

That was the end of their first meeting and it wasn't long before Professor Granger called on Marion Simmons for their second get-together.

Mr. Simmons returned to the Professor's office one late winter evening after the campus had become eerily quiet and blanketed with fresh snow brightly lit and glistening from the full moon. Rays of yellow-orange light from dorm windows shown as ribbons of warm color on the bluish snow as students studied in their cozy abodes.

"Now that you've brought me into this project, what did you want me to do? I'm a biologist; how can I contribute?"

"It's about those creatures you saw during your last visit. I wondered if we were looking at the past on our own planet or elsewhere in the universe."

"How could it be from—?"

"I have one."

"You what?"

"In the basement. It's for real. I succeeded in crossing the frame barrier and I brought one back."

"I can't believe…show me."

Professor Granger led Marion Simmons down several flights of fire stairs and entered a dingy, seldom used basement of Building 16. A long hallway of chipped paint was punched with rusting steel doors on each side. The professor came to a door with a padlock on it. He drew a key from his vest pocket and unlocked it. The door squeaked open and they entered. Granger led Simmons through a couple more doors and there in a three meter cube of steel bars was the strange creature they had seen in another lifeline. Simon's took a step back, his eyes wide, his brain fighting his body to take flight.

"Oh, my god! This is out of a 50's monster movie. It's some kind of stage effect."

"No, it's perfectly real. I'm not into special effects, Mr. Simmons."

Simmons stood there in suspended animation, collected himself, and then spoke as if what he was looking at was nothing special: "What do you feed it?"

"I tried different things until I hit on something it devoured with enthusiasm—"

An alarm clock went off. Marion Simmons slowly reached the threshold of consciousness. He was in his bed and it was 6:30 A.M. Simmons slammed the button down—the ringing stopped. Beads of sweat ran down his brow. He sat up. It was a dream, just a dream, no horrible creature in a cage in the basement of Building 16. Simmons took a big sigh of relief and lay slowly back down. He had worked with the Professor for almost six months, but then had not heard from him in the last three. Granger was not an easy man to work with; it was his way or no way. And he had become more and more obsessed with his discovery. Simmons was happy he hadn't called—

The phone rang. Simmons reached for it on his bedside table,

"Hello?"

"This is John Granger. Can you come into the lab today? I'm ready to do the next test of the *RotoGen Embalizer*. I've built some new equipment."

"Uh, yeah, sure."

"Nine?"

"I'll be there."

It was nine months since Marion Simmons first saw the *RotoGen Empalizer* at Building 16. They had done several more experiments that handed them some more images of other worlds, or at least past events of this one, but Granger still chose not to go public with it. He wanted to know more, he wanted real proof. The *RotoGen* was still there in the lab, sitting inert, but the way it sat there at one end of the room, all by itself, towering over everything else with its shiny black finish, spoke an evilness that dominated the room. Simmons wasn't sure he wanted to enter that room. The Professor was pacing and smoking like a soot-choked chimney.

"Are we going back to twisted trees and barren landscapes?" asked Simmons.

"They're gone," said the Professor solemnly, "All we've seen so far—gone. We need a root directory so we can find our way back to the same frame "walls" we've been to before."

"We can't go back and look at a place we've seen before?"

"Not at this stage, but come with me."

Granger led Simmons down a hallway where he had hung several photos of the alien landscapes he had captured with the *RotoGen*. They were amazing sights, beautiful works of art in their own right. They could have been the works of a science fantasy artist, and others in the building who saw them probably thought they were: a barren sea of red sand with a violent yellow sky, a tortured world of dense dilapitated housing that could have been a Detroit of the future, and a lush forest of alien vines and trees so deeply green even the Olympia National Park would be envious. The Professor said no one yet knew what he was up to. He had graduate students and engineers building parts for his equipment, but no one person knew the whole story.

From there, we entered another laboratory that backed up to the first. A hole had been cut in the wall and a second vessel had been connected to the first *RotoGen* with a two-meter bellows-like tubing. The second vessel was similar to the first, but several meters larger in diameter, and a meter taller, but instead of a window, it had a small doorway in one side just big enough for a man to pass through.

"What is this?"

"We can do more than just look at other worlds, John. Before you sits the world's first time machine."

"Time machine? I thought we were working on a way to see into other lifelines?" A time machine? This was too much for Simmons. Granger, he thought, had gone way over the top, his research aims gone astray.

"We have seen into other worlds, but we haven't met Albert or Newton yet. We can't do it sitting in this lab."

"Have you got all your records up to date?" Simmons asked. "Before we go further—"

"With what I've done, I've got the Nobel in my pocket and I'm working on my second one, but I need you. You're the only one I can trust." The professor put out his cigarette in the palm of his hand and didn't flinch, but Simmons did.

"You said it was a time machine, but you know we can't go forward in time, only backward with this device, only to randomly view things that have already happened, and if one was to actually go there, he could never return."

"That's not true, and I'm going to prove it to you," said Granger as he circled the room, his head down, a trail of smoke making the largest smoke ring Simmons had ever seen, well, except maybe in the Cyclotron.

Marion Simmons was still standing in front of the doorway to the new vessel as the Professor approached. "I'm not going in there."

"I don't expect you to Mr. Simmons, I just need you to run the program at the computer console in the other room."

"I think you need to stop and get some system engineers to go over your figures," Simmons replied. "You need programmers, not me."

"You'll do just fine."

The Professor sat Simmons down at the console and showed him what he would need to do.

"You just wait for my command."

The Professor, with a burning cigarette still in his hand, carefully entered the portal into his new black vessel. "Okay, start the routine," he yelled to Simmons. Simmons clicked the mouse and the aluminum cylinder started to turn and picked up speed. The centrifugal forces it created as it rotated at a very high vector speed was felt as vibrations in the floor. Glass flasks danced across the lab tables. The room lights dimmed for a second and an eerie purplish-green light emanated brightly from the vessel door. Simmons watched on the computer monitor. He knew Granger would never return. He knew he would then go quietly back to his office in the biology building and the FBI would come to him and ask him questions about the disappearance of Professor John Granger. He knew they would not find any documents about his research—he would make sure of that. Granger's lifeline and the history he created would come to an end right here in Building 16. Suddenly a blast of white-hot flames shot out of the doorway and a big black blob was blown from the vessel. It landed tangled and contorted on the lab floor. It was Granger, now nothing more than a big lump of grimy ash. The black polished steel vessel then shattered into lethal pieces of shrapnel as something bigger and more powerful than the vessel emerged. It was a multi-legged, asymmetrical creature of strange proportions with shiny reddish skin, like the skin of a cooked turkey, but crawling and undulating over its skelectical structure—if it had one. Three meters high, two in girth, it stomped over the ashes of Granger and then ripped apart an MIT student that had entered the room. Blood splattered to the walls and ceilings. A second student found himself thrown through a second-story plate-glass window. Simmons sat at the console, stunned. Seeing it on the monitor, it didn't seem quite so real to him, like being numbed by violence on television—just a science-fiction movie from the 50's, that's all.

Then the creature crashed through the wall between the two lab rooms, sheetrock and metal studs flying everywhere. It was the last thing Marion Simmons would ever see. The creature, with its wildly flaying appendages came to a sudden halt, freezing in time and space. The sheetrock remained hanging in the air. Simmons sat motionless in front of the console, abject terror frozen on his face. Students on the sidewalk outside stopped moving in mid stride. Birds hung motionless in the sky.

Due to a system error, the application that ran the universe had crashed. On seeing the creature, if someone could have asked, "What is it?" the professor would have simply replied, "It's a glitch, just a glitch."

But unfortunantely, no one was left to reboot.

Stairway to Hell

By Don Kirk

THE STAIR SQUEAKED UNDERFOOT. Each woolen-socked foot was carefully, very carefully, placed on the next tread of a long run of slippery stairs in an old Victorian mansion, a marvelous home that had been saved from the wrecking ball because of years of loving hard work—hard work that was all now for naught. The stairs had never seemed this long before. *The architect should have added a couple of landings along the way,* Jason thought, as he shifted his load, trying desperately not to move his center of gravity so far forward that it would tilt him off balance and send him catapulting down to a world that he darn well knew would no longer be made of key lime pie and 300-thread-count satin bedsheets. He could see himself falling head over heels, his arms flailing, the stairwell spinning, his head hitting a solid-oak stair nosing. A crack, a terrible aching sound coming from within his head, bright blood oozing, thinking of all the people that would look on in dismay, a massive load crashing down on top of him, and finally the world going black. Jason tried to lift his right foot against the heavy load he had chosen to saddle himself with, and stepped out into thin air—like stepping blindly off a mountain cliff—hoping there would be another solid ledge just seven inches lower. He would be glad when he could get this lading off his shoulder; when everything could be put back to normal, at least the normal that Jason had known: a contented family, a loving wife, two wonderful kids—and a gambling habit. His wife had said it was the last straw and that she wouldn't put up with him anymore. He lost it and pushed her; it wasn't intentional, just a temporary loss of self control. He was so very sorry. His stomach tightened and his heart pounded out a rhythm unfamiliar to him. It was different from the feeling he frequently got when he lost his entire stake at the tables. Why had this happened? Was God punishing him for his sins? Not an accident, he told himself, just fate, and as such maybe he could do something to correct it—that's what he intended to do as soon as he could get to the basement, just one more flight of stairs to go. She would understand and forgive him; she knew it was an addiction and he couldn't be blamed. He had to hurry; his two young daughters would be home soon, home from school on the last day before summer vacation, and surely they could not face this, surely they could not forgive him, surely they would find out that he had overstepped his bounds. But it was not to be. He was halfway down the first flight of stairs when a key in the front door—the door facing him like the gates of Hell—popped a bolt open, and he could see the door latch rotating ever so slowly. Jason froze, both feet on a single tread, a tread too narrow for his big feet and the dead weight he had wrapped like a rolled carpet about his shoulders. The door inched open, and his two, smiling, rosy-cheeked girls, their brightly-colored backpacks in hand, looked up at their father in disbelief and said:

"Daddy! It's mom's job to do the laundry."

Curiosity Killed The...

By Don Kirk

IT WAS AN OBSESSION. Like an addiction, he did it for the pleasure of it and could never get enough. He enjoyed it and nothing could stop him from doing it. I don't know how it all got started, but I remembered that first night I played poker with him and his wife Maybell Biddle.

It was a regular event in the Biddle household. Tuesday night was poker night and new players were always welcome. In fact, Maybell invited new blood on a regular basis. I supposed it was to get new money into the game. I had met Maybell at Winford's Grocery at the checkout lane. She was the Aunt-Bee-of-Mayberry type in physical appearance with that down-home country in her warm-hearted personality. There was nothing about her not to like, but she was always dressed in an oversized, flowery day dress to conceal what I didn't want to know, and was painted with enough makeup for me to think she had just come back from a black Lutheran funeral. She was a good cook and always had something for us to munch on at the game table—not raw carrots and pork rinds, but homemade cream cakes, cherry pie, and apple strudel. She was a chatterbox during the game, but could bluff with the best of them. Her husband, Benny, was another breed, quiet and reserved, a meek, slender man of a height that would make him invisible in a sidewalk crowd. He played cards with us on occasion to fill out a foursome, but often disappeared into the basement to play with his trains, the Lionel O-27 gauge variety with the silver track and that unrealistic third rail. He had rolling stock that automatically did things on the sidings, like loading milk cans and dumping logs.

Benny's home was a modest, chocolate-colored bi-level on a street bordered with aging poplars in a quaint old suburb west of Chicago. The inside of the house was covered with flowery wallpaper and worn furniture hand-me-downs from some previous generation and they were covered with thick layers of greasy lemon oil and wax. A few steps led up from the living room to two bedrooms and a bath, and a longer run of steps led down to a half-basement with a laundry, furnace room and a large game room—filled now with Benny's prized Lionel train set. We played our card games in the kitchen breakfast nook on a well-worn 1950's Formica table with aluminum edging.

The house felt warm and cozy on this bright snow-laden winter's evening. The moon was full or near so and the blanket of crystalline snow reflected eerie bluish light into the house and across the ceiling. Floor registers on the oak floors radiated a homey, dust-smelling heat.

"Two pair," I said.

Maybell lay her hand on the table, "Ace-high straight." One side of her mouth turned up ever so slightly as she raked up her winnings.

"You seem to be weighing down your side of the table with all those coins, Maybell. You might want to push some over this way."

"You'll have to take them with a better hand, Mr. Green."

"You're drawing all the good cards," I replied lightheartedly.

"My grand-mammy woulda lopped you side 'o the head with her walking stick if you'da said that to her."

"I was just joshin' you, Maybell, making no intimations about your character."

"I didn't think you was. Iffin I had, you wouldn't still be sittin' in that chair."

Everyone laughed.

"Seein' as how your poke is near empty, why don't you go down to the basement and see what Benny is up to. I reckon he could use a little company other'n that gawd-awful smoke-belching steam engine o' his. And tell him to stop with that damn steam whistle."

"I'll do that Mrs. Maybell, and you shuffle those cards real well now, I'll return to win my money back."

I grabbed the handrail and carefully made my way down the steep basement stairs. Benny was in a large room off to the left, his simple train set laid out on a sheet of green-painted plywood sitting on sawhorses in the middle of a dirty-white linoleum-tiled floor. The track was laid in a simple figure eight with two short turnouts. Several *Revell* plastic-model structures kits had been screwed to the board including a signal tower, water tower, and train station. As I approached, I could see that green flakes of something had been glued to the board to represent grass. How could Benny spend so much time on this unassuming layout, I couldn't imagine.

"Did you win the pot?" asked Benny.

"You know I didn't."

"Well, maybe next week."

"Don't know that I'll come back. I've already turned my trouser pockets inside out."

"You'll be back."

Benny backed his black, Western Pacific 4-4-2 steam locomotive, with white smoke puffing from its stack, into a siding to hook up the milk car. The coupling closed magnetically and he pulled the engine forward, but the pilot wheels came off the track at the switch. He bent down to place them back on the track when I heard a guttural bellowing noise coming from behind a small, four-foot-high door in the wall behind me.

"Did you hear that, Benny?"

"What?"

"That noise in there."

"Huh, no, maybe you just heard the furnace."

The train stopped at the little Victorian railroad station and took on invisible passengers.

I didn't reside more than six blocks away from the Biddle's and developed a genuine friendship with them. Maybell continued to invite new players to the game and I was beginning to fear that our entire town might end up in the poor house.

On Friday, our local paper, the Gardendale Gazette, reported the bizarre disappearance of numerous cats and dogs in our neighborhood; the story brought to their attention by Dr. Raymond Raimondo, our town's only Veterinarian. He had received an unusual number of calls from pet owners asking if he had heard from anyone who had found a lost pet. Raimondo had placed dog tags on his patient's collars with the pet's name and veterinarian's phone number etched on them. He told the Gazette that none of the missing pets had turned up, and this was a small community situated between a fenced commuter rail line and a man-made drainage creek that was always full of water. There was some undeveloped swampland within the city limits, but there had never been this many missing pets at any one time. There was such an uproar that the city council got involved and made a promise to the taxpayers that their pets would be found, or promised the mayor, "I'll personally see to it that we get to the bottom of this thing."

It was as if the pets had disappeared into thin air—abducted by aliens—with only plush toys and paw prints left behind. At one point, the town's highway department drug, poked, and fished the swamps for signs of something that could be eating the pets. Nothing was found, but they stopped short of trying to drain them. A few weeks later, Bob Gillings, a grocery store clerk, also turned up missing. This ratcheted up the tension in town by several notches.

"I can't believe Bob is missing," muttered Maybell, "He was my favorite clerk at Winford's." She threw out three cards and drew three to fill out her hand.

"Three cards? Your hand's not so good, huh, Maybell?"

"I'll make do," she replied with the conviction of a jailbird intent on making an escape.

"I hear the FBI is going to get involved."

"We don't need 'em," blurted Maybell, "we kin take care o' our flock."

"It's a shame about all of those pets," I said trying to change the subject as I threw out just one card. I had the chance for a straight, was delighted by the possibility, and tried to turn my face to stone, with poor results I'm sure.

"I don't think there's nary a one left. No sweat off my keister, though, I never liked none o' them—turning over my trash can, pooping in my yard."

"Some folks," I said, "need the love of an animal."

"That sounds a might kinky, you sure you don't wanna rephrase that, Mr. Green?

"Now don't get testy, dear," interrupted Benny, softly.

"Go play with your trains," Maybell replied harshly.

"As you wish, dear." Benny bowed his head, slowly pushed back his chair, rose, and opened a nearby kitchen cabinet and removed an old skeleton key on a ring and disappeared down the basement stairwell.

"Call ya, Mr. Green, what'a you got?"

I laid out my cards. "Unfortunately, I'm one card short a straight."

"Bless you. I've a lowly pair." She dragged the pot to her.

It was about two weeks later when the Gazette reported another missing person from our neck of the woods. And it turned out the man was a nice gentleman Maybell had had over for cards some weeks prior. A portly man with graying sideburns, he played a good game, and always threw out a few sacrilegious, but sidesplitting, Catholic jokes for our consumption. Benny had even laughed at them. But now Clarence Keggle, that was his name, appeared to be missing, his wife of thirty years totally beside herself. She had spoken discourteously to Maybell about his disappearance and the county sheriff decided to pay her a visit. He questioned Maybell about her relationship with the missing man. She said she had him over just once, that he wasn't a very good player. The sheriff conceded they didn't have any good leads; Keggle and Bob Gillings' disappearance were a mystery of the first order. He said there might be a connection between the two of them. Soon, the town was in an uproar and the FBI was ruffling a lot of feathers as they tried to turn over all the rocks.

Meanwhile, the quiet, unassuming Benny played with his trains. He always seemed to be down in the basement when I came for a visit. I didn't just come to play cards on Tuesday; in fact, there was not always a seat for me. Maybell was always inviting new people to take to the cleaners; some enjoyed the game and came back, some didn't. When I did come to play, there was usually a new face at the table. I had the privilege of meeting a lot of people that spring and Maybell's poker parties became the talk of the town: *have you had the pleasure of playing cards with Maybell Biddle? No, how can I get a seat? I hear her cooking is divine.* On this day, I was there to give Benny a gift for his birthday and found him in the basement…as usual.

The steam locomotive puffed around the track pulling several box cars and a red caboose.

"Benny? I brought you a present. Where are—"

Benny came out of the small four-foot door that probably accessed the sump pump. He closed and locked it behind him. "So nice of you, Mr. Green."

"Nothing, saw it in Chicago, thought you might like it."

"Nice." Benny carefully opened the white box with orange graphics and pulled out a Lionel self-loading reefer car with blocks of ice. His eyes sparkled like a kid's on Christmas morning. "Thank you, Mr. Green."

"No sweat. You and Maybell have been so good to me. Good company you both. I thought living alone here in Gardendale would, well, be lonely, but it's a good friendly town, Benny."

"It is I suppose."

"I don't see you out much Benny. Your complexion's looking a little pale. You spend a lot of time in this basement."

"I do."

"How about I take you to see the White Sox next week? We'll make a day of it, maybe even spend the night in Chicago."

"I uh, couldn't do that Mr. Green, I mean, spending the night. I don't think Maybell would go for it."

"Oh sure she would."

"No, I—"

"I'm sure she'd love to get you out of her hair for a while."

"She wouldn't."

"Okay then, just for the day."

"Maybe."

"Good then. It's a date."

"I didn't' say…"

Just then, a bang rattled the sump room door behind me. I turned to look at the door. The door was secured with an old padlock. "There's something in…" I blurted out, but without sufficient air in my lungs I couldn't complete the sentence. I took a deep breath.

"No, Mr. Green, it's nothing, I have been trying to brace up one of the floor girders. The living room floor is sagging a bit; my temporary brace must have fallen against the door."

"I can help you fix it."

"Oh no, not now, please, you'll soil your good clothes." Benny turned back to his trains. "Besides, I want to work now on my 4-6-2's electric motor. I'll get to that girder in due time."

"Okay, you call me when you need help and don't forget about the ball game." I turned to leave when I eyed a large glossy white, rectangular box. "I see you and the misses bought yourself a new freezer."

"It was given to us by our nephew in Minneapolis. He knew we needed one. Maybell prepares so much venison, freezes berries, peaches, pecans, jam, everything—we needed more space."

I left the Biddle's that day with an uneasy feeling. I had walked on the living room floor to the front door and it felt solid, no bounce. Benny was hiding something and I wanted to know what was behind that locked door. Then an image popped into my head. The skeleton key. I had seen Benny—weeks earlier—take a key from a kitchen cabinet and go to the basement. That had to be the key to that locked door. I needed to get that key and get to that basement when Benny—and Maybell—were away from home, but that would be a trick.

I conjured up a plan to unlock a basement window the next time I was there and then I'd send the Biddles two winning tickets to a popular play in Chicago. They would appear to be from a fictional non-profit organization.

I executed my plan and when she got the tickets, Maybell was overjoyed, but skeptical at first, disbelieving she had actually won something. She called to verify the legitimacy of the tickets. They were good of course; the only address and phone number on my prize-winning letter was to the playhouse ticket office. When that day came for them to go, they were off to Chicago and I entered their house by the basement window I had unlocked earlier, dropping five feet to the floor below. Over in the corner, I could see the freezer. I had to look inside. I carefully raised the heavy lid, a mist of cold condensation rose into my face. The freezer was already chock full of frozen meats wrapped in white butcher paper—and they had just recently purchased the freezer! Planning a huge barbecue maybe? I lowered the lid, climbed the stairs to the kitchen, found the key in the cabinet, and returned to the basement. I took the key in my right hand and palmed the old padlock in my left. I inserted the skeleton key and turned, the key spun around, but wouldn't catch on anything. This was not the right key; it was too small. I had assumed…there had to be another key around here. I began to look high and low, over the doorjamb and under the carpet. I looked behind the railroad pictures hanging on the wall and felt under the only chair in the room. I turned to the train layout, looked at the track, looked at the buildings and the rolling stock. I grabbed up the plastic maroon-colored boxcar, opened its sliding door and shook it. Nothing. I looked again at the layout. Where would he hide it? I grabbed the octagon roof of the water tower and lifted it. And there, in the tank, was another larger skeleton key—this had to be it.

I grabbed the padlock on the door again and slotted the key with a grating noise and turned it and worked it. The lock snapped open. I removed it from the iron hasp and opened the heavy, wooden, inch-thick plywood door. Rushing into my face was stale putrid air, musty with mold and scum from stagnated water. I jumped at a grinding noise as the sump pump kicked in. Without the pump, the basement would fill with the water that slowly seeps in from the substrata as the result of melting snow. The beams and joists that supported the floor above lay just above my head and I had to duck as I carefully stepped across the muddy ground. The under-the-floor cavern was damp as an icy morning in spring. A packed-down path led me to a stagnant pool of water. The sump pump was apparently not doing its job.

The pond extended off into the darkness; I couldn't quite see the concrete perimeter foundation wall in the distance. The only light was coming from the open doorway. I could see a few bare light bulbs strung between the joists and looked for a light switch. I heard a bang, the light bulbs began to swing, and footsteps fell on the oak floor just over my head. They were back early. Much too early. I made my way back to the four-foot door, climbed out, closed it carefully, and replaced the lock. I returned the key to the water tower, then hurried to the basement window and closed it. It was too high for me to climb out of and so I went into the furnace room and closed the door behind me. I listened for footsteps on the stairs. I stared at the light seeping under the door. The key! I had Benny's other key. He'll look for it in the kitchen cabinet and it won't be there.

I heard Maybell raising her voice to Benny, chewing him out for something. I could imagine her swinging her big leather purse at him, or worse. He wasn't yelling back. Then I heard her say, "You're not going down there anymore. You can stay up here with me."

"I'm going down there anytime I please," replied Benny with a backbone I had never seen before.

"You left the tickets here on purpose, didn't you!"

"I'm sorry, dear."

"If you go down there, it'll be your last time."

At that, I heard a loud thump and the sound of a body tumbling down the stairs. A shadow interrupted the hall light that was bleeding under the furnace door. And then everything was quiet. The only sound came from the fire in the furnace.

I stood there frozen. And waited.

Then I heard footsteps coming slowly down the stairs.

My heart pounded so loud I was afraid she would hear it. She was a big and brawny gal and I doubted I could overtake her. Maybe she had a knife...or a gun. I chose not to confront her. My legs and feet ached. The concrete floor was cold under my feet and beads of sweat dripped from my forehead.

I saw shadows moving under the door and then heard Maybell as she struggled to drag Benny across the floor. Oh, poor Benny.

He didn't bother anyone, just wanted his little space here in the basement. I heard the lock being opened on the door to the sump room. She was going to bury him under the house!

What could I do?

I decided to wait.

Soon the padlock was returned to its hasp on the plywood door and Maybell turned off the hall light and, after a few moments, went back upstairs. I cracked open the door and dared to venture out. How would I get out of here? The basement windowsill was too high and I didn't dare go upstairs. I would have to wait until she went to bed. So I waited and waited and thought of Benny laying in the damp muddy basement, going stiff and bugs crawling all over him. Maybell hadn't spent much time in the sump room. She would need to come back and burry Benny before he began to go ripe. But maybe…could he still be alive? I had to get the key and open that door and make sure.

In the dark, I located the water tower and removed the key. Putting it in the lock, I turned it, jiggled it, and the lock came open. I removed it from the hasp, lay it on a bookshelf, opened the door, and flipped on a light switch by the door. The dangling string of light bulbs came on. I went in and could see the beat-down path across the mud, but I didn't see Benny's body. I started down the path and noticed a bed of twigs and hay in a patch of sand off to the right. I stepped over to it and kicked at the twigs. Some white eggs, hen eggs maybe, came into view. As I reached down to pick one up, I heard the plywood door behind me slam shut. And the lights went out. Maybell knows I'm here! Adrenaline coursed through my body. I hurried back to the door and pushed on it. It stood fast. I hit it hard with my shoulder. It didn't break open. The lock must have been put back in the hasp. Maybe she didn't know I was here. Either way, I was trapped. Then it occured to me that Maybell knew right where the key was kept in the water tower on Benny's train set. So why would the key be kept hidden? Who else would he hide it from? At that thought, I tripped on something, almost falling into the mud, catching myself with my hands. A big rock maybe? I reached down with my mud encased hands and felt a blubbery mass—and I felt breasts—it was Maybell laying there in the mud! So it wasn't Benny who had been pushed down the stairs. Then I heard sounds behind me. Something was coming up the path. Crawling toward me. I couldn't quite make it out, but there was more than one of them. Small four-legged creatures with black and yellow banding. Fear welled in me like never before. I turned back toward the door and between me and the only way out was a huge—maybe ten to twelve feet long, blackish-brown body, and leathery armor plating—a freshwater predator capable of killing almost any animal entering its domain. I stared, frozen in my tracks by its powerful broad snout as it opened wide, displaying rows of menacing teeth. My last thought was that Benny, poor Benny, was raising alligators as pets and was having a hard time keeping them fed! Poor Maybell. Poor me.

The locomotive whistle blew as the train raced around the track.

A Lover's Lair

By Don Kirk

THE BURLY, JIM TREACHERY pulled the rumpled white bed sheet away, slid out of bed, and pulled on his tattered jeans. A chained, black billfold snuggled itself in his back pocket. His muscular torso glistened with sweat. An ironworker on a new high rise going up nearby, Jim was on his lunch break. He flung on his faded-red plaid shirt; sleeves still rolled up to the elbows, and tucked it in.

"You're leaving so soon?"

"Back to work. The hardhats won't give me no slack."

"Coming back tomorrow?" asked Jenny softly.

"You can mark it on your calendar."

"Don't think I'd better do that, my husband might see it."

Jenny lay there, half under the sheets, with smooth pearly-white skin and a disheveled hairdo. A well-endowed redhead, but a little on the heavy side, with tiny, size-5A feet, she and her Wall-Street husband lived on the fourth floor of a restored brownstone in New York City, a nice little one-bedroom apartment. A modest kitchen adjacent to a cozy breakfast nook opened through an archway into a small art deco living area. A wall-hung plasma screen television with a slightly askew couch sitting close to it was all they needed, or could afford.

Jenny heard a key turning in the lock of the front door, and startled, she sat up in bed and whispered forcefully: "that's my husband!"

Jim was immediately panic-stricken. He searched for his work boots, but didn't see them.

"Go out that way. There's a fire escape, oh no it's..."

Jim bound barefoot through a pair of French doors that opened onto a small balcony facing the alleyway. He closed the doors behind him and quickly discovered that the fire escape was broken and wouldn't draw down; he instead squeezed his brawny body into a small area beside the door.

"Jenny, are you here?" came a voice from the living room.

Jenny could still see Jim's arm through the glass doors and jumped out of bed and closed the white lace curtains that still let a soft, soothing light penetrate the room, but sucessfully hid Jim from view.

"I'm in here sweetie, ready for you," replied Jenny as she hopped back into bed and pulled the bed sheet over her. She tried to organize her mussed hair.

"There you are."

"Here I am." Jenny raised her arms and threw a sweet, come-hither smile.

"Baby, I've missed you this week," replied Roland Lane as he began, frantically, to unbutton his shirt. A thin sandy-haired young man with narrow-rimmed dark glasses, Roland worked as a messenger boy on a ten-speed bicycle, skirting through the beleaguered city traffic with lightening speed.

"You're early aren't you?"

"Couldn't wait any longer, baby."

"Even though I gave you a key, dearest, you need to knock first. I might have someone else in here."

"Someone else? Oh, you're just kidding, aren't you?"

"Of course, sweetums, you're my special only one. Come to me."

Roland put his glasses in his shirt pocket, removed his black baseball cap, and placed it carefully on the nightstand next to a bawdy-looking lamp with a tasseled, crimson shade. He shed his uniform and hopped into bed. The afternoon light bled through the sheer curtains and speckled the pair of lover's with soft invigorating light. Jim waited on the balcony, patiently, as a vagrant rummaged through the trashcans below and a chilling breeze gave him goose bumps the size of highway buttons.

Soon, Jenny heard another key in the door's lock; she was attuned to the sound like a submarine radar operator.

"Oh, my god, it's my husband!" bellowed Jenny. She was wishing now the landlord hadn't waited so long to fix the fire escape.

"Your husband?"

"Yes, you have to get out of here."

Roland jumped up and grabbed his clothes.

"Honey pie, I'm home."

Roland spun around and then headed for the French doors. Jenny's eyes widened and the terror of a subway train barreled toward her.

"No, not there, dear, there, over there, in my wardrobe."

Roland bound to the large antique cherry-wood cabinet on casters and turned the latch to open one of the two paneled doors. He slid in among Jenny's gaudy dresses, his uniform cradled in his arms. As he closed the door, he saw his cap on the nightstand. Jenny understood the significance of what he was looking at and grabbed the cap and slung it under the bed.

"Honey, where are you?"

"I'm in bed dear, feeling a bit under the weather."

Jenny's husband, Ralph Crutchfield, entered the bedroom. He was wearing smartly, a dark, pin-stripped suit with a bright red tie with a Windsor knot, but the tail was hanging much too short. He had a large body frame and wore a graying, well-trimmed beard, but he still had the look of a truck driver. He didn't fit the stereotypical Wall-Street analyst.

"What's wrong dear?"

"I've got a bit of a fever. Feel a little down today."

"You do look a little flushed."

Ralph slowly unbuttoned and removed his jacket and laid it on the bed.

"You're home early?" inquired Jenny.

"I had thought we might go out to dinner, at *Barrymore's,* but since you're so down..."

"I am." Jenny turned on her side as if trying to go back to sleep.

Ralph stood up and walked around the bed to the French doors to open the curtains to let in more light. Jenny's blood pressure jumped; if she had been flushed before, bright pink was the new color of this normally fair-skinned girl.

"Darling, I need it dark so I can sleep."

"Oh, okay, honey-bit, I'll let you..." Ralph saw something peeking out from under the bed and reached down to pull it out—"A work boot? What is this doing...Jenny?" Hair began to stand up on Ralph's neck. "You've got a man in here, don't you? And he's still here, isn't he?"

"No, there's no one..."

"Where is he, Jenny? You promised...I'll kill the bastard!"

Jenny sat up in bed, but made sure the bed sheet covered her breasts. "Darling, no, there's no one here."

"Then explain these boots under the bed—dirty, scruffy boots, I might add."

"I can't."

"No, you can't."

Ralph pulled the curtains aside almost tearing them from their moorings and peeked out. He looked from one side of the balcony to the other. Only a small, white, wrought-iron table with two matching chairs and a potted fern needing water, stood on the balcony.

"Where is he? I'll find the bastard. Come out wherever you are." Ralph tore into the living room and looked into the entry's coat closet. He looked in the kitchen pantry and looked in the refrigerator, where he picked up a tall, 20-ounce *Michelob*, all the while cussing her and the egregious interloper he knew was there, somewhere. Jenny leaped up and went to her wardrobe, opened it, saw Roland's face peering fearfully behind her dresses and grabbed her housecoat, closed the door, turned the latch, and wrapped her naked self in the robe. She then charged into the living room.

"Let me fix you something for dinner, something special. I've got a leg of lamb, sweet potatoes, greens—there's no one here, Honey Pot."

"Sure there is. It's not as if this is the first time, Jenny. You promised. This is the last straw." Ralph's suspenders were tensed and ready to snap from his torso. "He's here and I'm going to kill the son of a bitch."

Ralph stampeded to the bedroom like a charging bull—slinging the frothing bottle of beer along the way—and crouched down to look under the bed. He pulled out a black baseball cap with the insignia of one of the city's bicycle messenger services: *The Trojans*, with its slogan printed underneath: *There Before You Can Say Slam-Bam-Thank-You-Ma'am.*

"The bicycle on the stoop! The damn bicycle!" roared Ralph. "He's here, Jenny, and he's a dead man." Ralph was blistering under the collar. "Where's that son of a mother's son?" Blowing with liquored breath, Ralph had apparently made an earlier stop at *Randall's*, the corner bar.

Ralph stood up and eyed Jenny's wardrobe. "That's it! He's in there."

At that, Jenny catapulted into the bedroom and stood defiant between Ralph and the wardrobe.

"You need show me no more." Ralph pushed her aside, and as Jenny grabbed at his suspenders and beer-soaked pin-stripped silk shirt, he pulled the wardrobe out from the wall and pushed it toward the balcony. The French doors were still open and the wardrobe rolled through the doors and out onto the balcony.

"What are you doing?" scorned Jenny.

"I'm within my rights."

"No, please don't!"

Ralph banged on the wardrobe door, "You're history, my friend."

The latch rattled as Roland tried to extricate himself. Ralph pushed the wardrobe against the stone parapet. Jenny jumped on his back. Ralph grabbed the bottom of the wardrobe, grunted, and lifted. Roland screamed and pounded the cabinet with his fists. Jenny let go of Ralph and stepped back, struck with disbelief. The wardrobe now teetered on the top of the parapet wall. At that Jim Treachery came out from hiding and tried to stop Ralph from doing something he might regret.

"Who are you?" demanded Ralph, "Ah, no, not another? Jenny!"

Jim pulled on the wardrobe and Ralph pushed on it.

"You son of a bitch," screamed Ralph as he swung Jim around with unregulated adrenalin and slung him over the parapet wall, but Jim caught a ledge just below the wall with his fingers, his body dangling four stories above the alleyway below. The outraged Ralph lifted the wardrobe and gave it a final push, and as the center of gravity shifted to the outside, Jim stared helplessly up at Ralph. The wardrobe slipped over and hit Jim, knocking him from the ledge. A caster of the wardrobe caught on Ralph's suspenders, tore into his shirt, and pulled him over the railing. The three men fell, the four long stories, to their death.

Jenny took a step backward, smoothed down her tangled red hair, turned around sharply, and headed back into her bedroom mumbling to herself: *I must get ready for my 3:00 appointment.*

So what's the moral to this horrific tale? God won't necessarily wait to send you to hell—or maybe, just maybe, God's a woman.

Available at
lulu.com/sweetwater

For information regarding special discounts
for bulk purchasers, please e-mail the publisher at
kirkwest@sbcglobal.net.

Please send me ____ copies of Cool Short Stories.
I am enclosing $ 12.95 plus $3.50 to cover
postage and handling. Please send check or
money order, no cash or C.O.D.'s please.

Name ____

Address _______________________________________

City ____

State/Zip_______________________________________

Send orders or comments to:
Sweetwater StageLines, Dept. DM03,
5118 Village Trail Drive,
San Antonio, Texas, 78218-3831

Prices and availability subject to change without notice.

DM03 2006v4

RATE THESE STORIES

		WORST	BEST

1. Grave Sight...1 2 3 4 5 6 7 8 9 10
2. Monster in My Room 1 2 3 4 5 6 7 8 9 10
3. The Inanimates 1 2 3 4 5 6 7 8 9 10
4. Be Quiet Now, Dear 1 2 3 4 5 6 7 8 9 10
5. Air Pocket..1 2 3 4 5 6 7 8 9 10
6. Dogcatcher's Catch 1 2 3 4 5 6 7 8 9 10
7. Henry...1 2 3 4 5 6 7 8 9 10
8. The Cyst 1 2 3 4 5 6 7 8 9 10
9. The Contrarian's Husband 1 2 3 4 5 6 7 8 9 10
10. The Department Store 1 2 3 4 5 6 7 8 9 10
11. Redemption in a Watery Grave 1 2 3 4 5 6 7 8 9 10
12. Where Time Stopped 1 2 3 4 5 6 7 8 9 10
13. My Darling Tilley 1 2 3 4 5 6 7 8 9 10
14. 100 Ways to Dispose of a Body 1 2 3 4 5 6 7 8 9 10
15. Night Flight..1 2 3 4 5 6 7 8 9 10
16. I Carried It in My Pocket.................1 2 3 4 5 6 7 8 9 10
17. The Visitor..1 2 3 4 5 6 7 8 9 10
18. Marberger's Syndrome 1 2 3 4 5 6 7 8 9 10
19. Printer's Ink.......................................1 2 3 4 5 6 7 8 9 10
20. Hello Goes The Fizz 1 2 3 4 5 6 7 8 9 10
21. Top Secret 1 2 3 4 5 6 7 8 9 10
22. Prime Beef..1 2 3 4 5 6 7 8 9 10
23. Last Stop 1 2 3 4 5 6 7 8 9 10
24. A Frame In Time 1 2 3 4 5 6 7 8 9 10
25. Stairway to Hades.............................1 2 3 4 5 6 7 8 9 10
26. Curiosity Killed the Cat 1 2 3 4 5 6 7 8 9 10
27. A Lover's Lair.....................................1 2 3 4 5 6 7 8 9 10

Sweetwater Stagelines™
5118 Village Trail
San Antonio, Texas 78218